LUKE CHRISTODOULOU

TWELVE MONTHS OF MURDER

A COLLECTION OF SHORTS

VINCI BOOKS

Vinci Books

vinci-books.com

Published by Vinci Books Ltd in 2026

1

The publisher and the author have made every effort to obtain permissions for any third party material used in this book and to comply with copyright law. Any queries in this respect should be brought to the attention of the publisher and any omissions will be corrected in future editions.

A CIP catalogue record for this book is available from the British Library.
Paperback ISBN: 9781036713638

The EU GPSR authorised representative is Logos Europe, 9 rue Nicolas Poussion, 17000 La Rochelle, France contact@logoseurope.eu

By Luke Christodoulou

Greek Island Mysteries

Dedicated to my siblings
You have formed me more than you know...

JANUARY OF DECEIT

His bare foot sat in a wet puddle of red wine on the floor. Michael awoke naked on his living room sofa. The breeze from the slightly-opened kitchen door carried a scent of freshly brewed Colombian coffee. He struggled to sit up. His head felt heavy. His familiar intense migraine lingered behind his sore amber eyes. This time at least he could blame the alcohol running through his veins. Around him evidence of a successful New Year's Eve party lay with him. His OCD kicked in as he observed the random objects that had invaded his three-bedroom beach bungalow. Beer cans, bottles of wine, lipstick-smeared champagne glasses, confetti, deflated balloons, Jack's tie, Anna's woolly hat, multiple dirty plates, his brown pair of trousers.

'Why am I naked?' he asked aloud as he placed his palms upon the leather sofa and pushed himself up. The window blinds were wide open; the Greek sun was blinding. He dashed across the high-ceilinged room while keeping an eye outside. Midday was Mrs. Papadaki's favorite time to walk her four dogs; just before cooking time. 'Old ladies and their routines,' he mumbled as he gazed at the deep blue sea that filled his horizon.

He pulled up his trousers and zipped them up carefully. His body ached as he put them on. A peculiar pain rode below his back. He walked towards the kitchen and popped his head into the small room. A smell of fried bacon pervaded the air beating out the rich aroma from the hot beverages. His wife, Joan, turned and smiled. 'Good morning, sleepy head. Breakfast, or better, brunch, is nearly ready. I turned on the heat as I didn't want to wake you, Mr. Nude.'

'Please tell me that I got naked *after* all our friends and neighbors left,' he said and walked towards her. His arms travelled around her waist and he gently kissed her neck.

'Fortunately, yes. As soon as my sister left last, you shredded your clothes and fell dead asleep. Snoring in seconds. I was going to clean up with her, but I thought fuck it, chores can wait,' she said as she cracked an egg on the hard counter. 'I'm not spending the first day of the year cleaning!'

Michael pulled out a wooden chair and sat down. His face shrivelled up in pain. He exhaled deeply.

'Something a matter?' Joan asked as she cracked another egg.

He stared at her. 'Don't laugh. My ass hurts... Hey! I said don't laugh!'

'Sorry, babes. Sorry,' she apologized as another egg met its fate. 'You probably banged into something while dancing last night.'

Michael scratched his eyebrow and agreed. Soon, he was diving into a delicious full English breakfast and shortly after, into a steamy bath. The hot water stung. He pulled his mind away by thinking of their years living in London, where the young Athenian had met the island beauty during their studies. They stayed fifteen years in the city, earning 'good money' in real estate as his deceased father liked to say. The downside was their failure to have a child. He was officially diagnosed sterile. When both were a step before forty, Joan's grandmother passed away due to a third stroke and Joan found herself inheriting a beach property on the picturesque island of Naxos. They packed their clothes and knowledge, and relocated to the town of Chora, the capital of the small island, opening their own real estate office, selling beach properties mostly to elderly Brits.

'What the...?' he whispered as he noticed the red dots swimming in the water before resting on the porcelain bottom of the tub. 'I'm bleeding...'

'Jesus, that's one hell of a hit,' he thought as he stood up and rushed to the bathroom mirror, dripping water all over the floor. He turned around, checking his buttocks. No sign of a bruise or wound. He felt dizzy again. He had had this feeling quite often lately. Always in the morning. Always accompanied by a funny rumbling in his stomach. His wife's breakfast always beating the strange feeling away.

'I need to book a doctor's appointment. No risks at forty-five, Michael.'

The following day, they kept their promise and cleaned up. And right on schedule, they argued, agitated by doing something they both despised. Every now and then, they would bring in a cleaning lady from the village behind the hill, though both hated it. Michael couldn't stand things being touched and placed in the *wrong* spot and Joan disliked the idea of trusting someone else to clean as thoroughly as she.

Joan blamed their arguments on their 'too many hours together' while Michael pondered on how things went wrong. They had no serious issues. They argued over the silliest of things.

January was a slow month for business. Second quietest after February. Their business boomed all up to Christmas. Last year, they took turns going into the office during winter. This year, Michael insisted on closing for a couple of weeks.

'I'm not all that well, lately. I need a break,' he said in response to his wife's despair. He thought she feared all the free time they would have with each other. If he only knew.

———

Sickly mornings became frequent over the next couple of weeks. A known germophobe, Michael postponed a visit to the doctor. As Joan had informed him that she would be taking the ferry to Athens the following morning to visit her mother and sister for a few days, Michael planned to do all the things he put off doing when he had her company. He found himself knocking on Thomas's door just hours after her departure from Naxos's small quaint port. The handsome fisherman that lived next door shouted out. 'Who is it?'

'Michael,' he yelled back. The television set was blaring out the sports news.

'Mike, my man. It's open.'

He entered to find his gigantic bodybuilder neighbor curled up on the sofa, under a checkered blanket with a hot mint tea between his hands.

'You look comfortable,' he said, approaching his friend.

'Sshh, give me a minute,' Thomas replied and leaned forward, apparently bringing his ears nearer to the TV.

Michael stood quietly, his eyes travelling around Thomas's bachelor pad. Thomas married young and divorced young. He was married to the sea he joked. Michael smiled at the thought that even if he was single, he would never be as untidy as Thomas.

'Tell me. What's up?' Thomas said, switching off the news, pulling Michael out of his thoughts.

'Are you going fishing tomorrow?'

'Does Jennifer Lopez look fine?'

Michael forced a smile. 'Can I come?'

'Sure, man. What's up? Fight with Joan?'

'No, no. She's gone to Athens to see her mum. I'm bored, to be honest,' he admitted.

'Cool. Hey, let Nick know, on your way home. He's been asking for a fishing excursion, too. Be down at the harbor at six.'

'Aye, aye Captain,' he joked and saluted.

Closing the main door behind him, Michael took a deep breath of cool winter sea air. He was feeling much better. No migraines or upset stomach for days. He looked up at the clear sky and smiled at the lack of clouds. Only rain could ruin his fishing trip with the boys. He rushed along the conquered-by-weeds path and hopped down the narrow steps that led to Nick's bungalow. His last jump landed him in a shallow puddle.

'Watch it!' a man grunted.

Michael turned to see Yianni, a scruffy-looking neighbor in his late fifties. Yianni was for Michael, the black sheep of the small beach bungalow community. Yianni wiped a few muddy drops from his face. 'You splashed me,' he said.

'Sorry, Yianni but to be fair, you were laying on the grass...'

'It's a cozy place to sleep!' he retaliated, standing up.

Michael noticed that his neighbor's two top trouser buttons were undone. Yianni's round bulge stared back at him. Michael hated to think what he was doing hiding by the steps, among the tall wavy grass. He had a clear view from there into Mrs. Toula's bedroom. Yianni buttoned himself up, ignoring Michael's surprised look. 'Heard you had a party last night.'

'Yes, a few close friends...'

'Heard everyone in the neighborhood came.'

'You must have heard wrong. Sorry, Yianni. I must be on my way. I'm late,' he replied and dashed along the path, exhaling deeply. '*God, what an awful man.*'

'Yeah, I'm sure you are,' Yianni whispered from behind closed teeth and hid back behind the steps; his right hand travelling down into his pants.

Michael sighed in relief to be away from Yianni. '*And he wonders why we didn't invite him.*'

Michael pushed open the freshly-painted white fence and walked along the bricked path that led to Nick's house, admiring the blossomed garden. Nick's wife had died of cancer just two years back. She had been so proud of her roses and geraniums, and Nick had decided to maintain her legacy by taking care of her plants and each month, on the fourth -the day she died he planted something new. A few months before fifty with his son married and living in Athens and his daughter off at college, Nick retired early from teaching and took up gardening and drinking.

Michael pushed the doorbell button twice before looking through the dusty window. No one seemed to be home. Michael pulled out his cell phone from his right pocket and texted Nick tomorrow's fishing plan. By the time he had reached home and settled on the sofa ready to enjoy an old horror movie, Nick had replied to count him in. Michael was a great horror movie fan, yet Joan not only did not find them thrilling, she despised the genre.

At night, he devoured a delivered pizza, drank a glass of whisky and with the help of his thick coat, enjoyed a cigar in his back-garden hammock.

'You crazy fool, you'll catch a cold,' he mimicked Joan's high-pitched voice. 'Do you know how many calories a pizza has? I'm so glad you gave up smoking. Those cigars smelled awful,' he continued and blew out an opaque cloud into the winter air.

Back inside, he undressed down to his black boxer shorts and dived into bed. 'Aren't you going to have a shower?' he continued to mock Joan's voice with her particular pronunciation of the word shower. He switched off the lights and took his phone in his hand. As he typed in *Pornhub*, his mind thought of his vexatious morning sickness. Especially with fast food and alcohol swimming around his stomach. But such thoughts vanished quickly as his selected video began.

———————

The winter sun is a painter. An array of bright orange rays running from the flaming sphere phenomenally rising from the dark restless sea welcomed Michael as he trotted down to the pebble beach. He nodded good morning to a pair of seagulls resting on a neglected fishing boat, left to die on land. His hands were full. A blue cool box in his right, his fiberglass fishing rod in his left. He whistled as he gazed up at the clear sky. A weak rainless winter was detrimental to the farmers, but for Michael it meant days at the sea and nights in the yard. His nemesis, his morning sickness just like January's clouds, also had taken the day off.

Nick and his two packs of beer had arrived before Michael. He stood enjoying a hot Greek coffee and an American cigarette on the long wooden pier.

'Good morning to the bachelor for a week,' Nick said and embraced him.

'Morning, Nick,' Michael replied, unable to hug him back.

'Here, pass them up,' Thomas's deep voice came from FISH AND CHICKS, the name given to his boat. According to Thomas's account, the name was coined by an ex-girlfriend who caught him cheating. 'All you care about is hunting, fish and chicks, you filthy jerk!'

Michael passed the frozen lunches and his rod up to Thomas. 'Bachelor, huh?' he asked, turning around to face Nick.

'Well, she is away...'

'What's with the sneaky smile?'

Nick shot a guilty look towards Thomas.

'Save a surprise, Nick! Let him get on the boat first before scaring him off,' Thomas replied, threw his head back and let his notorious uproarious laughter loose to echo around the tranquil harbor.

Nick pretended his lips were a zip, closed them with his fingers and mimicked locking them and throwing away the key. He winked to Michael and jumped on board. Michael shook his head and followed. 'You nutters!'

Thomas turned the key and the boat's engine roared to life. Soon, FISH AND CHICKS was sailing upon the clear, pure waters of the Aegean at top speed; the thrashing of the waves drowned out by AC/DC booming from the ship's speakers and Thomas's lungs. An hour later, they reached their destination. A natural bay on the nearby island of Donousa, home to waters occupied by seabream and small barracudas.

The sun had revealed itself in all its morning glory as the boat came to a halt. Thomas killed the music and all breathed in the cool, unpolluted, salty air while preparing their rods.

'So?'

'So what, Michael?'

'What's the surprise?'

Thomas patted him on the back. 'Hookers!' he said and his dark eyes widened.

Michael looked around frantically. 'Where?'

Nick laughed out loud. 'Sshh! You will scare away dinner!' Thomas told him off. 'No, dickhead. Later. Tonight, at my house,' he continued.

'We thought to have a proper men's day,' Nick added. 'Fishing, a barbeque with our prey, more beers, then we shower and Thomas has arranged for a couple of working girls to come around his house later tonight!'

Michael looked at them both in disbelief. 'You are pulling my leg, right?'

Thomas placed his right hand upon his broad chest and swore that he was not kidding.

'Only you could find hookers on an island of twenty thousand people.'

'It's two girls from Moldova that work at summer bars. During the winter, they are unemployed and thought of ways to kill cold lonely nights and make a buck or two.'

'You should have been a lawyer, Tom. You always present things the way you want. The poor girls are probably forced into prostitution by a fat sick fuck of a sleazy boss with a thick porn moustache...'

'And you should have been a yellow paper journalist.'

Hungry seagulls flew above them, squawking at the smell of their bait. Their shadows playfully sliding upon the still turquoise waters of the bay. The sun had fully risen out of the horizon and light fought back the remaining darkness.

'Not hot, not cold. God, I love this weather,' Nick commented as he stood up and stretched his arms, cracked his waist and knuckles, and then burped before settling down on his plastic green stool again. With his rod firmly in his hands, he announced, 'let the boredom begin.'

Thomas stroked Nick's hair the same way he petted his dogs. 'You're a special kind of lunatic, boy!'

The following hours passed as a dull relaxing fishing day should. Mostly silence, interrupted by a few exchanges of 'want another beer?', 'this is the life' and 'these sandwiches are the bomb.'

Thirteen fish, three squid, a piece of a plastic bottle and a ripped yellow bikini top summed up the catch of the day. Thomas stood behind the wheel, pressed play on his Bluetooth speaker and hits from his favorite singer, Mitropanos, filled the air and covered the boat's rather loud old engine.

Back at Thomas's house, barbeque duties were shared by Nick, and Michael found himself inside, making the salad. A chore both Nick and Tom admitted to 'suck at'. Thomas made an extra comment about his big manly hands being unable to peel cucumbers and eloquently cut up the tomatoes. 'You're domesticated, Mike,' he continued. 'I'm sure you make a terrific salad. All the veg and whatever you need are in the kitchen. I went shopping yesterday.'

As Thomas poured the charcoal out of the bag and Nick cleaned the fish in the garden sink, Michael whistled away as he washed the green peppers. A sudden movement on the floor to his right caught his eye; a tiny shadow dashing across the floor.

'A cockroach in winter?' Michael whispered and slowly walked to the end of the kitchen counter and leaned towards the hallway, just in time to see the roach clearly as it disappeared under Thomas's bedroom door.

Michael stood on one leg and removed his white trainer. Shoe in hand, he followed the creature. Thomas's bedroom was dark and smelled of his cheap cologne. Michael switched on the lights and saw the cockroach up on the Playstation. '*Yeah, I'm not hitting that,*' he thought and slowly, tiptoed closer, raising his weapon in the air. As soon as the roach moved, the shoe came banging down. Grey juices came out of the squished bug and a pile of camcorder tapes tumbled to the carpet floor.

'Shit!' Michael swore and quickly kneeled to pick up the mess. 'September 25th. First time,' he read the label on the first tape. 'Halloween banging,' he read the next. His eyes ran through them all. 'Solo jerk! You're nasty, Tom.' One caught his attention the most. 'New Year's Eve. *After party!*'

Michael sneezed and swiftly looked up. No one heard him. '*After party? Why is it written in italics? An innuendo? After my house party? With whom?*'

His curiosity got the best of him and he picked up the camcorder from the shelf below the Playstation. He pressed the button to open the lock and placed the tape inside. His heart was pounding and he could feel his blood racing below his shivering skin. His index finger landed on play and he closed his eyes, took a deep breath and prepared himself to see his friend naked. He just wanted to see with whom he had hooked up with at his house party. Thomas had spent most of the night drinking with the boys. He hadn't seen him even talk to any of the ladies there. '*Maybe it's a prostitute?*' was his last thought as his eyes opened up wide. He recognized the room well. It was his own. And there he was, fast asleep while two shadowy figures kissed beside the bed.

The faint light provided by the bedside table lamp fell upon his peaceful face. His mouth was open and he was drooling on his overpriced microbead pillow. Michael knew he was gullible, -yet could not resist believing everything promised on the shopping network. The sound of passionate kisses broke the recorded silence. *'How come I'm not waking up?'*

The couple fell on the bed beside him and a familiar giggle echoed in his ears. 'That's Joan! Fuck!' he grunted, the curse escaping his lips. He looked up, remembering where he was. His eyes returned to the tiny screen as he witnessed Thomas take off his wife's pink top and begin to lick her nipples. Just then, they both stopped and turned their attention to the door. Joan placed her finger on Thomas's trembling lips.

'Yes?' Joan called out. *'Why am I still sleeping?'*

A female voice came from behind the door. 'Give me a minute, Maria,' Joan replied to her sister and turned towards Thomas. 'You better go. We have many days ahead of us,' she whispered. Thomas shook his head, but she pushed him off her, put on her tank top and exited the room by opening the wooden door slightly.

Thomas followed her towards the door and laid his head upon its surface. His right hand pulled out his erection and he started to masturbate. As he locked the door, his eyes turned towards the bed. He dropped his clothes to the ground and slid into the purple satin sheets. Michael watched in horror as his friend curled up behind him and pulled down his trousers. Michael felt a storm in his stomach and fought back throwing up as the satin sheet was pushed back revealing Thomas raping him. Michael remained with closed eyes and an open mouth while Thomas pounded away. Michael could not see no more.

With shaking hands, he took out the tape and returned it to its plastic home. He wiped his sweaty hands on the faded-blue carpet and picked up the stack of cassettes, ready to return them to their initial place. '*What's on the others? Me again? Joan? Others?*'

Once again, he found his curiosity getting the best of him. He stood up and tiptoed speedily back to the kitchen. From the open window, he saw both men enjoying a beer while spreading out the flaming charcoal. He dashed back to Thomas's bedroom and one by one played the tapes. Just for a few seconds on fast-forward. All in his bedroom. All with Joan and Thomas having sex while he slept by their side.

A changed man returned to the kitchen counter and continued cutting up the vegetables. With a blank mind, his hands meticulously proceeded with the task of a Greek village salad; escorted by dips and all.

Ten minutes later, Michael emerged from the house with the goods laid out on a cafeteria tray; his bare feet gently caressed by the freshly-cut grass. The cold wind carried the mixture of smells released by the crackling of the fish as the heat from the charcoal below attacked them.

'There he is, Mr. Slow-Cutter. Go for a shit?' Nick joked as he poured Michael a beer.

'Jeez, man. Aren't you cold?' Thomas asked, his eyes fixed on Michael's feet.

Michael placed the tray on the foldout picnic table, walked up to Thomas, placed his arm around his shoulders and said, 'real men don't get cold. Real men fuck anything. Right, Thomas?'

Thomas smiled. 'Damn right, bro.'

'Someone's ready for the whores,' Nick said and passed Michael his Greek-brewed beer.

'Can't wait,' Michael replied, the usual cheery tone of his voice making his friends laugh. Michael chuckled, too. His eyes, though, remained still. A mirror of the thoughts inside.

The next couple of hours rolled out just as expected. Three neighbors having fun in their back yard, with good food, alcoholic drinks and fine music from decades long passed.

Tales, anecdotes, football, women, politics, movies, the meaning of life. A fire, cold beers, a clear sky and a few good friends. It could have been a perfect day; could have... if one was not plotting the death of the other.

With the spectacular red sunset behind him, Michael walked home with his eyes on the ground; the day's last rays making his shadow one of a giants. 'Fee-fi-fo-fum, I smell the blood of an island man. Be he alive, or be he dead, I'll grind his bones for fucking in my bed!'

Michael surprised even himself. He expected more rage, yet a wave of calmness swallowed his initial shock and even as he fast-paced home, his heartbeat remained serene.

At home, he showered and dressed. Tonight was a party he did not plan on missing for the world. Michael stood in front of the mirror and smiled while he splashed on his Montblanc cologne. He squinted his eyes and licked his lips. 'You've got this.'

As he locked the front door behind him, he gazed up at the starry night. He exhaled loudly and brushed his fingers through his thin hair. The hairs on his arms stood at attention as the icy air invaded his bare skin. Michael pulled down his hoodie's sleeves and rushed down the path to

Thomas's house, stepping on stubborn winter weeds that surfaced from the deep cracks. 'Not deeper than the ones on my soul,' he whispered. *'Yes, this is the time to swing into poetical mode!'* he thought, took his hands out of his jean's pockets and began to jog.

The lights in the living room were on, yet all curtains were shut. Four pale shadows moved about and music and laughter faintly echoed outside of the warm house. He was last to the party of five.

'That must be Michael,' he heard Thomas's bass voice as he rang the doorbell. 'There's my boy! Come in. It's freezing outside. The girls are here to heat you up,' Thomas continued as he opened the door, hugged Michael and pulled him into the room.

With the door slammed behind him, introductions followed.

Ludmila and Ruslana could not have been more differ-ent. Though both Moldovan -as Thomas had explained, and both with slightly less make-up than the Joker, their outer appearance was diametrically opposed. Ludmila stood a good foot above him, dark black silky hair fell to her bare shoulders, emerald eyes shone amidst her glittery make-up and mascara, and she was the skinniest woman Michael had ever laid eyes upon in the flesh. 'A pork chop too little,' as his grandmother liked to say. On the other hand, Ruslana stood a foot shorter than him, short platinum hair lay as a crown on her round face, baby blue eyes fought against her provocative clothes to convince you of her sweet nature and she definitely enjoyed a good Greek pork chop.

Drinks flowed down dry throats and music covered all other sounds. The group of five found themselves dancing in the middle of the spacious living room. Thomas pushed himself up against Ludmila, while Nick caressed her from behind. Soon, Ludmila was on her knees and both men lowered their trousers. Ruslana led Michael to the sofa, her right hand on his genitals, her lips on his neck.

'Give me a second,' Michael said. 'Toilet,' he added as he rushed off.

Ludmila undressed and by the time he returned, she was bare from head to toe. 'Hey Nick, let Thomas go have his fun. Come help me out with this one,' Michael said, placing his hand on his friend's shoulder. A mischievous grin graced Nick's face as he pulled up his boxer shorts, failing to cover his erection, and followed Michael to the nude lady calling out to them. Thomas picked up Ruslana in his strong hands and with his trousers around his ankles, he wiggled off to his bedroom.

Michael smiled as he saw Thomas disappear into the shadows of the hallway, before closing his eyes as Ludmila's teeth bit his nipple and pulled down his trousers.

Back in the bedroom, Thomas's vanity helped to cover the little red light hiding behind The Hobbit on the black wooden bookcase. Thomas insisted on lights on, sure about his athletic build, his manly looks and his quite-above-average penis.

The following morning found them all in the hands of Morpheus; all but one. Michael carried the same beer in his hand all night, pretended that he kept on drinking with the others, poured Ruslana's offered glass of vodka in Thomas's Aloe Vera plant and spat every shot into his beer bottle. He had slept before the party and waited patiently for the tired drunks to fall asleep.

When the girls woke up, he was long gone. They dressed

and tiptoed out, happy to have been paid upfront and thus avoiding morning confrontations with customers demanding more sexual favors, before paying up.

At home, Michael kept his frail mind busy with house chores. Joan was returning to the island in the evening.

'Be at the port at six, my love,' Joan said over the telephone.

'Of course,' he replied. 'I've missed you.'

'Maybe I should go away more often, then. Make you miss and appreciate me more,' she said and giggled.

'Oh, my dear. Trust me. I appreciate everything you've done to me. See you soon,' he said and closed the phone.

Hours later, he parked his AUDI 3, next to the closed-for-the-winter ice-cream parlor and gazed out of his open window. Menacing grey clouds had gathered above and timid thunder could be heard. A fat drop of rain fell on his windscreen and Michael watched as it snaked down the glass leaving behind it a shiny, wet, river-like line.

'That's all we are. An insignificant drop. Thrown into life, sliding along, leaving a path behind us. Soon, both to be forgotten and gone forever...'

More drops followed and the gust carried rain into his car. He did not bother to close the window. He kept on gazing at the dark horizon. A figure of a ferry formed upon the startling deep-blue waters.

'What a fitting return for your black soul, queen of sluts, Joan...'

The ferry swung slowly to its side and approached the concrete pier with the old tires hanging from its sides. As it came to a halt -as much as it could master against the powerful waves, people rushed out of their parked vehicles, umbrellas held high, to welcome their loved ones. Michael exited the car, closed black umbrella by his side and strolled casually down the long dock.

'Baby?' he called out and waved as he saw Joan standing under the last dry haven offered by the boat. He ran towards her and passed her the umbrella. Her eyes smiled and her lips blew out a kiss. She opened it and reluctantly stepped off the ferry, small luggage in hand. 'You're soaking wet!'

'It's raining? I haven't noticed,' he replied, raindrops racing upon his face.

'You're a fool, but you're my fool,' she laughed and kissed him gently on his damp lips.

'Oh, I'm great at being a fool, that's for sure,' he said, laughed and took her pink bag.

Back in the safety and warmth of their home, they dined and Michael heard Joan's family news as they drank dry red wine.

'I can't believe you cooked,' she said. 'I was expecting takeaway pizza. Boy, this chicken curry is amazing,' she continued and took another mouthful of rice. 'So, as I said, my mother had no idea that her auntie had passed away and kept on asking poor Helen about the village. Oh, it was tragic. Funny, but tragic. But, don't let me blah blah blah all night. What have you been up to?'

Michael continued sipping his wine until his glass help no more. 'Oh, you know. I pretty much told you everything over the phone. Movies, fishing and such...'

'No news at all?' she asked, cutting into her chicken.

'Now that you say it. I opened your car yesterday. Was looking to check your car insurance's expiry date and I noticed a small package addressed to you.'

Joan's hands came to a stand-still. She squinted her eyes and looked straight at him. 'A package?'

'Yeah, a small one, wrapped in brown paper and taped. It just had your name written on it.'

'Did you open it?'

Michael continued to chew his meat as he shook his head. 'Nope. Left it on your bedside table,' he finally said after swallowing his forkful.

'Oh, now I remember. It's been there for ages. Katerina at the stationary gave me something for the office,' she lied. 'So, did fishing go well? What did you catch?'

'It went great,' Michael replied, scratching his nose. 'Caught so much.'

'Happy for you, dear,' she said rather apathetically. 'I'm full. I think I need a good shower and a rest, if you don't mind.'

Michael shook his head as he took another juicy bit of meat and watched a lonely pea free dive off his fork.

Joan stood up and rushed to their bedroom, closing the heavy door behind her. Minutes later, running water could be heard. Michael was positive about what she was up to. He licked his lips as he pictured her watching Thomas fucking someone else. *'Revenge. Sweeter than my curry chicken. If only I could have drugged you and placed you next to them.'*

Michael snuggled up on his living room sofa, under his favorite green blanket, and started streaming the latest Westworld episode when Joan approached him with a steaming cup in hand.

'What's this?' he asked, taking the hot beverage in his cold hands.

'Your favorite. Cadbury's hot chocolate with a touch of ground Arabica coffee beans. The least I could do. You cooked and I'm awful company. This migraine is killing me. The ferry trip did a work on me. I'm off to bed,' she said and pecked him on his cheek. 'Hope you're not disappointed. Horny after me being away for days.'

'I'll try and cope. You can make it up to me tomorrow,' he commented; his eyes never leaving the TV screen.

'Sure,' she replied, having already walked towards their bedroom door. 'Good night,' she added and closed the door behind her.

Twenty minutes later, Joan stuck her head out of the room and called out to Michael. 'Babe? Babe?' she repeated, louder each time. Michael's eyes were shut and his mouth hung open. She walked up to him, placed her hands on his shoulders and shook him. She placed her phone to her ear. 'Yeah, he's out,' was all she said and seconds later, there was a slight knock on the door.

Thomas rushed into the house as she opened the entrance. 'I can't believe you texted me that tonight I would be seeing you. I've missed you, too,' he said, picking her light figure into his strong arms. Joan forced a smile. 'Come in the bedroom,' she said, pushed him back and walked off towards her room.

'Oh, he's here.' Thomas took off his jacket and threw it on Michael's head. 'Who's a good coat hanger, who?' he said, mimicking a baby's voice and kissed Michael on his cheek.

'Hurry up,' Joan's voice came from inside the bedroom. Thomas scurried cheerfully from the living room, dropping his shirt onto the floor before entering his lover's bedroom.

'What's wrong?' he asked as he noticed Joan standing by the window, cigarette in her right hand, wine in the other and a frown upon her face.

'You! You stupid bastard!' she shouted, throwing the glass of wine towards him. Thomas ducked and replied, 'What the fuck, Joan? You just got...'

'Shut up, you cheating bastard!'

'What? That's rich coming from you!'

Joan screamed and ran towards him, her hands hitting him on his bare chest. Thomas grabbed both her hands and fell upon her, both of them landing on the bed. 'Is this a weird scenario or something? Want me to rape you...'

'What are you on about? You sent me the video...'

He looked puzzled. He let go of her red wrists. 'What video?'

Joan's hand slid across the bed, reaching for the camcorder on her pillow. She handed it to him and the note that came with it.

'Found a new partner for our game,' he read and pressed play to see him having sex with Ruslana.

'I believed you were different! I was going to murder my husband for you! We said in March, during our camping trip, but no, you couldn't keep your cock in your trousers long enough. I was going to risk everything for you. I loved you...'

'Joan, wait. I didn't send you this.'

Both stood staring at each other.

The sound of the cocking of the gun broke the silence between them. Thomas turned to see Michael standing by the door, revolver in hand. Thomas took a few steps back.

'Whoa, mate. Wait...'

'For once in your life, shut the fuck up, Tom,' Michael said calmly.

'How...' Joan tried to form a sentence.

'Your little drug bag? I found it. As if I would drink anything made by you. Kill me, huh?'

'Babe, I...'

'Don't call me babe!' he shouted and raised the gun.

'You know, I was just planning on scaring you two. Maybe just hurt Thomas for raping me...'

'What?' Joan's jaw dropped on her ashen face.

'Oh, yes. He raped me on New Year's Eve, as you sat with your sister. That's the kind of sicko you were going to leave me for. Leave me! Now, I hear, you were going to kill me. House, life insurance, real estate office and a lover. Joan would have had it all!'

'I'm sorry...'

'Too late!' he replied and shot her straight in the face. Her body shook violently and dropped to the ground. Blood sprayed across Thomas's face and parts of skin and brains crushed upon the white wall behind her.

Thomas let out an animal-like scream. 'This can't be happening!' he yelled. 'Stop!'

'Too late!' Michael repeated and shot him between the legs. Thomas's eyes opened wide as he fell to the cold floor; blood oozing from his genitals. The pain registered by his brain was unimaginable. Michael sauntered towards him. 'Suck on this,' he said, placing the gun into Thomas's screaming mouth. He took a deep breath and pulled the trigger.

When the police arrived, they found Michael, covered in blood, sitting relaxed in front of the television, watching The Shawshank Redemption.

'You know what? I've seen this over twenty times, but this is the first time that I truly believe he *did* murder his wife!'

FEBRUARY OF SANITY

-Something like an intro-

Reality eluded me.

It was a concept my frail mind never conquered.

I travelled in and out of it with the same ease you, my dear reader, travel to work, to school, to the market, to the next room.

Labels.

I had many labels growing up.

'Hyperactive.'

'Has problems focusing.'

'In his own world.'

'Autistic.'

'Weird.'

'Strange.'

'A.D.D.'

'Schizophrenic.'

The label 'danger to himself and to others' came much

later in life and you could call it *the final straw* for my hard-working, religious, 'fed-up' parents.

I remember my last day of freedom well.

It ended with me standing on top of the roof of my high school. Not a single piece of clothing upon my wet body. Blood dripped from my wrists as I prepared to jump.

My name is Jonah.

I was eighteen years old and this is my story -or should I write this is my warning? A plea to keep your sanity?

I know it sounds quite Lemony Snicket of me, it is not something I have thought of doing, but this is my time in an asylum and the glimpses of my life leading up to my *imprisonment*... if you're looking for a feel-good story, please look away.

Stop reading these words.

Go back to your blissful ignorance (I wish I could); to not knowing Jonah Petraki's life.

I will probably die before the end page...

February, 2004

Fluorescent light illuminated the small white-walled room. Seven o'clock sharp. All lights set to a timer, forcing my life into a fixed routine. You could choose to fight. To hide below your bed sheets and tightly close your eyes as if a sleepy child refusing to get up for school. The battle, though, would be fruitless. The nurses came knocking a quarter of an hour later.

I awoke with apathy. My colorful mind awake in an environment of faded white. My body dressed in white, warm between white sheets; all as white as cheap detergent would allow. My body awoke in a tired state, even after having enjoyed eight hours of slumber.

My vivid dreams evanesced as I stood up, my bare feet cooling on the cold tiles. I ambled to my lone, wish-it-was-bigger window and like Moses, I pulled the ripped curtains apart. Like dark waves they rolled back and the Promised Land filled my horizon. The city of Rhodes. My home town.

I longed to return home. I longed to go back to what I considered my norm. But, my parents and the strict judge with the well-trimmed grey beard had other plans for me.

The next twenty minutes could have been a perfect replica of the previous day. A fine copy-paste of each of my precursory ninety-six mornings in the gloomy mental institution that was now my home.

Pee, brush teeth, get dressed, say good morning to my roommate Matthew, head to the breakfast room, saying good morning along the way to fellow patients and to members of staff. Routine.

I never understood the need to say good morning, yet I always did. Two words encoded in my labyrinth of a mind. I uttered the set of words and kept on going, never answering the moronic and oxymoronic question, nurses always asked after the exchange of greetings.

'And how are you feeling today, Jonah?'

I'm schizophrenic. What exactly are you asking?

Could I be a happy schizophrenic?

Oxymoron. Same as a jumbo shrimp. Dreadful as a beautiful funeral.

Matthew limped along behind me, a smile spread upon his pale face. He loved answering The Question. He lived for the moment. Born with an extra chromosome of wicked humor, he came up with various ways to reply. He would even stay up late at night, jotting his ideas down to paper.

'And how are you feeling today, Matthew?'

'Moo, moooooo,' he would reply.

'Good morning, Matthew. Sleep well?'

'Woof, woof,' he would bark.

Juvenile silliness from a grown man of nearly thirty, yet he found it amusing and anything that helped cope with the long monotonous days ahead was okay in my book.

The breakfast room which transformed into a lunch room, then a dinner room and occasionally into a general gathering room, was a vast rectangle of a room with lights running along its high ceiling and a generous view of the institution's grounds. On fine Greek sunny days, patients would enjoy their first meal of the day, swallow their first set of prescription pills and spread out into the well-maintained gardens of the asylum. Under the watchful eyes of the medical personnel, the Herculean guards and the security cameras lingering above, of course. Not that you could get far, even if you avoided being seen. A tall brick wall featuring barbed wire on its top, ran around the land. The first time I met the wall, I told my mother that it reminded me of Uncle Stanley. She just exchanged a worried look with my father and forced a smile in my direction. That lousy excuse of a smile. The smile that hid her sorrow. Sorrow born from my 'condition' -her word, not mine. All I meant was that the tangled barb wire resembled Uncle Stanley's thick curls.

I stepped into the scrambled egg-smelling room and let my nose be tickled by the aroma of crispy bacon. I loved eating. It was one of my favorite pleasures. One both my body and mind could understand and enjoy. Matthew's pleasure came from getting to see the girls from the building opposite our own. He would stare at them, his small eyes following them around; his photographic memory making imprints of them in the back of his mind. Images he would later recall as he pleased himself in our bathroom while trying -and failing- to control his grunts. I was a firm believer that every single human being had beauty. Maybe I focused on different aspects than others did. I found it fascinating how seven billion people all looked dissimilar. Other shades of skin, hair color, scars, freckles, eye shape. Thousands of details that formed a face. I could think of nothing more exciting. All beauty. However, I often heard poor Matthew being called ugly. Ugly! Even the word sounds ugly. That extra chromosome did not help with his face symmetry that people tend to label as attractive.

Matthew and I took trays and stood in line, slowly passing in front of tired workers complaining about Monday. I wish *Monday* was my biggest problem. Cold sweat on my forehead was my issue at the moment. One hundred and thirty-two patients meant two hundred and sixty-four eyes were watching me. And that is without taking into consideration the kitchen staff, nurses and guards that varied in numbers. All watching me. I could feel their eyes roaming the back of my head. Running freely along my body. Studying me...

'Bread or toast?' the question from the kind elderly lady with the red glasses, pulled me out of my thoughts.

'Toast,' I whispered and stared at the floor. Matthew's shoes were dirty. I cleaned all my belongings before sleeping and re-arranged them either by size, color or first letter of their name.

As I raise my eyes, there she was. Standing still in the moving chaos around her. Her red locks dancing in the breeze that lived between the entrance and the veranda's sliding doors. She had green eyes, like mine yet brighter, more mysterious. She awkwardly licked her coral lips and exhaled deeply. Her starved body remained still, a thin flower in a room of weeds and parasites. It was my turn to stare. My brain washed away everything around her. She stood in the center of my mind, rainbows dancing around her, stars shining down upon her pale face, planets colliding in the background and supernovas dying, fading away, ashamed by her stunning beauty.

'Orange or apple juice?'

'Oh, for freaking sake!'

'Excuse me?' the tall lady raised her voice.

'Sorry, Mrs. Petrou. You woke me from a dream. No juice, thanks,' I mumbled and rushed along the line. My eyes stayed on the petite girl. A nurse came to her side and pointed her to the food queue. She was new.

The new girl.

It felt like high school. I was in love with the new girl.

John was not at breakfast.

I decided to seek where my best friend was.

John was a mute who resided in the west wing of the building. The *notorious wing* as many referred to it. It had maximum security due to the list of crimes committed by many of its patients. Killers, rapists and other criminals without a sane mind, occupied its narrow rooms. Most without the privilege of free pass. Most not allowed to mingle with the rest of us 'crazies'. John was not one of them. Often, I would see his tall figure in the garden, in the TV room, in the dining hall.

I guess his crime was not as severe as others.

A crime I was unaware of. I never asked, he never told.

I met John at a common group session with Dr. Stephano. Sitting in a circle with a bunch of others was never the highlight of my day. Too many eyes, you see. However, John was the first that I met in here whose eyes remained permanently glued to the floor. It was a wonder how he never bumped into walls and furniture. I for sure, would at least have a neck ache from his lowered head posture.

I first spoke to him by the coffee table.

'Hello, I'm Jonah,' I managed to say.

His eyes never moved from the task his hands were preoccupied with. He stirred his milky coffee and watched as the sugar vanished into the hot brown beverage. He placed the spoon on the white tablecloth, leaving an oddly-shaped stain behind. He took out a small notepad from his pocket and with his sharpened pencil he wrote 'I'M JOHN. I'M 25. I LIKE MOVIES. I'M A MUTE.'

'But can you hear me?'

He nodded. 'I like movies, too. I'm only eighteen,' I continued.

And that was it. A friendship was born.

To someone who constantly felt all eyes crawling on him and with voices living permanently in my mind, a mute friend who kept his eyes to himself was the ideal friend.

Daily we would spend hours together. Playing table tennis in the recreation room, coming up with weird nicknames for the nurses and silently sitting on a garden bench reading. I was a huge Agatha Christie and Stephen King fan, while John preferred magazines and comics. I guess he needed the pictures. The only activity he enjoyed that I could not follow was his passion for late night TV. Doctors recommended I stay clear from the escapism of television.

My mind was too frail and my Hollywood passion too large. Ever since I was a child, I was infatuated with movies and TV series. The downside was that I had trouble separating what I saw from reality.

I must have been just a few months older than a perfect six.

My father had an important business dinner plan and as he said, my mama 'had to be with him.' Maria, my mother, was reluctant to leave her restless six-year-old son and her nine-year-old daughter under the care of her degenerate seventeen-year-old son. Mark, my brother, was a free teenage spirit. His good looks and his daredevil sense of a good time usually landed him in trouble.

'It's time we gave him some responsibilities,' Panayiotis, my father, said. 'No wonder he doesn't give a shit about anything. He is spoiled. My father used to force us to...'

'Okay, okay. I'll come with you. No after-wartime stories about how many chores our generation had to do, please!'

That night the three of us sank into our living room sofa; pizza on the table and soft drinks by its side. Batman Returns was my brother's choice of a movie. Definitely not the movie my mother had agreed on.

Needless to say, my parents were shortly alerted by my brother and came home to a fire truck parked by their home. Firemen were approaching their house's roof as to get close to the young boy, dressed in all black, with a sheet for a cape, running around upon the orange roof tiles shouting, 'die, Penguin, die!'

Rain plummeted down and crushed against Dr. Stephano's rather large oval office windows. The olive-skinned man sat in his usual posture. Leaned back, relaxed, one leg upon the other, with his notepad lying on his right leg. I believe his blue Parker pen was permanently glued to his left hand as were his thin-framed reading glasses that hung on the edge of his Roman nose, giving him the ability to stare at me clearly and jot down my non-sense of answers with the aid of the special lens.

I, on the other hand, sat curled up on the armchair opposite him with my arms wrapped around my shaking knees as I jumped with every thunder February threw at us.

The tip of his tongue caressed his upper lip. The sign that a question was coming.

'So, a new girl you say?'

I nodded.

'And you saw her in the cafeteria?' his low smooth voice continued with the questions.

I nodded again.

'You've gone quiet, Jonah. You came in here ten minutes ago chatting about your perfect day...'

'Sorry...'

'No need to apologize,' he said, leaning forward. 'I'm just interested in your day. It's nice to see you smiling for a change.'

I smiled widely. No teeth. 'Well, Matthew was good. More lucid. His new meds seem to be helping. I fell in love with the new girl and I spent the evening with my best friend, John. What more could I ask for?'

His pen dashed along the empty lines of his pad filling it with Dr. Stephano's hieroglyphics. I could not be convinced that his scribbling was proper English words. More like my grandfather's cardiogram.

'How is your new medication?'

'Different shade of blue,' I muttered.

'Excuse me?' his eyes raised from behind the black frame.

'The new pills. They are the same size as before. Same pharmaceutical company, yet a shade lighter in the color.'

'And how are they helping with your dreams?'

I scratched my thick hair. 'They seem normal to me?'

'What was your last dream you remember?'

'Erm, being free, I guess. Sitting in literature class at school, having fun. But not with my classmates. I was with friends and staff from here.'

'Hmm, interesting,' he commented and continued writing. 'Was John there, too?'

I nodded. 'He was the teacher,' I said and burst out laughing. 'A mute as the teacher!'

Midnight came yet the rainfall did not call it a night. The pouring not only continued but grew into a raging storm. Palm leaves sang in the attack of the squalls and flower pots rolled around freely, adding bass to their song.

Inside, few hallway lights remained.

'Off for my rounds,' Miss Violet, the young French nurse said.

Mrs. Angela nodded, her eyes never leaving the repeat episode of her favorite Mexican soap opera. 'What a glorious life you're living Violet! Definitely worth leaving the French Riviera for!' she joked.

'There was no Vasili on the French coast,' Violet replied, pulling her red hair back into a high ponytail and walking off down the long corridor. As she distanced herself from the nurse's office light, she switched on her flashlight.

'Tout le monde est sage, dans le voisinage. Il est l'heure

d'aller dormir, le sommeil va bientot venir...' she sang as she went along, checking doors were closed and eyes were shut.

Thunder pierced the haunting silence of the dark TV room. 'What shitty weather...' she whispered as the light from her flashlight danced upon the walls and grounds. The room was empty. She turned to leave. Lighting followed the thunder and illuminated the room, revealing an inky figure standing right in front of her.

The man grabbed her by her wavy hair, his fingers twirling inside her scarlet hair, and he pulled her down. Miss Violet landed on her knees. She opened her mouth, yet the knife allowed no sound to be released. The blade came down in force, piercing through her cheek; the kitchen knife visible inside her opened mouth. She fell to the cold dirty floor, twitching in pain; blood was oozing out slowly. The man sat upon her torso.

'Please... don't! Je t'en supplie...'

With crimson blood dripping from its end, the knife came down again, shining in the darkness and penetrated her chest, puncturing her fast-beating heart. A silent cry escaped her trembling lips and with hollow eyes, Miss Violet's head fell back and hit the ground.

'You met me at a very strange time in my life...'

By the next thunder, Miss Violet's lifeless body was dragged away.

Dawn came; sunrays were emerging from behind weak white clouds. They had given as much rain as they could. Soon, they dispersed. Like a menacing gang of juveniles wrecking their local park during the night and running home to safety before cockcrow.

Morning routine followed, reminding me of my brother's cherished T-shirt. 'Same shit, different day' was printed on its black fabric, in bold yellow letters.

The exception to the day's fixed pattern came with Elizabeth's manic screaming. Her croaky yells for help followed. 'Help! The dead are here to kill us! It's a zombie apocalypse! Take cover. The blood demon is in the bathroom!'

If it was anyone else from us Looneys, the staff would have smiled and tried to calm us, but Elizabeth was not your average institutionalized mad woman. On the verge of a catatonic state, she spoke to no one. Self-inflicted alalia.

The sound of her previously unheard of voice in combination with the terror in her eyes, made the staff rush to the direction of the girls' lavatory.

'Did she say blood?' the male nurse asked his colleague, running by his side.

She nodded. 'I hope it's not someone cutting herself again.'

Neither was prepared for the macabre sight waiting for them behind the scratched burgundy door.

A dead body stood before their eyes. Her arms tied against the cubicles. Her head leaned back and her bloody legs crossed.

'My Lord...'

'Is that Violet?'

In a matter of minutes, staff was alerted and Dr. Spanos, the institution's director, ordered that every patient be counted for and returned to their rooms.

'Locked rooms all around until the police arrive...'

'Sir? Sir?' Dr. Andreas tugged on his white robe.

'What?' he asked, more stressed than angry.

Dr. Andreas leaned forward, bringing his lips an inch

from Dr. Spano's right ear. 'Mrs. Angela, the other night nurse, is also missing!'

Dr. Spanos swallowed his cough and his neck veins twisted as he found himself lost for words.

Dr. Andreas placed his hand on his shoulder and leaned forward again. 'Don't worry. I have people looking around for her. I'm sure she is fine,' he whispered, trying for the last line to sound convincing. 'Now, go be your fabulous self and be in charge. You've got this!'

Dr. Spanos forced a flatline smile and carefully stroked Dr. Andreas's hand with his index finger. Relationships at the workplace were difficult to maintain a secret.

'I'll go help in the search,' Dr. Andreas continued, fixed his thick-framed glasses on his fleshy nose and dashed down the wide corridor.

Dr. Spanos exhaled and walked to the main entrance to meet the police.

'Can I have your jello?'

Matthew banged his palms on the white table, three times. Our trays shook and my fresh orange juice nearly spilt over. Nearly. I took my eyes off the institution's staff gathering by the doors and caught my wobbling glass.

'Huh?'

Matthew giggled. 'Where's your mind, man? Can I have your jello?' he raised his voice.

'*Good question. The mind one, not the jello!*' I thought and passed him the plastic cup with the cheap dessert that pretended to be strawberry-flavored. Too much pretending in this world.

'Why are you worried?' Matthew mumbled with his jello-filled mouth.

'The new girl isn't here and something serious is going on... and... and...'

'What?' More giggles followed, drowned out by the slurping sounds of fake-strawberry dessert being devoured.

'And, I'm worried about John. He stays up all night watching movies. Something happened last night,' I raised my voice, wiped the sweat forming on my wide forehead and licked my dry lips.

'Everyone back to your rooms! Now! In order!'

'Room check, in ten minutes! Quickly!'

Tensed voices echoed around the vast cafeteria. Nurses wheeled away the patients confined to wheelchairs, and assisted elders. The rest did as they were told. Following orders was easy for simpler or if you prefer, more complicated minds. Tomato, tomayto.

I hid under the table, taking with me a chocolate-filled bagel, stuffing it in my pocket. Breakfast is important after all.

'What are you doing? Matthew asked as he stood up, ready to get in line and plod back to our room.

'Sssshh! Go ahead. I'll be there in ten. I have to find John. I sense he is in danger.'

Matthew shook his head. 'You're mad. Bye. See you later!'

Being called mad in a mental institution, where I was sent by the court, by the craziest person I have ever met is an understatement of irony.

Below the surface of the plastic tables and the yelling by staff, I crept to the kitchen. Safe away from wandering eyes, I lifted myself from the lemon-smelling tiles and rushed to the back door. I sneaked around the buildings, hid behind a dying plant imprisoned in a large peat pot and when I was sure the coast was clear -or I missed the coast, the carefree waves tingling my toes as my feet sank into the sandy beach, I made my way to the TV room.

John was nowhere to be seen.

'*He's probably safe. Gone back to his room as told. Where do the criminals sleep by the way?*' I asked myself. I still didn't know John's crime. My gut retaliated at my decision to leave and return to my cell of a room. I couldn't shake the notion of John being in danger. My eyes looked down. Something was out of place. My mind came with many features. Photographic memory being one of them.

'That carpet does not belong there. The red carpet is always under the Lego boxes,' I spoke aloud as I turned to see the see-through storage boxes filled with building blocks in their rightful place, below the second window. They sat on the bare floor. I knelt and stroked the carpet. Same feel as my deceased cat, Tiggy. It was without a doubt the Lego rug. I picked it up by its sides and decided to return it back to its home.

I stepped back in fear to dirty my white laceless shoes. A faded pool of red paint, lines scrubbed into it like a Van Gogh painting, spread out on the floor.

'The TV room is just around the corner,' a male nurse stated.

I turned towards the direction of the voice. No one was to be seen, but echoes of multiple footsteps marched towards me.

I dropped the carpet from my quivering small hands, feeling its loose threads sliding through my icy fingers. I ran and leaped over the LEGO boxes and sat down behind them; my head between my knees.

Through the plastic boxes, I saw a tall detective walk up to the pile of a carpet and kneel besides the paint.

'Oh, Lord,' I heard the director say, standing behind him with two officers of the law by his side. 'Is that blood?'

The tall detective waved to him to be quiet and his piercing blue eyes turned towards my direction. By the time, I place my hands upon my beating heart, I was being ordered to stand up and put my hands upon my head.

'Am I being arrested just like on *that* day?' I asked as I obeyed.

Both cops had their guns pointed towards me.

'Come out,' the detective said calmly.

'Jonah? What are you doing here?' Dr. Spanos asked.

'So, you are Jonah,' the detective said with a hint of satisfaction coloring his smooth voice. His smug face worried me. 'Come on, Jonah. Let's go have a coffee.'

With my head pointing towards the ground, I replied that I did not drink coffee.

'Hot cocoa, then. Even better,' he continued.

'Is my friend John okay?'

I received no answer. I wish I knew the new girl's name, to inquire about her, too. A murder had taken place and I had no idea where they were. As they say in the movies, 'I fear the worst.'

Both cops held me under my armpits and led me back to my room. Neither paid any attention to what I was saying. I began to doubt if I was talking aloud. 'What's in the box?' I shouted my favorite movie line.

Dr. Spanos, who was following them, squinted his eyes and exhaled through his nostrils. A sign that he was disappointed. I decided to be quiet, close my eyes and listen to his conversation with the scruffy-looking detective.

'Is he an adult?'

'Barely. Eighteen, but we should bring in his parents.'

'Can I interview him?'

'Let's talk to his doctor first.'

I opened my eyes with the unlocking of the heavy door. 'My room!'

My eyes lit up with joy. I was not in trouble after all. I was just being taken back to my room. Probably for my safety. My joy continued as the door closed behind me and I found John sitting on my untidy bed.

'John? John!' I said and rushed to hug my friend. 'I was so worried. Why are you here?'

He took his pencil and began to write. I watched line after line as the tip of the pencil ran along the thin white paper. He passed me the note and lifted my pillow. A VHS tape slept under it.

'What's that?' I asked. John pointed to the note in my hands.

I read it in a whispery manner. 'My ward is closed off. Our nurses put one of us in every room in your ward. I did something bad last night. The tape is from the security cameras. I don't know what to do.'

I sat down beside him. I placed my hand on his leg. 'Oh, John. Not again.'

We sat in silence, gazing across the room at the mound that was Matthew curled up under his sheets and fast asleep.

'How can he sleep at times like these?'

John wrote down. 'He said it was an opportunity to catch up on lost sleep.'

I swallowed a lump in my throat. 'That's why I sleep for

eight hours. To feel fresh and energetic in the glorious mornings.'

John passed me another note. 'Really!'

I laughed. He had a point. I was drained, morning in, morning out.

The banging on the door killed my laughter. I felt the swift breeze hitting me as the door swung violently open. 'Jonah, come with us,' the police officer with the red lipstick and silky black hair ordered.

The empty corridor had never appeared so long before. Its once welcoming walls, seemed dark and hollow. I had only been to the building's main offices once before -during my first day. Glimpses of my crying mother flashed through my fragile mind. My dad signing the various papers needed for my court-mandated stay.

For a split second, I could swear I could hear her breathily sobbing as I was led into a bright room and instructed to sit in the lone chair behind the wooden table. Opposite me sat the white-haired detective of the Hellenic Police and Dr. Stephanos who welcomed me as if in session. A camcorder sat high upon a tripod behind them.

'Is this an interrogation?'

'Could be,' the tall man replied. 'I am Lefteris Hadjis, police captain. How are feeling today, Jonah?'

I straightened my posture. 'Okay, I guess. A bit worried.'

'Worried about what?'

I did not dare mention John and his tapes. He had confided in me as a friend. 'The stormy weather. It scares me.'

He tapped his fat fingers upon the table. 'Did you sleep well last night?'

I nodded. 'Watch any movies?' he asked; his eyes looking down at his noted.

'No movies for me. Doctor's orders.' I smiled at Dr. Stephanos who had never seemed distant before. A slight sweat grew on his short forehead. 'They confuse me,' I admitted.

'Then what were you doing in the TV room last night then, Jonah if you weren't watching a movie? Did you go to play LEGOs? That's where we find you.'

'No, sir. You are mistaken. I sleep in my room every night. I never go out. I read...'

'Jonah?' Dr. Stephanos voice interrupted my fast flow of words. I felt warmth to hear his familiar voice at last. 'Relax. Concentrate. Close your eyes. Picture yourself leaving your room. We know you left your room. Miss Violet noted that you were missing during her rounds. That's why she came to find you. Think, Jonah. Picture last night.'

I closed my eyes.

'*I did leave my room. Why? Why did I go to the TV room? To find John?*'

'Jonah?'

'I think I might have gone to find John.'

'Was John there?' the police captain asked.

I nodded. 'Alone?' I nodded again.

'Did John hurt Miss Violet?'

I covered my face with my hands. 'Jonah, did John hurt Miss Violet?'

'I think so. He is my friend and I... I don't want to say something that would incriminate him.'

Dr. Stephanos leaned forward. 'Did John write something to you?'

'He showed me an old tape.'

The detective placed a VHS on the table. 'This?'

My eyes widened. 'You searched my room?'

'Do you know what's on the tape?'

I shook my head. 'How would *I* know?'

'Mrs. Angela says you took the tape, Jonah. And that you locked her in the closet with the brooms and mops. We found her an hour ago. You taped her mouth and tied her...'

'Lies! Lies! It was John,' I yelled and stood up, banging my palms upon the hard surface of the table. 'It's always him. He... he...'

'What, Jonah? What? Say it!' Dr. Stephano urged me, hoping for a breakthrough.

I stood motionless. I ground my teeth. 'He is the one that got me into this mess, this place. I'm innocent. It was John who attacked Mary!'

'That' day - June, 2003

Prom day had finally arrived. A hot Greek summer day faded as night time fell and fresh sea air dominated the gentle breeze. Unfortunately, neither the dropping weather degrees nor my protective-promising deodorant managed to prevent me from sweating.

'Stop pacing up and down, honey,' my mother said, smiling proudly at her white tuxedo-wearing son.

'Stand still,' my father's voice came from the stairs. He rushed down with his camera in hand. 'Let me take a picture of my handsome boy.'

That was my last happy moment with them.

The honking from the bus outside ended our family scene. Both quickly began repeating their advice for the night. Their *different* son, out alone at night with a bunch of drunken teens frightened them.

'I'll be fine,' I repeated for the twelfth time. If only I knew then, how right they were to worry.

I exited the door, waved them goodbye and dashed to the parked old-fashioned school bus. My senior class, all nineteen of us, decided to rent our town's former school bus and ride together for one last time. The choice was a relief to me. I had less friends than ears and there was no way, I was going to walk up to a girl and ask her to be my date. This way I was part of the group. A silent, shy, awkward part, but still a member. I smiled at the driver and jumped at the sound of the doors automatically closing behind me. With eyes lowered, I walked down the bus corridor and settled in an empty chair.

A scene pulled from an American teen movie unfolded before my wandering eyes. Everyone was so pretty. Handsome Greek guys all dressed up with perfect smiles and athletic builds. Stunning island beauties with curvy figures dressed with lavish clothes. '*Are we going to our senior party or to a magazine photoshoot?*'

The air conditioning was turned on; blowing out much needed cold air at full speed. June's first heat wave, with humidity as its ally, attacked the Aegean islands with fury. The hot thick air stuck to your skin, closing your pores, suffocating your attempts to breathe. '*I hate this weather. I wish it was February...*'

'What you looking at? Anything worth looking at is inside the bus. Jesus, that Martha is fine!'

Jacob Aspri. The chattiest, most sociable boy in school hopped on the chair beside me, waving and smiling at everyone in the rows behind us.

'Yes, she is. If I may say so. Is she your date?' I asked, trying to sound normal.

'You bet ya! I can't wait to get her alone,' he said and licked his lips.

He must have noticed my rosy cheeks and my lowered eyes, as he asked, 'you're still a virgin, right? Don't worry. The first time comes for us all. Do you want a condom? I brought loads.'

I was lost for words. My mouth opened, yet no sounds came out. My knees began to meet in the middle.

'Don't worry, my strange man. Jacob is here. I'll explain things to you.'

I exhaled deeply and replied quietly, 'I know what to do. I know I am inexperienced, that's why today, I saw porn for the first time.'

'First time? Wow!'

'Ssshhh. Please don't embarrass me.'

He placed his arm around me and pulled me closer. 'I know you get bullied a lot, but I just wanted you to know that I respect you. You're different and that's your right. So, what did you watch?' he asked, rubbing his hands together. 'Give us some details. And, who would you do it with?'

'The blowjob excited me the most. Seems nice...'

'Nice? It's freaking amazing!'

The commotion ongoing in the vehicle provided me with enough security to have such a conversation. People were drinking, singing and yelling out slurs about our teachers.

'I kind of like Mary. Her red hair... turns me on!'

Jacob laughed, slid a condom into my pocket and wished me luck.

The hot air invaded the bus as it came to a standstill

outside our school's freshly-painted gym. One by one, the class of 2003 exited the bus and rushed to have their photo taken. I passed the photo booth from behind and entered the vast building. Lights, music, magic. I chose a dark spot in the stands and sat there for most of the night. The dance swung into its second hour and the dance floor was filled with people moving around carefree and joyful. All four senior classes scattered under the disco lights. That was the moment, Jacob and a bunch of the so-called cool kids decided to ditch the chaperoned party and head for the nearby lake. As the group made its way towards the gym's side exit, Jacob noticed me.

'Jonah! Get up. Come on, we're going to the lake.'

Peter placed his hand on Jacob's shoulder. I read his lips. 'Don't invite the freak.'

'I feel sorry for him,' he replied. 'Move it, Jonah. Mary is coming, too!' he continued, raising his voice and winking at me.

I stood up and followed the group of screaming teenagers, running down the hill to the small lake. As they ran, clothes came off and were thrown to the side. With only their underwear on, they dove in.

The tranquil oil-green waters welcomed them. The towering oak trees hid them from the country road above. The slice of a moon provided them with enough light. The crickets sang to them. The fireflies danced for them. Nature opened her arms and embraced them.

The night sky above us and its myriads of stars waited for me. I stopped a foot away from the lake's edge. I undressed at my own pace, folded my clothes and placed them carefully in a neat pile. With my hands in front of me, I entered the warm waters. Soon, swimming and splashing gave way to kissing as most coupled up. Others exited the lake and lay in groups of three upon the wet muddy grass; beer cans and bottles of vodka stood by their side.

I sat alone, under an old fig tree, the night breeze as my sole company.

I shook my head as to make sure my mind was not imagining another movie scene in my brain's theatre. An obviously drunk Mary clumped towards me. She raised the bottle in her left hand and devoured the last drops of Russian vodka.

'Get up,' she said, offering me her pale hand. She pulled me up.

'Hi, Mary,' I managed to say.

'You're cute when you smile. Come on,' she said, urging me to follow her. Water dripped from her black underwear and her fire-red locks. I shadowed her to behind the school's abandoned warehouse where the groundskeeper used to keep his garden tools. She leapt on the first step of the outside stairs.

'Now am at your height, kiss me.'

I moved forward. Our lips met. My fingers journeyed through her hair and I held her close, just like the man in my afternoon porn. John was his name. I wasn't as qualified or well-endowed as John, the pizza-delivery guy, but I was eager to please Mary.

'Slow down cowboy,' she said and pulled away from me. I pulled down my navy-blue boxers and revealed my erection.

'I have a special delivery for you,' I said the line from my evening entertainment.

'Hey, Jonah, I know I'm dru... drunk and all... and... and Jacob said you liked me... but... but you need to slow down,' she stuttered.

'Ssshh, no more talking!'

My hands entered her hair once again and I forced her to her knees. I ripped off her bra. 'No biting,' I warned as I brought my genitals to her face. I closed my eyes in delight. The next memory I have is Mary choking and turning to vomit. 'Sex time!' I declared. She wiped her lips and ran away. Her yells for help shook me back to reality. '*Oh, John! What have you done?*'

I dashed up the creaking steps and stood on the edge of the rusty tin-top roof. There with a bare soul and a naked body, I decided to end my life. I picked up a fragment of a broken wine bottle and began to cut through my left arm.

'Don't!' John begged. 'It will all be alright!'

I can't recall how long I listened to him pleading me to not kill myself, but flashing lights dancing through tree gaps informed me of the police's arrival. Soon, I was being pulled off the roof and placed into the back of an ambulance.

A month later, *we* entered the asylum.

February, 2019

I am thirty-three years old today.

Fifteen years have passed since the moment the police showed the footage on the videotapes in court.

I watched myself kill poor Miss Violet.

I witnessed as I attacked Mrs. Angela and threw her in the closet.

I did those crimes.

I heard in Dr. Stephanos statement how there was no new girl. It was Mary's image, I was seeing.

The tall detective showed covers of movies. 'This is Stig-mata. You can see the similarity in the posture of the dead body. This is Fight Club from where the killer's line above the dying nurse came from...'

My mind had failed me.

It took me a while to realize and accept that John was also a fiction of my vivid imagination. Every night I would sneak into the TV room and stay up until late, waking up exhausted the following morning.

Sentenced to prison for fifteen years. Sentenced to a cocktail of pharmaceuticals. Sentenced to sessions with various professionals and of course, Dr. Stephanos. My parents visited every Sunday. Routine.

I was freed on Christmas Eve, 2018. Everyone up for parole in 2019 was pardoned by the new prime-minister. Holidays with our families.

I fought hard to show that I was cured. Rid of my insanity.

Two months later and I could not pretend anymore. I still saw Mary. I also saw Miss Violet quite often. John now spoke to me. He was no longer a mute. His voice was roaming the dark corners of my mind. I admitted none of this to my treating doctors.

It came to me on a fine warm winter day. I could not trust my mind. I could not continue living as a burden to my growing-old parents. My mind always fought me. I decided to strike back.

It's amazing what you can buy online these days. Thank you, Breaking Bad for the tip.

I did warn you in the intro.

I will probably die at the end.

Ricin is already in me. The poison eating me from

within. This is my last line. I can't write any more. I love you, Mum. I love you, Dad. Thank you for being there. Enjoy your peace without me...

Good bye world...

MARCH OF REVENGE

PROTARAS, CYPRUS

March, 2018

Murder in paradise is as hideous as everywhere else.

Fig Tree Bay's warm hug embraced few swimmers this time of year; its high season beginning in a month or so. The island's best waters lingered in the small bay. Clear, pure, caressing the golden sand beach and carrying the freshness of the Mediterranean Sea.

The Bay's prominent fig trees glowed as they welcomed the rising sun's first rays of the day. Few workers had parked on the hill overlooking the bay and were busy opening up their restaurants, souvenir shops and ice-cream parlors.

A rental car parked between them; its red number plates separating it from the others. Tourists.

'I can't believe you woke us up so early,' the teenage girl whined, rubbing her eyes below her dark shades.

'We don't even wake up this early on school days,' her younger brother added.

'Well, if we were back in England, that's exactly where

you would be going in an hour,' his mother said, stepping out of the vehicle. 'Remember, this is all about your father celebrating his promotion. We promised to go along with whatever he wishes,' she continued, massaging her husband's bare back as he stood in front of her enjoying the view offered by Greek Mother Nature.

'What a glorious sunrise! Come on. A quick, cool morning swim and then... breakfast. Mmm, I can smell the bacon and hash browns already.'

The girl rolled her eyes. 'The shops haven't even opened yet!'

Her father ignored her remark and began to jog down the covered-in-beach-sand wooden-plaque path.

His wife remained smiling as she followed him and settled their beach bag, their *borrowed* hotel towels and her straw hat on two sunbeds, just meters from the tranquil sea. Her smile vanished as she dipped her toes into the pool-like waters.

'Jesus Christ, it's freezing!'

Both her children laughed as they rushed by her and dove in. Their father joined them and soon, the gang of three splashed away; attacking their matriarch as she ambled past them, acting brave, accepting their usual attack of cold water.

With a deep exhale, she plunged out of their sight and resurfaced away from them.

'Anyone up for swimming to the island?' she asked, pointing to the uninhabited islet that dominated the waters of the cove.

'Too early for exercising,' her daughter replied and swam out back to shore to add more sunscreen to her pale skin.

Her son shook his head. 'I'm hungry.'

'The restaurant hasn't opened yet,' his father replied. 'Want to build a sand castle?'

His son nodded with a smile and rushed out of the sea to fetch his beach toys.

'See you later, dear,' his wife said and began swimming away, soon to be standing on the first rock, covered with low vegetation. The squawking of the colony of seagulls caught her attention. Her blue beady eyes squinted as she tried to focus among their thin legs and long beaks.

'Is that a seal? What are they eating?' she asked aloud as the breeze carried over a stench that reminded her of the miasma that had hung around her run-over cat.

She hopped from rock to rock until her wet feet landed upon the plectrum-shaped island. She turned to see her family. All three covered in sand, building away their Never-land. Other swimmers had made their appearance, too, while the restaurant had finally opened. Her tummy was rumbling, yet she would never admit such a thing as it would set off her kids.

'One look and I'm heading back.'

Steady step after steady step, she approached the birds. Her presence scaring enough of them as to reveal their feast.

Quiet Susan -as her family and friends often referred to her by, never knew she could scream that loud. She fell back and sat in shock as she covered her eyes. That is where her husband found her and wrapped his strong arms around her trembling body. Together they swam back to shore and asked the Cypriot waiter, standing at the restaurant's entrance, to notify the police.

The lifeguard boat danced upon the waves of the open waters by the islet. Chief Inspector Demetriou stood on the bow of the twelve-meter boat, ready to disembark onto the rocky island. She watched as her partner, Sergeant Nick Nicolaou swam the short distance from shore, in full uniform. She shook her head, strikes of blond hair escaping her black sports cap, exhaled and whispered to the forensic officer behind her. 'Why do I get all the weirdos?'

'He says he is afraid of boats and gets seasick,' the young man in full white uniform explained. Demetriou bit her bottom lip, rolled her eyes, tucked away renegade hair and jumped off the vessel. With arms wide open, she did her best to scare away the seagulls. The corpse lay naked. She approached the body, hoping the eyes were shut. She was new to homicide; only seven months in the department after years in internal affairs. Three bodies with open eyes so far and all three stalked her nightmares. As she placed a white rubber glove on her right hand, the young forensic officer's voice came from behind her.

'I thought they said it was a female body,' he commented, looking at the manly chest and hairy left leg before him.

'His genitals have been cut off,' Demetriou said. 'That and his long hair must have confused the tourist lady. She did say, she did not come *that* close.'

'I don't blame her,' he replied, squatting by the mutilated dead man with the multiple stab wounds.

Demetriou pulled the man's black hair from his face. 'Holy Mary, protect us,' she said and placed her right hand on her necklace's silver cross. 'His eyes have been removed, too!'

'The seagulls?'

'I doubt it. The sockets look stabbed. Look at the knife marks here...'

She paused, sensing a presence behind her. A shadow moved alongside and then covered her. She could hear the drops of sea water falling from her partner, landing on the dry rock, living just for seconds under the sizzling and merciless Cypriot sun.

'Isn't that Thomas Keravnos?' he said, breathless and soaking wet.

'Who?' they both asked.

'The Ayia Napa mafia drug lord,' he replied, squeezing the bottom of his white shirt, releasing a short-lived pour.

Demetriou gazed at the ashen, bird-bitten, eyeless face of the fifty-something man. 'You're right,' she said, feeling slightly guilty at the tones of joy coloring her voice. She was not the type to wish the death of anybody, but she did feel relief that this was not some poor family man and was probably the result of a drug deal dispute.

News nowadays did not have to wait. Not for the evening news, nor the morning papers. Stories of interest spread like a digital wildfire; online flames jumping from device to device. Thomas Keravnos's death was such a story.

A notorious business man, he was also a popular sports figure on the eastern Mediterranean island. For his fans, he was a former footballer who made a fortune in tourism and bought his beloved team, leading them many times to the league title. For his employees at his hotels, casino, bars and night clubs, he was a generous boss who offered hefty bonuses on top of above-average wages. However, for society, the media and the police, he was as dirty as they came.

Human trafficking, illegal prostitution and drugs were known activities of his. Yet none ever proven in court.

Prestigious lawyer Adonis Stylianou already felt tired that morning. With only two clients down and twelve to go, he locked his office door, stepped out onto the little side balcony on the 17th floor of Ayia Napa's Marina West Tower and lit a much-needed second cigarette of the day. His right hand snuck in his robe's pocket and he lifted out his iPhone. 'Let me check my bets,' he whispered aloud. As he activated his Wi-Fi signal, multiple notifications flashed across the top of the screen. 'Death of gangster?' he read the title that caught his attention. As the link opened, his knees felt weak. He stumbled back a step or two and sat down upon the air conditioning unit that occupied a third of the small balcony. His eyes watered up. He exhaled deeply. 'Got what you deserved, you fat bastard!'

He lit another cigarette with the dying end of his previous one, ignoring his office telephone. His mind could not be further from his socialite client's divorce papers. He looked down at his wedding ring. A year as a widow had gone by and it still decorated his index finger. Love, guilt or both, he could not find the courage to slide it off. Unable to move on, once again, his mind drifted to *that* night.

Protaras, Cyprus
March, 2017

Adonis paced up and down his hotel room. His wife, Kate, was still getting ready. His green eyes fixed on his black Rolex. Cold sweat was forming on his wide forehead and conquering his armpits. The room was cool; his heart was not.

'*What the hell are you doing, Adonis?*'

His wild thoughts were driving him crazy. His hands, unable to remain still. He headed over to the mini bar. 'Famous Grouse and Jack Daniels. Great,' he whispered and opened both miniature bottles, devouring their contents in seconds.

He wiped away his tears and headed to the bedroom's door. Kate looked stunning in her red dress. Her short brown hair caressed her bare shoulders as she placed on her gold earrings.

'I have no idea,' she said, leaning closer to her cell phone.

'Well, whatever Adonis has planned for you tonight, have a good time,' her sister replied and with the sound of kisses, Kate ended the call.

Adonis could not bear to step into the room. '*Maybe I should call it all off? She's my wife!*'

Kate swung the leather chair round with her legs and stared at her nervous-looking husband. 'Okay, what's the matter with you? You've been acting weird all week. At first, I thought, oh no, he's lost more money on gambling, then you told me that you booked a remote motel for us to have a quiet weekend getaway and I thought, okay, all is good. Now, we are here and you haven't said a word to me all day. I don't even know where we are going tonight.'

Adonis swallowed the lump forming in his throat; his Adam apple bouncing like a yo-yo as he searched for words. Outside, a car could be heard driving into the empty car park. Headlights danced upon the motel's thin curtains and light fell on Adonis's guilty face.

'We're not going anyway,' he managed to say with a

weak voice. Kate squinted her eyes and tilted her head slightly to her right. 'I did lose money. A lot,' he continued, raising his voice. The slamming of car doors outside adding haste to his words. 'I won a few rounds and got cocky,' he added louder, interrupting his wife as she stood and started to complain about his addiction. 'I went into the high-ballers room. I kept on winning and ended up on the main table in the back... with Thomas Keravnos.'

Kate sat back down and placed her ashen face in her cold hands. Thomas Keravnos. Her ex-boss. 'How much did you lose?'

'The house, the office...'

'What?' she yelled, looking outside, unable to face him.

'But, I made a deal. A last bet. He gave me a chance....'

Kate stood up. 'Go on, what chance?'

Footsteps could be heard outside their door. Adonis exhaled, closed his eyes and unleashed his heart. 'A night with you.'

Kate stood motionless for a second or two. A smile was born upon her coral red lips. A smile that grew into a giggle and then laughter. 'You're joking, right? Pulling my leg? Is this one of your sick jokes that I am supposed to find funny?'

The knocking on the old wooden door came as her answer.

Kate's eyes opened wide. 'You're mad! I'm your wife, you dumb weak cunt!'

'He always fancied you. Had a thing for you from back in the day when you worked for him. It's just sex. Ten minutes and we save our house and our savings...'

'Then you sleep with him! I'm out of here,' she said and walked past him, spitting at his feet. 'I'm done. We're done.

I'm going to my mother's and on Monday, I'm divorcing you!'

Another thud was heard from the door. The sound of keys followed and the motel door was pushed open.

Kate stood in the middle of the room. Three men entered the room. Thomas and two hefty bodyguards.

'Close the door,' he ordered in his distinct croaky voice.

'*He owns the place,*' Kate thought, looking as his bodyguard used the motel's master key to lock the door. 'Mister Thomas, there has been a misunderstanding. My fool of a husband does not own me. I am not up for this. I'm sorry he wasted your time. Take our house, take his money, take him and break his legs. I don't care, but I am not sleeping with you...'

'I won you fair and square.'

Kate bit her bottom lip and stepped back as he approached her. 'This is illegal. You can't win a person. If you touch me, I'll scream.'

Thomas smiled and his eyes glowed. All he said was 'boys', and both men came at her. They picked her up by her arms and forced her into the bedroom. Kate shrieked, kicked and even managed to bite one of the men. He replied with a strong punch to her face. She fell back onto the cheap bed, her nose spraying it with droplets of crimson blood.

'Don't hurt her,' Adonis cried and turned to leave.

'Where are you going?' Thomas said, blocking his way. 'Sit!'

One bodyguard grabbed him from behind, forced him to his knees and placed his head on the mattress. Thomas squatted by his side. 'You're watching the whole thing. You have to see how bets are paid.' The second bodyguard tied Kate's wrists to the bed post and ripped off her dress and underwear. He placed his large hands over her mouth and nodded to his boss. Thomas climbed upon the bed and untied his belt. Kate shook her body to fight him off, only to receive another punch to her face. She felt drowsy as Thomas entered her. Tears ran freely from her beaten eyes. The bed shook and Adonis closed his eyes.

With a grunt, minutes later, Thomas Keravnos fell upon her. Kate could not breathe with him on top of her and her face covered by the bodyguard's hands. She gasped for needed air. Thomas's breath smelled of strong cigars.

Finally, he arose from her. 'Lock him up and have some fun, guys. I'll be enjoying a smoke in the lobby. I've got some business to discuss with the manager.'

'No, no. No more! Leave her alone,' Adonis begged. Thomas kicked him between his legs. Adonis fell to the dusty floor, only to be picked up by the hair. The tall body-guard with the curly hair dragged him to the closet and locked him in. There, in the darkness, Adonis continued to hear his wife's ordeal. With his head between his knees, he waited. He lost track of time. He placed his ear on the crack of the closet doors. Silence lingered outside the confined space.

Adonis brought his eye close to the dimly lit line separating the closet doors. An empty old-fashioned armchair and a faded painting came in sight. He moved around, trying to broaden his view. Kate's bare feet hung from the old creaky bed.

'Kate? Kate?' he called out. No reply came. Her stillness scared him. He began kicking the thin-wood doors; his right foot opened a gap big enough for his arm to pass through and unlock the wardrobe.

He froze in shock before the double bed. His wife lay badly beaten; blood and bruises between her legs. He placed his hand over his mouth. He rushed to her side. She was not breathing. He slid off the bed, sat on the floor and cried. Cried like never before. The love of his life, raped to death for a stupid card game.

Voices came from outside. He recognized the high-pitched voice of the manager.

'Is he coming here? Could he be ordered to finish me off? Is that the business Thomas had in the lobby? What if he is with the police? Thomas owns half the department! They will frame me...'

In a state of terror, Adonis did not wait for his thoughts to be answered. His survival instincts kicked in and he stood up. He lifted his light thin wife and threw her over his shoulder. He made a run for the fire exit; car keys in hand. He plodded down the fire escape and metal screeching followed the thud of his steps.

He paused at the corner of the motel. The car park was deserted. His white antique Beetle waited below the tallest oak tree. He dashed out into the open, glad the aging motel had no security cameras. He bit his lips and avoided looking at her face as he dropped Kate into the boot of his prized Volkswagen. He ran back up to the room's window. No one was to be seen. He quickly collected their possessions, chucked them all in their blue Samsonite and crept back outside.

Funny how the brain can unbury memories when pressured. Adonis drove the dark country road at full speed, his headlights dancing upon tree to tree, scaring sleepy birds and squirrels with his engine's roar. In his mind, a school field trip from years ago played out. Mitsero village. Home to the famous Red Lake. A deep lake colored red by the acid waters provided from the closed-off mines surrounding it. Nothing managed to live in its waters, the tour guide had informed them.

'Perfect! No fishermen, no divers, no swimmers...' Adonis said aloud as he drove by the outskirts of the small village. Pure silence. Long after midnight and the hills stood quiet. He parked at the edge of the cliff with his lights switched off. He untied his brand-new mountain bike from the car's hood and with the gear in neutral, he pushed the vehicle off the edge. The Beetle sky-fell below, crashing upon the cliff's side and rolling into the dark waters with a loud splash. Adonis watched as it sank out of sight.

'Oh, God, what the hell am I doing?'

With three hours left until daybreak, he rode his bike through Mitsero forest back to his home. He stayed locked up inside for two days. The neighbors had to testify that he was away for the weekend. On Tuesday, he reported his wife missing. He stated how they argued on the weekend away and how Kate took his car, and drove off, leaving him there. He informed the police that he returned home by bus. With tears, he said that he waited for her to come home. How her phone was switched off and how she threatened to leave him for good as she walked out of the motel room.

Months later, the story of the missing woman was forgotten by the local media and became just another buried file in the overcrowded filling room of the police department.

Ayia Napa, Cyprus
March, 2018

Sotiris Andreou parked his black BMW in the underground parking off his apartment block, in the prestigious area near

Nissi beach, one of the island's most celebrated and awarded beaches.

It was his first day back at work after his boss, Thomas Keravnos had died six days ago. His feet ached after standing for hours as a bouncer at Castle Club, having to put up with girls trying to flirt their way in the crowded club and with drunken tourists arguing between them.

At five o'clock a.m., he was alone in the dark concrete maze. With slow heavy steps he made his way to the elevator on his right.

A noise from the shadows behind the thick columns caught his attention.

'Bloody rats,' he whispered before gasping for air as the pickaxe pierced his chest. He fell back, his eyes widened in shock. A slim shadowy figure stood towering him. He tried to focus as the woman came closer.

'Wait! What do you want from me?' he said as blood oozed out of his chest. He felt weak and each breath seemed more elusive.

'Don't you remember me, big guy?'

Her short brown hair and Greek nose came more into the light.

'Jesus Christ, you're that woman from the motel!'

'Bingo,' she said, pulling out the heavy pickaxe.

'Your husband said you died. He called Thomas and told him to cover up all evidence at the motel and had the manager back his story...'

Those were his last words. The sharp end of the tool came down with force, piercing through his bald skull.

Hours later, a doctor rushing to his car -late again for his morning shift, found the body. He calmly checked for a pulse, wiped the sweat from his bald head and called the police. For the second time in a week, Chief Inspector

Demetriou found herself examining a murdered body and contemplating her choice of a career.

'This has to be an underground vendetta,' she said to her partner who stood amazed at the pickaxe sticking out of the victim's head. 'He worked for Keravnos. We need to talk to other employees. Something bad must have gone down and I sense more death is on the way. Especially if Keravnos's men decide to retaliate.'

Her partner stood up straight and rubbed his lower back. His nose twitched, having inhaled the thick stale underground air that roamed the parking lot, now, carrying a scent of fresh death. 'That's if they have a clue about who's doing all this.'

The news of Sotiris Andreou's death fuelled the media who channelled their top reporters to the 'wiping out the mob' case. On a small island, everything is big news and these murders were huge to the public.

Just two blocks away, Chris Panayi, Keravnos's second bodyguard held his curly hair between his large hands and walked up and down his living room.

'Babe, relax...' his wife tried to reason with him.

'Relax? Relax, she says! I've got a target glued to my forehead and Agnes wants me to relax.'

The Swedish beauty stood up and hugged him from behind, laying her head on his wide bare back. 'Who has a target on you? The other nightclub owners? They all fear you,' she said and placed a gentle kiss on his shoulder.

Chris closed his eyes, his mind travelling back to that night. He held the pillow down too tight. He just wanted her to be quiet. That night changed him. He turned to his only living relative for help; his grandmother. The Cypriot granny with the silver hair sent him to her spiritual monk for guidance. Chris cleansed his soul and sought redemption, spending his days off helping out at the children's hospital in the nearby town of Paralimni.

'It seems you can't escape your sins. I have someone to see. It's either him or he lied that his wife died,' Chris said, picked up his white T-shirt from the back of the brown sofa and rushed out the door.

Agnes stood puzzled. 'Just be safe,' she managed to yell as the door slammed behind Chris.

———

Adonis spat out another piece of nail and watched it fall on the Persian carpet. His iPhone with the latest news on display sat by his side, keeping company to the opened bottle of scotch. Adonis lit another cigarette. Funny how he never smoked indoors before Kate's death. Now, he flicked the ash on the floor beside him. He remained laying down as the cigarette burnt down to his lips. He fought to maintain his mind calm and empty.

'This is not the time to panic, Adonis,' he yelled aloud as he thought of going to the Red Lake and swimming down to her body.

Twenty minutes later, he heard a car pull up outside. He drunkenly sauntered to the window and took a peek from behind the thick tartan curtain.

'Holy shit,' he said as he saw the tall bodyguard exit the vehicle; his curly hair blowing in the gust of wind coming from the hilltop.

Adonis rushed down the stairs and went down to the cellar. As he heard the doorbell echo downwards, he climbed out the narrow window and made a run for the hill, hoping for the evergreen pines to provide him with cover. Running up the hill he turned to make sure if anyone was following him. He froze in shock. There she was. Kate crawling into the back of the bodyguard's Land Rover.

He rubbed his closed eyes in disbelief. She was wearing her pink spring dress with the wild flowers printed on the back. She loved that dress this time of year. Adonis hid behind an aging fir tree and spied through its broken branches. The bodyguard walked round his property, knocking on doors and calling his name. Five minutes later, he gave up and returned to his car.

Adonis fell back into the dirt as the bodyguard drove out of his metal gate and vanished down the narrow road.

'How is she alive? I should have checked for a pulse... I should have taken her to a hospital... I deserve to die...'

Adonis stuck his fingers into the soft soil and pushed himself up. His head felt heavy; his eyes sore. 'Don't take this as disrespect. Thanks for the cover,' he spoke to the tree as he took a much-needed leak. He pulled up his jeans' zipper and scratched his head. 'Maybe the booze is playing tricks on me. I've been thinking about Kate all week...' he mumbled as he clumsily made his way back home.

Hours later, his answer came through his television set.

'I knew what I saw was real!' he yelled and jumped up from his bedroom's two-seater sofa.

Chris Panayi's death was announced by Chief Inspector Demetriou on the evening news. She was surrounded by reporters and a gang of microphones covered her up to her lips. The victim was shot in the back of his head with his own gun. He was found by the side of the road, dumped by two garbage bins. His car was found abandoned behind an old coffee shop, near a bus stop. Witnesses spoke of a tall, pretty lady with dark shades and a pink dress on. '... we cannot confirm an ongoing mafia vendetta, but we can assure the public that they are safe. Police are interviewing the route's bus drivers as we speak and in combination with our other leads, we are confident that arrests will be made shortly. Thank you,' Demetriou's last words came through his sound surround system.

Adonis exhaled and brought yet another cigarette to his lips.

'*I will not run. I want to see her. I will stay right here...*'

Last Day of March, 2018

Days went past uneventfully.

Adonis never left the house. In self-inflicted quarantine, he lingered through the dark house, living on delivered meals, alcohol and cigarettes.

Dawn came and found him still awake after a night of pepperoni pizza, cheese sticks, Mythos beers and a Lord of the rings movie marathon.

'God, this movie has way too many endings,' he complained as he got up to take another relief trip to the bathroom. He returned to his living room sofa -the new resting place for his pillow and sheets, before the closing credits. As he watched the hobbits sail off into infinity and the next scene cut back to Hobbiton, he leaned forward to take a closer look at one of the extras in the background.

'*He looks like the motel owner. Grumpy old man.*'

An idea came to him. '*Could he be on Kate's list? What if this is really just mob hits and executions? It has been weeks...*'

He switched off the movie, went back into the bathroom, splashed cold water upon his unshaved face, rubbed the black circles camping around his eyes and brushed his teeth. In his boxers, he rushed to his bedroom. He pulled up a pair of jeans and took a clean T-shirt out of the closet. Soon, with the morning sun rising behind him, he was in his car, windows down, driving back to a place where he thought he would never return.

An hour later, he scratched his short thick beard as he turned down the country road leading to the two-story motel.

Few cars were parked outside; only lively crickets breaking the silence of the morning. Adonis parked his vehicle near the entrance and got out of the car, unsure of what to say.

'*Hey, remember me? I'm the guy that lost his wife in a poker game and your boss with his goons raped her to death? Listen, what's going on with your mafia organization? Is it a vendetta? A drug war? Jesus! I'm a complete idiot...*'

His thoughts kept him company as he crossed the parking and stepped onto the patio by the motel's main entrance. A loud noise behind him made him jump. A well-fed, though stray, ginger cat leaped out of the overflowing dumpster below the outdoor staircase. His hairs standing straight up as he walked sideways, ready to fend off two approaching enemies. A woman's figure stood opposite him, in the shadows born from the stairs.

'Kate?' Adonis called out, taking a small step towards her direction.

The woman came into the light. 'Good morning, I'm Stella. I run the place. Was just feeding the cats. Looking for a Kate, huh?'

'Err, no. Not really,' he replied, scratching the back of his head.

The olive-skin woman raised her green shades from her eyes. 'A room, then?'

Adonis watched her right hand slide across her shorts and hide below her black tank top. 'No need to go for your gun. I'm not here for trouble.'

'A gun, sir? What are you implying? This is a legitimate business...'

'I'm not a cop. Nor a journalist. I know this place is where Thomas used to settle a lot of his dirty business...'

'Good morning, Mrs. Areti. How are you today?' Stella raised her voice to cut him off and waved to the old lady strolling on the first-floor balcony. 'Maybe we should take this inside?' she whispered to Adonis.

With the office door closed behind them, Stella exhaled and sat down on her black office chair. 'So, what's your deal?' she said, dropping her friendly tone and lit a cigarette. 'Sit!' she ordered.

Adonis sat in the high-back armchair opposite her. 'I'm looking for the manager...'

'That's me.'

'No, no. The old guy. Short with a long grey beard and long scruffy hair?' He left out the *'looks like a hobbit part.'*

'What do you want him for?'

'Questions about a night that could be connected to all these deaths.'

Stella blew out a thick cloud of smoke, leaned forward and placed her hands on the mahogany desk. 'Who are you? Did you work for Thomas? I haven't seen you before.'

Adonis shook his head. 'I'm nobody. A fool that got himself in a sticky situation. Please, can I speak to your manager?'

Stella fell back into her chair. 'My father died from a heart attack last Christmas. But, if you know anything about these murders, you need to tell me now. Someone is targeting us...'

Adonis placed his hand upon his forehead. 'You just answered what I wanted to know. I wanted to ask your father, if the murders are drug-related or a result of a vendetta or whatever that went sour.'

'What's it to you?'

'I believe my wife was murdered here last March or at least that's what I thought... I've been seeing her... I don't know... Maybe I'm crazy, but I thought maybe she was the one doing the killings.'

Stella looked at him hesitant of what to say or think of the bizarre stranger that showed up at her motel at the crack of dawn. She blew out another large cloud of smoke and dropped her cigarette to die in an empty ashtray by her phone. 'Did my father kill your wife?' she finally asked.

'No, no,' Adonis shook his head. 'I'm sorry to have wasted your time. It was a far reach, but I was hoping for any answers your father might have had about the three deaths.'

'You're scared.'

'To death,' he replied and forced a smile. He stood up. 'If I'm right, this story will close with my death and you and the mafia are safe. If I'm wrong, then I'm safe to live in guilt and you lot need to find out who is hunting you down.'

Stella did not reply. She watched as the sweaty man rushed out her office. She followed him and noted down his number plates.

Adonis returned home exhausted. His ankles cracked and his knees retaliated as he stumbled up the stairs. Fully clothed, he fell on his bed and in seconds, drifted off to dreamland.

Kate haunted his dreams. Every dream of his, she turned into a nightmare. She rose from the Red Lake and followed him through the dark forest, naked and abused. Blood dripping from her insides and a sharp knife in her right hand. Her eyes were missing. Adonis tried to run, yet branches moved around him, blocking his way. Tall gothic trees laughed and taunted him. The trees held him down. Kate sat upon him and raised the blade. As its end pierced through his eye, Adonis screamed and found himself awakening in cold sweat. He ran to the bathroom and splashed icy water to his face, wiping away sweat and tears.

'Adonis?'

He froze and looked behind him. 'Am I still dreaming?'

'Adonis?' the female voice echoed around the room. It was coming from downstairs. Adonis stepped back into his bedroom, opened his closet and picked up his baseball bat.

He descended the stairs with care. Barefoot, he looked around as he moved. A smashing sound from the living room made him jump. He noticed the clock above the door. Midnight. He had slept all through the day. He crept into the room and switched on the lights. His wedding photo lay surrounded by pieces of glass. He approached the broken frame and picked up the picture. The smiling faces raising memories of happy days long gone. His gambling addiction made sure their life together lacked joy. As he stood up, his bare foot landed on a tiny piece of glass. It cut through his flesh with ease. He hopped in pain to the armchair by the dirty fireplace. He sat down and pulled out the small glass segment from his skin. Just then, he felt the thin rope run around his neck and he was yanked to the back of the chair. A blow to the head made him lose his senses. He reopened his eyes to find himself tied to the chair, unable to move. The lights were out and only the lit fireplace provided light.

Kate sat in the shadows opposite him. Her feet rested in the light; he recognized her favorite heels.

'Kate... Kate... How? You're alive!'

'No thanks to you,' she whispered.

Adonis began to sob. 'I'm sorry, I'm so sorry. Whatever I say is not enough...'

'You deserve to die!'

'I know,' he replied, thought skeptic with the rasp in Kate's voice. 'Did you kill Thomas and the others?' he asked, hoping she would talk louder.

'All of them. Revenge really does taste sweet.'

Adonis titled his head. 'You're not Kate.'

Laughter came from the shadows. 'No, you dumb bastard. Of course not. Believe in ghosts, do you?'

'Eva?' he asked in surprise as Kate's sister came into the light.

'Is this where we have our movie scene where I describe my plan? Do you need such satisfaction, Adonis?' she asked as she came closer, butcher's blade in her right hand.

Adonis remained silent. 'Just kill me...' he said and bowed his head.

'Not before you answer me. What did you do with my sister's body? She's surely dead, right?'

Adonis raised his head. 'Wait... what do you know?'

The kitchen screeched slightly as he spoke and Eva turned around. *'Did I leave it open?'*

'Eva, believe me, I had no intention of causing any harm to Kate. I loved her...'

Eva yelled and brought the blade down, chopping off two of his fingers that rested on the armchair. 'Loved her?'

Adonis screamed in pain and looked down in horror at his two bloody fingers lying on the vinyl floor.

'I never trusted you. You made her suffer, day in, day out. The hours she spent crying in my arms, whenever you lost money and had drank your weight in alcohol. And then, you took her to that shitty motel to be raped. That's your idea of love? You sick fuck, huh?'

Adonis's tears snaked down his pale cheeks. 'How did you find out?'

'As I said, I never trusted you. Your smug face telling the police that she left you, that she disappeared. After months went by and she did not even call me, I knew something bad had gone down. She would run from you, but she would have let me know where she would be going. I visited the motel you said you stayed at and found the manager. I forced him to tell me the truth. I listened to how you sorted a rape night for Keravnos and his two bodyguards. I would probably have gotten more out of him, but I injected him with too much and he went into cardiac arrest...'

'You killed the old man? Well, go on, nurse. Cut me where you know I will bleed out. Guess your profession helped you become a murderer...'

Her laughter cut him off. '*You* are judging *me*?' she said and the knife came down again, chopping off another finger. 'What did you do with Kate? No one knew where her body was.'

'I found her dead. I put her into the back of the Beetle and drove her off the cliff, into the Red Lake.'

Eva screamed and frantically began cutting him. Blood shot up high as she slaughtered him; butchered his body.

Breathless and covered in blood, she dropped her knife and cried. 'I love you Kate... Sweet revenge for you, babe,' she whispered and turned to leave. She gasped for air as she saw the woman standing in the doorway.

'Hi, I'm Stella. Just heard that you murdered my father,' she said, raised her gun and shot Eva between the eyes. 'Don't know about sweet, but revenge is surely a bitch,' Stella said, walked over to the fireplace and threw lighter fluid into the flames and made a line leading to the sofa. As Stella drove off into the night, she saw from her rear-view mirror, the flames devouring the curtains.

The burnt house with the two murdered bodies was the second unsolved case in a row for Inspector Demetriou. She gave her resignation to Homicide at the end of spring. Murders just weren't for her.

APRIL OF ADVENTURE

EUBOEA ISLAND

1993

Twenty-seven children went into the woods that day. Twenty-six came back.

Christmas was not the ideal time of year -in most people's minds- for camping. Yet the state-of-the-art facilities of Edipso's camp combined with Greece's Mediterranean climate, made it a year-round destination.

Eleven-year-old Icarus was among the group that left his hometown of Chalkis and set off for the campsite on Boxing Day. Five days of adventure, the leaflet passed around at school had promised. Icarus and his friends had signed up the following day.

It was a sunny winter day on the 28th of December. The timid sun finally appearing in the Greek blue sky after two days of rain. After two days of indoor activities, the children and their pack leaders prepared for a hike to Pedoupoli through the pine-tree forest. Pedoupoli; literally translated to the town for children. The group camped for the night in an opening next to a colorful playground. The mountain, nature's tower, stood behind them, and the sea view on the horizon in front of them calmed them. It was a sweet winter night with ghost stories and snacks around the fire.

By midnight all were asleep.

Patrol leader Mario Karamanli blew his piccolo trumpet at seven o'clock sharp. The horde of children crawled out of their tents and like zombies moved around the site, washing their faces and brushing their teeth.

'Sir? Sir?' Jason Castellano raised his voice over the commotion to grab the attention of Mr. Karamanli.

'Good morning, Mister Castellano. What is it? The maid forgot to pack your toothpaste?' Mario asked, turning around with a wide smile.

Jason's bright blue eyes travelled sideways. His way of swallowing what he truly wanted to say. 'I can't find Icarus...'

'I'm sure he is around. Group assembly in five. You will see him there...'

Jason stepped in front of the tall man as he started to walk away, ticking boxes from his daily agenda. 'I woke up before your awful trumpet playing. He wasn't in his sleeping bag...'

Mario stood up straight and placed his hands on his sides. 'Now, watch your language, young man!'

Alexander 'Alex' Stamos was heading to the camping tables to check out what was on the breakfast table, whistling along the way, when he noticed Mr. Karamanli's index finger waving in his friend's red face. 'Good morning, Mister Mario. Lovely day, today, right?' he interrupted as he hugged Jason's shoulders. 'What's up, rich boy?'

'Icarus is missing!'

'Probably taking a dump in the forest,' Alex replied, and his signature chuckle followed.

Jason pushed Alex away from him. 'I'm being serious, dude!'

Mario rolled his eyes. 'Okay, stop getting agitated over nothing. Let's go find your friend.'

Nothing turned into something.

All the boys were accounted for, but Icarus.

Kids yelled out his name, yet the forest remained silent and unwelcoming.

'Maybe Iolaos ate him,' a boy with spiky hair joked, much to his friend's amusement. The two boys were watching Iolaos Veli devour half his sandwich in one bite.

'Shut the fuck up, Bill,' Alex said, looking back as he stood on a rock for a better view down the hill. 'Icarus is missing. Stop being a prick!'

Both boys looked down. Alex was the tallest, buffest and most popular kid in their school.

Iolaos took another bite out of his chicken and mayo sandwich and threw the rest in the garbage bin by the picnic tables. He ran up to Alex, his belly moving around like jelly under his green extra-large T-shirt. 'Thank you...'

'Don't talk to me in public,' he replied and jumped off the rock, calling out Icarus's name.

The minutes of searching turned into a whole hour. Activities organizer, Miss Julia stood by Mario. She stroked his icy ashen face. She loved it when he shaved. 'Babe, we have to call it in. We can't have these kids wandering in the forest looking for their friend. He is probably somewhere safe and sound.'

Mario reached into his pocket and pulled out his NOKIA 101 cell phone that the camp administration had bought for hikes and pulled out its antenna. 'Lousy reception,' he mumbled and jogged to a clearing to notify the authorities.

The hours of searching by the forest rangers and two police officers turned into a day. Nightfall was closing in.

Leading the evening expedition into the evergreen mountains were the lost boy's parents. His father angrily forcing his way through thick bushes and cutting hanging tree branches. His mother with a flow of tears, screaming out his name, followed behind her husband. Her only son, her precious boy, lost.

The days of searching turned into a week. Icarus's sweet innocent face with his golden short hair dominated the news. Weeks turned into months and hopes turned into despair.

Hopes that faded just like his *missing child* posters.

———

April, 1994

The school bell rang as it always did at half past one. Yet, on Friday the 22nd that year, its ringing vibes spread around the school halls and classrooms, causing an uproar to the student population. Easter break had arrived.

A sea of smiling youths ran outside the two-story building; out of the shadows and into the bright Greek sun and the eruption of spring flowers.

Jason stood on the top step of the Chalkis Primary School main entrance and hopped on Alex's back. 'Woohoo,' he yelled as they ran down the paved path and out of the school's fenced perimeter.

'Two whole weeks, baby!' Alex shouted as Jason jumped

off his back. 'Did your dad get you the new GameBoy tapes as he promised?'

'Sure did! Tetris 2 *and* Wario Land!'

'You lucky bitch.'

'Hey, I worked for them. Three projects. I had to turn in three ass-boring, *extra* if I may add, projects in history, geography and science,' Jason replied, punching Alex on his right shoulder. 'Dad says we always have to put in...' he paused, coughed and took in a deep breath, before continuing, mimicking his father's deep voice, 'our one hundred and ten percent. Just doing your assigned homework doesn't make you stand out!'

Alex whistled. 'Sweet, however you look at it. If my dad was as rich as your dad, I wouldn't even do my homework. I'd pay someone geeky as Athena Lazou to do it!'

Jason smiled. 'I'm sure you would,' he replied as they turned off the main road and strolled through the golden hay fields. Their favorite shortcut home.

Suddenly, long wavy hay rattled around and moved towards them.

'What the...?' Alex asked as Iolaos ran past them, his schoolbag jumping up and down on his back.

'Come back, Bacon cheeks.'

'Here, piggy-piggy!'

'Oink, oink.'

Voices from the group of four boys and two girls chasing him were heard from the road above.

'Alex, save me,' Iolaos yelled at his neighbor as he made a run to the outskirts of the small pine forest by their town.

'Shit,' Alex said and ground his teeth. 'This is getting ridiculous.'

Jason looked at the forest ahead and swallowed a lump in his throat. Ominous music played in his mind and sweat began to form upon his clenched palms. 'Iolaos, wait,' he yelled and chased after his terrified classmate.

Alex dropped his Jurassic Park school bag to the dirt, widened his shoulders and walked up to the group of bullies. 'Hey Mark. Lisa,' he nodded. 'Wassup?'

'That snitch deserves a beating,' Mark said and spat to the ground.

'Snitch? What did he say? Iolaos is good at keeping secrets.'

'Is he your boyfriend or something?' Antony asked. 'Like them fat, do you?'

'Yeah, that's why your mama and I are so close!'

Antony's face turned red as his friends laughed. 'My mama isn't fat...'

'Yo mama's so fat, every time she lies on a beach, Greenpeace throws her back in,' Alex said and prepared for Antony's attack. He looked behind his back just as Jason and Iolaos were consumed by the darkness of the forest. He had won Iolaos much time. He raised his arms. 'I'm sorry. Didn't mean to offend your mother. Just leave the kid alone.'

'He told Mrs. Christina that we stole his lunch money!'

'Well, stop stealing his fucking money, then, Lisa,' Alex replied. 'The guy has enough on his plate,' he continued and regretted his poor choice of words.

'Yeah, we can see how much he puts on his plate.'

'He probably eats the plate, too!'

The gang continued laughing at Iolaos's expense as they walked off. Iolaos wasn't worth missing the bus home.

Alex exhaled deeply, picked up his filthy bag and jogged to find his friends.

He found them sitting under a thick oak tree. An out-of-breath Iolaos was explaining how he left school from the back window of the science lab. 'I thought they would run out the front, celebrating the Easter break with everyone else, but that prick, Mark, followed me. He promised to kick my teeth in...'

Both looked up at the sound of twigs being stepped on.

'Alex!' Iolaos said with excitement, jumping up and running towards him with arms wide open. Alex stopped him by placing his hand on Iolaos's head. 'Whoa, cowboy. You're sweating all over.'

'Thanks... again. I know you hate it when people know we are friends.'

Alex messed around Iolaos's gelled hair and winked at him. 'Hate is such a strong word,' he said and chuckled.

'We're going over to my house to play on our Game-Boys, if you wanna join us...' Jason stood up and said; a strong eerie wind running through the forest interrupted him. Dirt, pieces of hay and a piece of ripped paper swirled towards them. The three boys closed their eyes and waited for the gust of wind to pass by and vanish into the woods. Iolaos picked up the poster that landed on his belly and raised it to eye level. 'Holy shit, it's Icarus.'

Jason took the paper from his chubby fingers. The poster had faded, weak under the mighty sun and nature's elements, yet those two blue eyes pierced through Jason's soul.

'I miss him. I miss him every day,' he admitted, bowed his head and his eyes began to water up.

'Me too, bro. Me too,' Alex said and placed his hand on Jason's shoulder.

'Easter was his favorite holiday,' Iolaos said.

Jason looked up at him. 'How do you know that?' he asked the one-year-younger-than-them kid.

'We were together in chess club. He was the kindest kid there. He chose me to be his partner in the finals. We lost, but it was the best time of my life. He was your best friend, right?'

Jason wiped away a tear with his fist. 'Together since nursery. Never met anyone as loyal as him. Always eager to help, to make you laugh, to...' Jason bit his lips and looked away.

'Why did he like Easter so much? Lamest holidays, in my humble opinion. No presents like Christmas, no beaches like summer,' Alex said, trying to change the subject.

Iolaos was dusting off his clothes and mumbling how his mother was going to kill him. 'If it's not the bullies, it will be her. Either way, I'm dying young...'

Jason spoke without turning around. 'That's exactly why. He used to say, there's no pressure on us at Easter. Christmas is family dinner after family dinner. He hated the whole forced festive mood. That's why we signed on to that damn camping trip in the first place. Easter, he felt, there were no plans. His folks aren't religious, so he felt like he had like two weeks to chill and write.'

'Write?'

'Yeah, he wrote these weird messed-up stories. With murders and rapes and all,' Jason replied, turning around. 'I see him in my dreams, you know. Not in a gay way, obviously. He haunts me. I see him in those woods. He screams to me to save him and I wake up in a cold sweat.'

'I miss playing football with him,' Alex said, kicking the pile of leaves to his left. 'You suck, dude.'

'Icarus!' Jason yelled and then cursed.

'Do you think he is dead?' Iolaos asked.

Jason grabbed him by his white collar. 'Don't you even say that!'

'Calm down, Jason,' Alex said, pushing away his arms. 'The police found nothing. It has been months...'

'And what the hell do you think happened?'

'Well, I'm not going to pretend he is alive. Safe and sound and all. I don't believe he ran away. He probably went for a leak and fell down a ditch or something. Bad luck. Bad shit happens to the best of people, my grandfather used to say.'

'Then, where's his body? The police, the rangers, his parents... they searched every inch of those mountains.'

'Why don't we go look for it?' a voice came from behind them, making them jump.

The three boys stood shoulder-to-shoulder as Athena Lazou came out of the darkness. Their jaws dropped at the sight of the lit cigarette in her left hand.

'You smoke?' Jason asked. Athena nodded and her silky pitch-black hair fell forward. 'You're eleven!'

Athena shrugged her shoulders, brought the cigarette to her pale lips; lighting up its end as smoke travelled down her youthful lungs. She blew out smoke and laughed at their shocked faces.

'But, you're a straight A pupil. Top of our glass. You never speak to anyone,' Alex said. 'Your nose is ducked in a book all the time. Where are your glasses, by the way?'

'I don't really need them. My father likes them,' she replied.

'Do your parents know that you smoke?' Iolaos said, slightly stuttering. Girls made him nervous.

'My mum died when I was four. Of course, my father doesn't know.'

Silence fell on the forest opening. Jason and Alex realized they didn't know their classmate at all. 'So,' she continued, 'Why don't we go look for him? His body at least. It's called closure in psychology, you know.'

Alex was ready to laugh when Jason replied. 'Sure. Let's

do that. Let's go back to that stupid camp site and follow his last steps. He has to be somewhere.'

'Dude, our parents would kill us.'

'Not knowing is killing me already. Come on, man. One last adventure before high school and exams and shit.'

Iolaos came close, whispering as if someone could hear them. 'That's an hour on the bus away and another hour hike, what will we tell our parents?'

'You coming, too?' Alex asked, his eyes open wide. 'You agree with this madness?'

Iolaos tilted his head and raised his hands. 'Nothing better to do. You're my only friend and you grew too popular. Besides, Icarus was a great kid...'

'The greatest!' Jason said, his eyes sparkling as the adventure unfolded in his mind's private movie theatre. He envisioned finding Icarus alive, caught in a bear trap and having survived by eating cockroaches and drinking frog's blood. 'We have to go as soon as possible.'

Alex stood behind him and placed his chin on Jason's shoulder. 'Why? Going skiing in Switzerland on Monday?'

'No, butt face,' he replied, pushing Alex's head off him. 'We're going to lie about our whereabouts. No way are our parents going to let us stay away from home over Holy Week. This will have to go down tomorrow!'

Synchronized alarm clocks went off simultaneously at eight o'clock. The three boys awoke with mischievous smiles engraved on their youthful faces.

Jason kicked back his X-men sheets, beating Wolverine to the ground. He ran into his en-suite bathroom and clumsily brushed his teeth. In a matter of six point two minutes -

as he later described it, he was dressed to go, standing in the mansion's main kitchen.

'Well, well, well. You are up early, little master,' Besjana, their maid said, laughing at the sight of the young boy eating leftovers out of the fridge. 'Shh, don't wake them up. I haven't mopped yet.'

'I'm on a mission, Mrs. Besjana. I don't want to wake them up, either,' he replied and grabbed a carton of orange juice. 'I'm off. Tell mama, I went to see my friends at the arcade. Street Fighter tournament. Bye!'

Besjana shook her head. 'Good bye and be careful,' she said, and watched him creep out the kitchen door and ride his bike down the road of the prestigious neighborhood. Sorrow colored her eyes as her mind travelled to Albania and her now grown-up children. 'Patience Besjana, patience. A couple more years of saving money and you can retire. Back in your village, surrounded by grandchildren and cats!' she whispered to herself as she picked up her broom and headed outside.

Jason sped down the hill with his Walkman headphones placed in his ears, Ace of Base keeping his mind from stressing. He turned his bike past Saint Paraskeuis church and gazed at the bright sun shining down on Chalkis Bridge; a golden passage over the Euripus strait, connecting the island to the mainland. He then rode away from the business center and headed into the rundown part of the town. Scattered country houses with overgrown-with-weeds gardens and gates begging for a brush of fresh paint welcomed him.

An old man sitting outside a dark convenience store caught his eye. 'A penny for an unemployed widow?' his sign asked shoppers.

'*Perfect!*'

Jason dropped his mountain bike to the ground. He

fixed his hazelnut hair with his hands, wore his meeting-parents'-friends smile and with his Greek chin and Roman nose held high, he sauntered up to the sickly-looking man with the faded, ripped jeans and scratched-up, brown sandals.

'Good day, my fine sir.'

The man placed his hand above his tired hands as to block the rays that the sun offered so freely upon Greece. 'Huh? Who are you? Got five hundred drachmas to spare? I'm very hungry...'

Jason's smile grew. 'I can do you one better, sir. How do you like the sound of ten-thousand drachmas?' he asked, pulling the deep purple bank note out of his pocket. 'It's got Asclepius on it. The God of medicine. Could bring you luck with your health, too,' he continued. Jason was a great mythology fan. Anything to escape the boredom of his business logistics-oriented home.

The man struggled to stand up and starred at the boy in disbelief. 'You serious?'

'Never been more serious, sir. I have a proposal for you.'

'Hey, no weird shit, okay. I can't get into any more trouble and...'

'No, no. Nothing like that. All I need you to do is come with me to the phone booth up by the gas station. Three phone calls and the cash is yours.'

The man held on to the railing and limped down the steps. 'It will take me a while to walk over there. You better not be pulling a silly joke on me, young man or I will curse you by the saints.'

Half an hour later, Alex and Iolaos high-fived each other as they stood by the phone booth and witnessed Jason slowly riding along next to the homeless man.

'I knew that rascal could do it!'

'So, we call our parents and lie that we are sleeping at Jason's house tonight,' Iolaos said as he dug deeper into his bag of Vinegar-flavored chips.

'And after the homeless dude acts as Jason's dad, he will pretend to be my dad and Jason will lie that he will be sleeping at mine!'

'Bulletproof plan, my friend. Bulletproof,' Iolaos said, giggling and crunching away the last pieces of potato chips.

The afternoon bus came to a halt at the stop opposite the bowling alley. Smoke clouds came up from its exhaust as the driver left it running. He dashed out and ran to the kiosk for a packet of Assos smokes. The boys -all with backpacks, turned and watched as Athena appeared through the black cloud with her school bag hanging from her right shoulder. She cat-walked the pavement with her army boots, jean shorts and black tank-top. 'Ready for adventure, boys?' she asked and stepped up into the bus.

'Never seen so much skin of hers before,' Alex commented as he watched her sit down in the back seats. 'She's always dressed like a nun at school.'

Jason slapped him on the back of his head. 'Concentrate, man. We are on a mission.'

'Yeah, yeah. Got our tickets, Mr. Sponsor?'

'All four of them!'

'Edispos, here we come,' Iolaos said. 'All aboard!'

Soon, the group of four sat side-by-side in the back row, enjoying a bag of Jelly babies.

The driver threw his bud on the sidewalk, grabbed the steering wheel and pulled himself up. He squeezed into place and turned the key. With the engine's roar, the children were on their way.

'Look,' Jason said, pointing to Icarus's house. The once-flourishing garden had died, all curtains were shut and a certain air of gloom lingered around it.

'I heard his mother hasn't got out of bed yet,' Alex said, rubbing his nose. 'Or so my gossip-crazed mother says.'

'His sister is failing her lessons in high school, my brother told me,' Jason replied.

'Any green ones left?' Athena asked, catching Iolaos off guard.

'Here you go,' Iolaos said, giggled and passed her the last two jelly babies. He hated the green ones. 'So, what excuse did you use?'

Athena bit the head of the candy and looked down. 'The usual. Anyway, my father doesn't really realize I'm gone most of the time. He's a drunk, you see?'

Iolaos nodded with a flat-line smile and lowered his voice. 'Must be hard being just the two of you. My father left us when I was like five. Just me and my mama since then. That's why she is so overprotective. All she does is cook for me and clean the house since then...'

'Yours left. Cancer took mine. There's a difference. And I wished *all* my father *did* was chores,' she replied, each word enwrapped in bitterness.

'Sorry, didn't mean to...'

'No sweat,' she replied, forced a short-lived smile and gazed out the window, watching their hometown vanish into the horizon. Like miniature cardboard boxes, the houses stood dark in front of the sun. And in minutes, only green fields filled her view.

A flock of swallows swirled around at the foot of the hill. Their nests cleverly hidden in the first line trees of Edipsos forest. The four children stood at the edge of the dirt track.

'Well, here goes nothing,' Jason said and took the first step off the sidewalk.

'How far is it?' Athena asked, walking by his side.

'An hour's hike to Pedoupoli,' Alex replied, rushing to her side and nodding to Jason to go talk to Iolaos.

'Your athlete hour or normal people's hour?' she replied and laughed out loud when he opened his mouth to reply.

With the sun getting lower on the horizon, the group - fuelled by youthful energy and a desire for answers, reached the campsite.

All four dropped their bags to the ground and picked up their water bottles.

'Thank God, it's Easter and not summer. Cheers, Icarus,' Alex said, wiping his forehead and raising his water into the air.

'So, where did you see him last?' Athena asked.

Jason ran over to a fallen log. 'Right here. Our tent was right here. I woke up and he was gone.'

Iolaos came closer. 'Don't get angry, dude, but what if he did run away?'

'Why would he?'

'We all have our reasons,' Athena mumbled and looked around; only trees in sight.

'Then why run away from here and not from home? And leave all his stuff behind?'

Alex picked up a stick and pointed to the dense forest behind them. 'Then, we go with my idea. He went for a dump. He walked into the forest to get as far away from everyone, to have a good shit in peace...'

'And something happened along the way,' Athena added.

'Off into the woods, then,' Jason said, picked up his bag and jogged into the cool darkness. The rest followed.

The group moved together; twigs dying into fragments below their feet. Crickets and birds provided their soundtrack as they walked in silence, thinking of where Icarus could have gone.

'Shh!' Alex said and raised his fist. 'Stop. Listen!'

A rattling in the bushes ahead, made them group closer and freeze.

'What the hell is that?' Iolaos whispered. 'You know, there are rumors of ghosts in these parts...'

'Shh,' Athena said. 'It better not be any rattlesnake. I'm running back to town...'

'Icarus?' Jason asked.

Two large tusks came out of the thick berry bush.

'What the fuck is that?' Alex asked and took a step back, his hand protecting Athena. She smiled at the hand touching her hip.

'It's a warthog,' Jason said. 'I think they are quite friendly.'

'Does he know that?' Iolaos yelled as the beast grunted and started to dig his feet in the dirt.

'Run!' Athena screamed and the group ran down the hillside. The hog ran after them, raising a large cloud of dust behind him. He stopped at the edge and watched as the four children tumbled down the hillside.

The four landed on the grass of the plain on the other side of the mountain. After the shock departed, they burst out in laughter.

Jason stood up first. 'Did you see it?'

'Yeah, what a pig...'

'No, no! The army bunker! There!'

The rest stood up and turned their attention to the small hidden bunker among the trees, in the middle of the mountainside. 'Icarus loved anything military. If he saw a World War Two bunker, he would go explore it.'

'I think these were built during the civil war,' Athena commented.

'I'm going to check it out,' Jason said.

'I need a break,' Alex said and sat back down. 'Me too,' Athena said, pulling out her cigarette package from her bag.

'I'll come with you,' Iolaos said with a smile. He picked up a pack of biscuits and trotted back up the mountain. Jason raised his eyebrows at Alex and rush to catch up with determined Iolaos.

Alex wiped his lips. 'Smoking at eleven? What went wrong there, Straight-A's girl?'

Athena blew out smoke. 'Twelve. I'm twelve.'

Alex moved up closer to her. 'My brother had his first kiss at twelve. And, I'm the fourth kid in my family. The youngest always do things quicker.'

'Is that your proposal for a kiss?'

'Well, we did nearly die,' he replied and licked his lips.

Athena leaned closer. 'Close your eyes, loverboy.'

Alex remained with his eyes closed for a whole minute before reopening them. He turned to see Athena sneaking off up the mountain.

'What?'

'You've never been kissed. I've never seen a bunker!' she laughed and rushed to catch up with the boys that stood disappointed by the large padlock on the bunker's small door.

Alex shook his head and got up to go pee. He wandered around the mountainside and found shade beneath an oak tree. With his back turned to the herd of sheep moving along the grassy plain, he pulled down his shorts' zip.

The sound of him relieving himself upon the tree mingled with the Cuckoo chirping above. As he pulled his zip back up, he jumped in horror as he noticed the old shepherd starring right at him.

'Nice to be a man and piss wherever you want, right?' he said, coming closer.

Alex nodded.

'What are doing out here this time of day? I'm taking the sheep back to sleep.'

'Camping on the mountain. With my friends.'

'Friends? No parents?' the old man with the crow's feet around his small eyes asked, coming closer. 'I wish I had friends. My son and wife died and I'm all alone out here.'

'Sad to hear,' Alex replied. 'By the way, did you see a blond kid in these areas a few months back?'

'Oh, the missing kid. Yes, the police came by here. I helped in the search you know,' he said and moved closer to Alex.

'Sorry, but I've got to go.'

'Stay, keep me company. Do you know chess?'

Alex turned and ran away; the old man's smell of animals blended with scotch nested in his nostrils.

Minutes later, he joined his friends who lay disappointed on the cement roof of the army bunker.

'Where were you?'

Alex tried to catch his breath. 'There's a creepy old guy down there. He watched me pee!'

The three laughed and giggled. 'I'm serious. There's something off about him. He's like those weird pedos our parents warned us about. He kept coming closer to me. I want to go check his cabin.'

Athena stood up and stroked his cheek. 'Relax. You're going to give yourself a heart attack or something.'

'Didn't know you cared,' he replied, lowering his voice. Athena shrugged her shoulders.

'So, let's go,' Jason said, jumping off the bunker.

'Wait, wait. Guys, that's breaking in. It's illegal and these farmers are all loaded with guns,' Iolaos said, wiping biscuit crumbs from his hands.

Alex pushed his fingers through his thick hair. 'He's old and lives alone. We camp here tonight, and in the morning when he takes the sheep back out, we go in!'

Nightfall engulfed the silent forest and a clear sky showed its jewelry in a display of beauty not seen in towns.

'I love sleeping under the stars,' Athena admitted. 'That's Venus. The brightest star. The only female-named planet in our solar system. And the most beautiful in the night sky.'

'Sure is beautiful,' Alex said, not taking his eyes off her.

'Good night, boys,' she said and closed her eyes.

Soon, Iolaos's snoring took over the mountainside, making sure no wild animals came close. Unfortunately, the same couldn't be said about the fierce Greek mosquitoes that fed on Jason for most of the night.

The first sunrays found him awake and scratching.

'How come they only bit me?' he complained as the rest opened their eyes.

'Cause you're gay,' Alex laughed. 'You like being pricked.'

'Actually,' Athena said, standing up and stretching. 'Only female mosquitoes bite. So, not gay. Just desired by the female population. I read somewhere that it has to do with your blood type. You're O, right?'

Jason nodded with a wide smile. 'I won't have any blood left if we stay here one more minute.'

Half an hour later, the four sat in the stomach of an Acacia tree, their eyes on the old shepherd as he ambled by his sheep and headed away from his wooden cabin. They waited for him to disappear from sight, before crawling through the tall grass up to his red door.

'It's open!' Alex declared and pushed the door open.

Stale smoky air welcomed them. The burnt frying pan housed two horse flies and the old man's plate was still on the round kitchen table. Photos of his son and wife covered every shelf.

'No TV,' Iolaos said as he crept around.

'Icarus?' Jason called out and headed to the cabin's bathroom and dirty bedroom.

Athena picked up an old photograph of the aged man in his youth. A tall man, wearing an army uniform. 'Old age really screws you up, huh?' she said and passed the photo to Alex.

'No one is here, man. Let's go,' Alex shouted to Jason, who was looking under the old man's bed. Only muddy boots and a spider's web.

'Shit,' he cursed and stood up to leave. That's when his eyes fell upon the lone key sitting in the middle of a clean ashtray on the old man's bedside table.

'Could it be?' he asked aloud, picking up the key.

'Dude, let's go,' Alex asked from the doorway, making him jump.

'Look, Abus.'

'What?'

'Abus,' he repeated and showed Alex the make of the key. 'Same as the bunker's padlock.'

Alex whistled. 'Well, fuck a duck and see what hatches.'

'Back to the bunker!'

The sun finally appeared from behind the trees and light sneaked through the branches. The children ran back up the hill and headed to the bunker. Jason took the key out of his pocket and watched as it slipped right into place. He turned the key slowly and eight eyes opened wide as the padlock unlocked. Alex took a deep breath and pushed the metallic door back. One by one, the children ducked and entered the cavernous space.

'Why are the lights on?' Athena asked. 'Why is the air fresh?'

'And cool,' Iolaos added.

Steps heard from the room in the back, froze their blood. A rattling chain echoed towards them.

'Dog?' Alex asked.

'Let's hope it's not another warthog,' Iolaos whispered in reply.

'Who's there?' a voice came from the room.

'Icarus?' Jason yelled.

'Jason? Jason!'

The children run into the small room and found a pale Icarus standing by an old bed. A chain to his ankle was connected to a hook in the center of the round room. An air conditioning unit provided him with air. An empty plate, a few books and some board games covered a wooden table by the wall. A potty filled with urine was beside the plastic tub. A shower head hung from the wall above it.

Jason ran straight to him and hugged him. Icarus stood in shock. 'Am I dreaming?'

'Dude, how long have you been here?' Alex asked.

'What month is it?'

'April.'

Icarus bit his bottom lip. 'I've been here since Christmas. The old man locked me up. You have to go get help.'

'I'm not leaving you,' Jason said.

'No, no. You don't get it,' Icarus yelled. 'He will be here soon with my breakfast. He is mental. He thinks I am his long-lost son.'

'I'm already here, boy!'

The children jumped back and watched as the shepherd came through the door. Iolaos shook all over. 'You bastard! You took our friend,' Jason yelled.

'That's my son! And now he has friends! He was so lonely down here. But, I couldn't let him out. I cannot lose him again!'

Athena took one step forward and kicked him between the legs. 'Run!' Icarus screamed as the old man fell to his knees. All the kids, but Jason, ran for the entrance. 'I'm staying with you,' he said and looked around for anything useful to cut Icarus's chains.

The old man stood up, laughed, walked out of the room and slammed the door behind him.

Hand in hand, Alex and Athena ran like crazy through the woods; branches cutting into their skin. The old man stumbled behind them.

'Shit,' Alex said as they reached the edge of a steep cliff.

'This way,' Athena said and turned, only to stop at the sight of the old man's rifle held to her face.

'You little bastards aren't taking away my boy!' he yelled and his finger slipped around the gun's trigger.

A wild scream came out of Iolaos as he ran faster than ever before, throwing all his weight on the old man. The shepherd fell forward over the edge and let out an animal-like sound that came to an abrupt end as his body hit the rocks below. Thick blood oozed out of the old man and the three children exhaled in delight.

Athena turned and kissed Alex on the lips. She giggled at his stunned expression.

'Thank you, Iolaos,' she said and kissed the young boy on his right cheek.

The news of the old man's death brought Icarus to tears. He fell into Jason's arms and remained there, while Alex, Athena and Iolaos made their way back to town to bring help.

'Local heroes find lost boy,' the midday news announcer read that day. Their heroic tale was narrated as images showed Icarus running out of the police car and into his mother's arms. She held him close and kissed him repeatedly while his father broke down in tears by their side.

Alex's, Jason's and Iolaos's parents came running into the police station to pick up their boys. Angry and proud they escorted their boys home.

'You're grounded and you can have whatever you want, my hero son!' Jason's dad said and all laughed.

Athena never left the station that day. She stayed behind and testified against her father for sexual abuse. After a whole day of freedom in the wild, she was not willing to go back to the hell she had been living in since her mother died.

The four grew up famous in their town of nearly one hundred thousand. They remained classmates and friends until college.

Icarus went off to study literature in the UK. After his

ordeal, he was never the same. His youthful joy vanished and he became a Goth during his teen years, writing dark poetry and horror stories. He never returned to Greece. He rented a studio in Kingston, never married and became a screenwriter for Black Hangar studios.

Athena was placed in her aunt's care. Her father was imprisoned for eight years. Enough time for her to become an adult, legally change her name and move away to Thessaloniki.

Alex stayed in Chalkis. A knee injury at eighteen killed off his millionaire sport's icon dream. He ended up where he didn't wish to be. Working twelve-hour shifts in his dad's DIY store. Realizing at twenty-eight that he was transforming into his unhappy father, he boarded the bus to Thessaloniki. He became a tour guide at the bear sanctuary there, taking children into the woods and teaching them about nature. He married nursery teacher, Melina Latsi - Athena's new name. They have two children together and fondly remember their first kiss.

Jason never reached his thirties. He overdosed on expensive cocaine while studying in New York.

Iolaos stood up to his mother and demanded a healthier lifestyle. He became a fitness addict and even studied the science of physical education at Athens University. He is the proud owner of three gyms today. He married and had three boys. Jason, Icarus and Alex.

MAY OF MAYHEM

The end of the world began as a joke...

—Melissa Onasi, May, 2023

May, 2019

Danny ran as fast as he could; his short legs leaping over the bodies that lay on the bloody grounds of Trafalgar Square. His speed and the cold breeze dried the tears running from his swollen red-shot eyes. Blood oozed out of his hair; the hit from his father still hurt. The strike from the silver candlestick came to his mind. His father had gone crazy. No easier way to explain it. As he leapt over another dead body on the sidewalk, a woman, he thought of his mother. She'd murdered his dad in front of his innocent eyes. Then, she turned on him; the kitchen knife in her shaking right hand. Danny did not beg. He did not try to bargain for his life.

Something in her eyes told him that his mother was no longer *there*. He ran out of their apartment block and made his way to the streets of London. Murder after murder unfolded before his light green eyes.

Gun shots made him jump; the hairs on the back of his neck stood at salute. He did not stop running. From the corner of his eye, he saw two police men shooting without aiming; shooting at the crowd of screaming people and the herd of *crazies* chasing them. Both were laughing.

Danny climbed up to the large black lion statue on the right of the square. He crawled along the beast's back and hid behind its massive head. He closed his eyes and prayed. His young body shook as each scream arrived to his ears. People were beaten to death all around him. People biting and digging their nails into each other's skin; excitement was vividly present in their hollow eyes as fresh blood sprayed them.

An hour went by before silence fell upon the square. The sun began to hide behind London's skyscrapers and orange light reflected from the tall glass buildings. Danny looked around him. Piles of bodies -some still twitching, filled his view. He gradually made his way off the animal statue and stood among the dead. He took a deep breath and made a run for his grandmother's house. The smell of blood and wild yelling followed him down narrow roads. Soon, he stood outside a two storey bricked house with thick rose bushes by its open white gates.

The streets were quiet. Danny looked left, then right and made a sprint to his grandma's door. He rang the door-bell. A whole minute went by before he tried to open the wooden door. It was unlocked. The house inside was dark and silent as the bat cave his school had visited the week before.

'Granny?' he called out as he walked into the house. Faint light escaped the gap from the living room door. Danny opened it and walked up to the television playing on mute. Large numbers next to the word *dead* ran along the screen. Images of people attacking each other flashed before his eyes. New York, Tokyo, Athens, Paris. Chaos. Mayhem. Murder.

The floor boards creaked behind him.

He turned with a smile. 'Granny, thank God, you're here…'

Those were his last words. Susan Smith, his loving grandmother, who held him in her arms for hours when he was sick, hit him with force with her brand-new garden spade. The boy fell to the floor. Susan stood above him and stabbed him repeatedly in his trembling chest with her sewing scissors. She howled like a wolf as she licked his warm blood dripping from the sharp end of the blades and Danny's last breath departed from his pale lips.

May, 2023
Island of Omfori, Ionian, Greece
25 meters below ground

Melissa Onasi awoke in her queen-sized bed and stretched her hands out high. Her back still ached from gym class the previous day. Her Persian cat, Tiggy, opened its eyelids and raised her right paw, begging for a tummy stroke. Melissa smiled and picked up the feline in her hands, enjoying the sound of her loud purring.

She dressed nearly as quickly as she shed off her night gown. Designer jeans and a pink tank top. 'I wish I had something new to wear,' she mumbled. She picked up her 2014 iPhone that was permanently plugged in the socket below her mahogany desk. She only used it for its alarm, calendar, viewing of old photos from the outside world and a few games that still functioned. *'Ten days until my birthday,'* she thought as she checked the date.

'Wake up, sleepy head!'

She walked into her sister's room opposite hers. The grey walls were hidden under printed movie posters. 'Wakey-wakey!'

'Day 1461 in this hole and I still see no reason at all why we have to go to school!'

Melissa sat down on the soft bed. 'Has it really been that long?'

Her sister, Eva, rolled her eyes and fell back into her pillows. 'You know it. You were fourteen when we last saw the sun.'

Melissa stroked her sister's blonde hair. 'Eighteen soon. No more school for me,' she said, giggled and messed up her sister's hair.

'I'm sure mother will come up with some sort of college for you!'

'Christ, don't give her any ideas.'

'As if she needs my help with coming up with ideas,' Eva replied, sadness coloring her words.

'Cheer up, three more years of school left for you! Anyway, we will probably be leaving soon.'

Eva sat up straight. 'You really believe that? I gave up hoping of seeing the outside world on day 467.'

Melissa stood up and forced a smile. 'Just get ready, weirdo.'

The beeping from the hallway speakers echoed around

the wide corridors informing the population of seven hundred and sixty-three that it was eight o'clock.

The facilities' psychologist, Aika Takahashi, advised on everyone maintaining a normal life while underground. 'Humans need their routine, as much as we seem to hate it. Inactivity is a killer,' she had said. Thus, a daily schedule was made up. School, jobs, chores for the mornings. A gym, a youth center, a swimming pool, a bar and a cinema for the evenings. Weekends were left free. 'Something to look forward to as we kill time down here,' the Japanese expert had continued during her presentation to the world's elite.

Of course, adults kept it up for the first year. That is how long they had planned on staying underground. Now, misery lingered in the man-made ant colony. It filled up the space like the fresh air blown out by the state-of-the-art systems that truly ran the place. Money bought them clean oxygen, but it could not buy them patience; enough patience to last four years with yet another ominous year underground ahead.

'Attention. Attention. Board meeting at half past eight. Board meeting at half past eight,' Eleni Latchi's voice came through the speakers.

At school, the two hundred and thirty-two under age citizens of Gaia City divided into their classrooms.

Senior class had three weeks of lessons left and as no examinations were on the horizon, their teacher, Rania Petraki, sat and listened to open projects presented by her twenty near-adult pupils.

After ten minutes of Aggelo Milona's presentation about how the Playstation 4 outranked the Xbox in every technical way, Melissa took the stand. She threw a side smile at Aggelo as he walked past her. He winked and his fingers brushed gently against her bare arm.

'The world before and why it needed a change,' the teen began her speech and pictures from wars and starving children flashed behind her on the classroom's projector. After numbering crime and rape statistics, Melissa made a dramatic pause for impact. 'That's where our city comes in. Gaia!' Colorful images of their underground city appeared behind her. 'Funny enough, the end of the world began as a joke...'

Her teacher stopped listening and looked to her left. Grey cement. Everywhere. She once had a window with a view. She missed her vacation home in Santorini. The sea, the sunsets, the cocktails by the caldera, the infamous Greek gyro. She missed her apartment in New York overlooking Central Park. The endless traffic, the galas, the country club.

That's where it all began. The country club.

A place for the rich and famous of Greek descent to gather. Over the years, other nationalities from multicultural New York were allowed to be members, but the club still retained its Greek character.

Five women sat around a table enjoying their Argyros Estate, twenty-year-old wine. Natalia Aggelopoulou, dressed in black, was talking about her late husband. 'Three years. It has been three years, already. Stabbed in an alley way!'

'It's a sick world out there,' her friend, Zoe, added. 'Back in Lesvos, my mother says that Syrian refugees keep showing up. Thousands by the day. Children covered in blood and fear.'

'You heard about the rape gang in Astoria?' Christina said. 'Just miles from our homes. From our daughters!'

'A gang?'

She nodded and took another sip of wine. 'Four men!

They raped three girls over the course of five days, before the police caught them. One is still on the loose.'

'This is not a world I want to raise a kid in,' Tina said, rubbing her pregnant tummy.

Andreas Onasi, Christina's husband, stood up from the comfortable high-back armchair by the marble fireplace. 'What this world needs is to start over. We give millions to charities and only shit happens. The UN is pathetic. Humans are like a virus and the planet should get rid of us!'

'That's a bit harsh,' his brother said, his hand digging into a bowl of mixed nuts.

'Not harsh at all. Imagine if it was Melissa who was raped. Our daughters deserve a better world.'

'Well, let's get rid of everyone and build our own world, then,' Christina said, laughed and raised her half-full glass.

Through laughter and giggling, a voice was barely heard. It was famed biologist, Alexander Vrahimi, the owner of the world's largest pharmaceutical company.

'What?' Christina asked.

'I said, it is easier than what you think. An airborne virus, unable to survive for more than a year, could defeat mankind.'

'And where will we be?'

'Underground,' he replied, straightening his thin-framed glassed on his Roman nose.

'I just bought an island, by the way. Between Lefkada and Kefalonia,' Andreas said. 'Omfori! One thousand acres of paradise. Perfect location to live out the year,' he added and they all laughed.

None would have guessed that Andreas and Christina would remember the idea when Christina's mother was the victim of a hit-and-run by a drunk teen. That they would meet up with Alexander and come up with a plan. How an *aggression* virus was manufactured and a list of who was going to survive the mayhem was drafted.

But the year after the virus was unleashed had come and gone. People were still killing each other outside and millions still survived. Four years later and the 'one-year' virus, having mutated from species to species, still carried on strong. Humanity, though hidden and aware, still existed in the post-apocalyptic world. And the names on the *survivor's list* still lived underground.

'And that's the story of our great city,' Melissa concluded, raising her adenoidal voice and Mrs. Rania shook her head as to bring her mind back to reality.

'Wonderful, Melissa!'

Late that night, Andreas Onasi was awoken by footsteps outside their door. His wife lay fast asleep beside him. His bare feet landed on his Versace checkered-patterned slippers and he crept up to his bedroom door. He placed his ear against its cool surface. Footsteps and whispering. Both of his daughters had said their goodnights hours ago. He opened the door slightly ajar; a slice gap for a peek into the dark corridor. A shadow moved around against the wall. He switched on the lights and saw his daughter moving around, looking down. As he prepared to yell at his daughter for sneaking out and returning drunk, he noticed that she was in her white nightgown.

'What the hell, Melissa?'

The girl raised her head. 'Tiggy is missing.'

'It's a sealed underground city. There's only so many places she can go. Please go back to sleep.'

The next day, as soon as the fluorescent lights signalled

morning, Melissa searched for him before school. The cat was still missing. She met up with Aggelo, like always, at the corner by the movie room.

'Babe, I need your help...' she began to say.

'Godzilla is missing,' he spoke simultaneously.

'Someone's pulling a prank on us.'

'Huh?'

'My cat is missing, too,' she replied.

Their teacher arrived minutes late that day. 'I apologize,' Mrs. Rania said as she walked into the classroom, her hair grabbed in a loose ponytail. 'I could not find my dog this morning. I do not understand how he got out.'

Melissa and Aggelo exchanged a worried look. The list of missing animals was growing fast. The missing pets became the subject of the day in the small town. A cat, a dog and an iguana proved hard to find. By night time, none were found. None were seen.

Aggelo Milonas did not sleep that night. He decided to crawl into the city's air vent system. He was positive that it was the only logical place for his iguana to be.

On the other side of town, Melissa had also come up with a plan. She was going to use her father's master-key to sneak out that night and search around off-limit offices and laboratories. Her cat had to be somewhere.

She tiptoed down dark corridors and made her way to the main building in the center of the city. She beeped herself into the reception area. Faint light came from bulbs along the floor; activated only during night-time. As she moved forward, heavy breathing echoed towards her. She swung around, only to see shadows scatter and then the sound of a vase falling to the cold ground came from her right. Melissa began to step back. That's when she heard the scratching upon the tiles coming from the darkness. She turned and ran; the seconds seemed longer to her. As if she ran in slow motion. She slammed the door behind her and beeped it closed. A sound resembling grinding of teeth came from behind the door.

'Jesus Christ,' she said, exhaling deeply. 'What sick security has mother come up with?' She dashed home through the darkness and minutes later, hid underneath her warm covers.

Aggelo, also, heard steps behind him as he crawled through the large air vent tunnels. His flashlight danced around the metallic walls. Nothing was to be seen. He continued forward, his hands shaking, cold sweat dripping from his forehead. He turned the light around again. A large shadow moved towards him. Aggelo opened his mouth to scream, yet no sound came out. His throat was slit. Multiple strikes followed.

The news of the missing youth came as a shock to the small community who, up to that point, thought the three missing pets were an extreme crime in their utopia.

Schools was cancelled and many stayed home with their kids.

An emergency board meeting was announced and by nine, all members had gathered in the vast oval office.

The discussion did not take long to heat up.

'I told you we needed cameras down here,' Christina complained, blowing a hazelnut streak of hair from her olive-skinned face.

'It was supposed to be our safe haven away from the world. What sort of freedom would we have if a few of us watched over the others? We needed no authority. As much as you would have loved that!' Aika fired back.

'And we are arguing again,' Natalia interrupted.

'It's the years down here. It's driven us mad. We need to get out,' Zoe added.

Christina stood up and pushed her chair against the table. 'Right! So, Mister Science, why is your virus still out there? If we could at least live *on* the island and *not* under it!'

'Do you think the pets and the boy found a way out?' George Onasi asked.

'I doubt it. It was designed with only one main exit and a tunnel from here leading up,' his brother, Andreas, replied. 'Both as you can see, are still closed and need security over-ride to open.'

'Exit! More like an entry to Tartarus,' Rania added and said she was okay with any decision made. 'I'm going to go search for my pupil and dog.'

Search parties were organized, yet once again night-time came and none were found.

Mrs. Rania closed her apartment door behind her. Her weak ankles had swollen up. She walked up to her bathroom mirror and splashed cold water on her wrinkled face. 'Time still eating me away,' she grumbled. She undressed and carefully entered her shower. Water fell down and she closed her eyes. The cool droplets ran freely upon her body. She looked down to find her shampoo when she noticed a few red drops swimming around her feet. She turned around and noticed a rivulet of blood originating from her air vent and snake-lining down her bathroom wall. Her right hand pushed back the wet curtain and reached for her brown towel. She turned off the running water, wrapped the towel around her body and opened the door to let out the gathered steam. She pushed her stool towards the vent and stepped upon it, placing her eyes inches away from the cover. Suddenly, a loud rattling noise came from the darkness and the cover came flying off, pushing her back. Mrs. Rania fell back into the tub, face down, banging her head on the hard porcelain. Disoriented and drowsy, she struggled to raise her body. In the silence, she heard breathing behind her; warm breath felt on her right ear. Her eye pupils moved to view her attacker. Her screams were short-lived. What remained of her mutilated body was found the next morning.

Zoe used the master key to open her door after Rania did not show up for school or reply to her intercom. 'Oh, Lord,' Zoe gasped as she saw the chopped off leg in the bathroom doorway. She took a brave step forward to take a look into the dark room. Four red eyes came from the shadows. Zoe screamed and ran for the door, the heavy thuds of steps getting louder behind her. She raised the master key into the stale air and beeped the door open. Nails pierced her thighs and Zoe fell to the ground.

'Heeeelp!' she yelled as teeth made their way through her neck. Her head rolled forward and stopped upon the feet of Andreas Onasi who was first to the scene. Zoe's attacker was nowhere to be seen.

Deafening sirens boomed through the city and red flashing lights signalled the lockdown ordered. All civilians were to remain in their private quarters until further notice. A task force was set up and for the first time in Gaia's peaceful four-year history, guns were given out from the locked warehouse, hidden behind headquarters. The armed group of twelve, stepped out onto the deserted steel streets, their rifles raised to eye level. Half had never held a weapon before.

'Four groups of three,' Andreas Onasi said and pointed around at the men and women standing in a half circle opposite him under the bright fluorescent tube that ran above the main streets to give a feel of real sunlight.

Two women followed Onasi, Aika who had tied her long, silky, black hair into a ballet bun, and Natalia Aggelopoulou who grew up in a family of upper-class hunters. She wore what she referred to as her 'Sarah Connor' set. Boots, army jeans and a black tank top. They began their search from Zoe's room. The lights in her room flicked as if the wires had been messed with. Her electronic front door was stuck half-way; grunting to close, yet unable to. Onasi stood by the bathroom door and waved his gun in the small room.

The body -well, parts of the remains, was still there.

Onasi knelt by the tub and observed the bite marks along the bloody torso that was once his secret lover. He wiped a tear from the corner of his eye and exhaled with a prolonged sigh. Suddenly, a tumultuous rattling noise came from above. Heavy steps were clearly heard in the tunnels above. Onasi yelled to his female counterparts to beware. Aika had no time to react as she was currently looking into the living room's vent. The howling beast jumped upon her, pushing her back. Its red teeth dug deep into her shoulder and Aika shrieked in pain. A loud gunshot echoed through the low-ceiling space and silence fell. Onasi ran to Aika's aid, while Natalia stood proudly above her kill. The dog's muscles were still twitching and its mouth still foaming. Natalia never took chances. She took another shot right to the canine's head and with eyes wide open she yelled, 'it's the fucking virus. Quickly out!'

Onasi let go of Aika and ran with Natalia to the door. Aika limped behind them. 'No, no, wait,' she begged as her white blouse turned red. Onasi kicked the door twice and exhaled in satisfaction as it finally closed. He used his override master key, punched in his secret code and sealed the door for good. As Aika banged against the metal plates, he turned to Natalia. Ashen, she nodded. 'We have to burn her.'

Onasi opened the main framework panel on the wall opposite them and closed all doors in Zoe's apartment. They had prepared for a possible outbreak.

Inside, Aika sat on the floor sobbing as she took off her top and looked at her deep wound. She felt her heartbeat accelerate and anger building up. She despised Zoe's taste in art. She dashed around the room, clawing at the paintings on the wall; foam dripping from her yelling mouth. A hissing sound made her look up at the cloud of pale smoke coming into the room. Soon, the cloud turned red as flames ran through it gathering strength. Aika yowled in excitement as her skin boiled and caught fire. Her black, smoking, burnt body fell to the ground in less than a minute.

Onasi sat back and placed his head into his hands. That is where Alexander Vrahimi found him. 'Task force was successful. One team killed the cat and another shot the iguana. We placed them in sealed bags and burnt them in the incinerator.'

Onasi raised his sweaty head. 'Then why is your voice so fucking miserable?'

Alexander knelt before him; his eyes looking sideways. 'Your brother was scratched. We sealed him off and decided to quarantine him. I know I haven't found a cure yet, but...'

'Shut it, Alex. Just burn him. Burn him now!'

News spread like wildfire around Gaia. People hugged

their children and decided to remain inside their homes. Only the church welcomed a few daring souls that wandered *outside* to find comfort in their place of worship.

Christina Onasi scoffed as her husband told her about the packed church. 'We should have banned religion, too. It's so primitive. I can't believe the majority voted to keep Orthodoxy in the new world. Our new world.'

'Christina, I'm tired and my brother has died. Please, give it a rest.'

Eva eavesdropped on her parents' conversation. She crept backwards and went to her sister's room. Melissa was nowhere to be found. Pillows formed hills under her pink blanket; her parents believing she was mourning her lost boyfriend.

Eva looked around and noticed the tiny metallic screw that lay on the floor by her bedside table. 'Shit, Melissa,' she said as she looked up at the air vent cover, slightly out of place.

Seventeen-year-old Melissa crawled through the dark tunnels in search of Aggelo. She was sure that her practical boyfriend was alive and stuck or scared into hiding by the virus. She had to notify him that all three infected animals were terminated.

The vents smelled of smoke as she approached Zoe's apartment. The sight of blood drops in the vent made her stop. She checked that the mask on her face was tightly glued to her skin and her bottle's level of oxygen was in the green. She passed above the late woman's home and proceeded onwards. She headed for their secret meeting place. Their so-called love nest. A confined place behind Gaia's storage rooms. The air vent cover was open. Feet first, she climbed down into the small room.

'Baby, I knew you were here! The virus has been dealt with, you can leave…'

Her last words died as he turned and faced her. His mouth dripping saliva and blood. He leaped forward with manic screams. He grabbed her by her wavy hair, his quivering fingers tangled in her locks, and he began to bang her head repeatedly against the steel wall. Melissa passed out and fell to the ground.

Task force Two, notified by Eva, found them there. Aggelo had eaten half her face off by that time. He was shot three times in the head and both were burnt.

Natalia announced the death to her parents who broke down in tears in each other's arms. Eva shook her head, wiped her left eye and then grabbed her father's over-ride key and ran out.

'Eva!' her mother screamed.

Her father, followed by the task force, ran after her. Eva locked herself in the main headquarters. Onasi hit his hands against the glass door and yelled to her to open it. Eva smashed the key card in front of his eyes. Onasi stared at his daughter, puzzled and confused.

Eva sat on the large office chair and turned on the speakers' microphone.

'Dear citizens of Gaia. I am Eva Onasi and I injected the animals with the virus…'

Everyone paused and gazed at each other. Christina stopped her crying and looked up at the overhanging speaker. Her right hand covered her mouth and she bit down on her bottom lip.

'… I can't live another day down here. We have been lied to. A year! One year! It has been four and I believe they never plan on letting us out. I wanted to scare my parents and those in charge, in hope of fleeing this Hades. And now, my sister is gone. I don't want to live no more.'

Onasi licked his dry lips and ordered Natalia to shoot at the window as he saw his daughter place the red key in place. The key used to open the main gate to the outside world.

The bullet barely scratched the bulletproof glass. The task force watched in shock as the main doors opened and fresh air roamed through the corridors.

Never before had a gust of wind caused so much terror.

In a matter of minutes, rage haunted Gaia. The first gunshots were heard and chaos began. Eva used the fire escape ladder from her father's office and headed up the one hundred steps to freedom. She struggled with the door. With a smile painted on her youthful face, she pushed the lid open. The sun burnt her weak eyelids; it took a while to get used to. She took off her shoes and ran barefooted to the beach below. The fresh sea breeze and the majestic palm trees welcomed her. Soon, her toes sunk into the golden sand. 'I'm sorry, Melissa. See you soon,' she whispered and sprinted along the beach. The cool turquoise waters of the Ionian crashed against her legs as she ran in. She began to swim around, the cold waters soaking into her clothes.

'At last, feelings!'

She stood up and opened her arms wide. 'The sun, the sea, the air. Life!'

Her body, suddenly began to twitch. Her spine shook violently from side to side. 'Goodbye, freedom,' she said and her right hand went under her top and behind her back. She pulled out her father's firearm and placed it to her temple. Her finger trembled upon the trigger.

Yelling made her turn. People came running out of

Gaia's entrance, hitting, biting, and punching each other. Her naked father appeared on her horizon dragging her mother's lifeless body behind him.

Eva's finger never pulled the trigger. Inexplicable anger clouded her mind. All she wished to do was shoot at the wild crowd. Screaming at the top of her young lungs, she ran towards them shooting; her father being her first victim.

The sun, the sea, the mayhem…

JUNE OF RHYMES

CHIOS ISLAND

The smell of salty sea air blended with the aroma born from her freshly baked apple pie. Helen smiled at her two kids dancing happily around her, eager to devour their 'dekatiano', known in the modern world as brunch, these days.

'It needs to cool down first,' she said and jokingly smacked her son's right hand as it approached the sweet pie. 'Go keep yourselves busy for ten minutes or so. Let my masterpiece settle!'

Her teenage son grunted and with his shoulders lowered, he made his way to the living room. Helen shook her head. *'First day off school and he will spend it on his Playstation!'*

'Mummy? Can I go play outside? On the swings?' her six-year-old daughter asked.

'Sure, Eleonora. Anything you want! It's summer time, at last,' Helen replied, a motherly smile spreading upon her face as she stroked her daughter's rosy cheek.

'Beach or pool tomorrow?' the child kept on with the questions.

'Beach, as daddy will be off work too. Pool on Monday.'

Eleonora danced her ballet routine around her mother and rushed out the kitchen door. The small park was attached to their home. Helen was reluctant to buy a home without a garden, but after she saw the view from her seafront home, with its large verandas and the park beside it, she was sold on the idea.

'Be careful. I'll be on the balcony if you need me,' Helen yelled, hoping to be heard. She picked up the blue laundry basket filled with her kids' summer clothes and headed upstairs. *With this sun and breeze, they will be dry in no time.'*

Helen placed the basket on a wooden chair with a straw back and leaned over the railing. 'Hi, baby!' she waved down to her daughter who screamed with delight as she leapt on the swing. 'Quietly,' her mother advised, noticing another mother sitting on a green bench, reading her book while her son played carefree in the sand-pit by the towering oak tree.

Helen picked up a wet pair of shorts and gazed ahead. An endless blue horizon welcomed her. The sound of the waves mingled with the ferry boats' engines as they entered Chios's port, carrying hundreds of tourists from the mainland. Both sounds were drowned out by the rattling sound of the swing beneath her balcony. 'Not too high,' she called out to Eleonora.

The strong Greek summer sun fell upon her laundry as she finished hanging them up on her two washing lines. Helen picked up the empty basket and took one last look at the Aegean Sea. '*Majestic,*' she thought, smiling at the notion that she would ever get used to having such a view. 'Look at the house, not the view! You're not going to look at the water all day! The kitchen should be bigger,' she mimicked her mother-in-law's raspy voice.

Just then did she realize the silence from the park below. She approached the railings and looked down at the green park, expecting to see her daughter playing on the slides.

Empty swings and vacant slides filled her view.

Her honey eyes moved quickly from side to side, scanning the area.

'Excuse me,' she yelled. 'Where did the little girl go?'

The woman with the curly hair placed down her novel and gazed up, squinting her eyes at the bright sun rays. She finally spotted pale Helen on the balcony. She raised her hands as to signal that she had no clue. 'Maybe she came inside.'

Helen's knees felt like jelly. The house was also quiet. She pushed back streaks of blond hair that escaped her ponytail and exhaled. She dropped the basket and sprinted around the house calling her daughter's name.

'What's wrong, mum?' her son asked, removing his headphones.

'Have you seen your sister? Did she come in?'

The teen shook his head. 'She's outside playing, isn't she?'

Helen ran by him, pushed her kitchen door wide open and jumped down the steps.

'Eleonora!'

Helen stepped through the thick rose bushes behind the swings, thorns ripping through her yellow dress and cutting her bare thighs. 'Eleonora,' she screamed, her worried eyes moving along the busy sidewalk. She was ready to start asking passersby about her girl, when she noticed a piece of white paper on the swing. With an accelerated heartbeat, she approached. It was stapled to the wood.

'Faith's Bridge is falling down, falling down, falling down. Faith's Bridge is falling down, my fair lady,' she breathlessly read the hand-written note.

The following morning came and found Helen broken and in tears as no sight of her daughter was reported. Her feet were swollen from roaming the streets all night with her husband and relatives. Police had launched an island wide campaign to find the missing girl -the second missing child that week, though yet without any results.

Elli, an athletic student at the Aegean University, lived on the outskirts of town. Cheaper neighborhoods and better paths to run with her three dogs. Elli awoke as always on a Sunday; seven o'clock sharp. A daughter of a priest, she never missed a Sunday service. Her routine continued with a change of clothes after church and a long two-hour jog with her Labradors. She loved the scenic route towards the rather naked hills behind town. With Ariana Grande keeping her company through her iPod, she quickened her pace and breathed through her nose as she ran by the old landfill. It was deserted on a Sunday, yet its gates never closed. The lemon fields behind it, made it a worthy shortcut in Elli's book. As Elli exited the dump site, she noticed Julie was missing. She took out her earphones and gazed around.

'Julie?' she called out to her oldest Labrador. 'Stay here. Sit,' she said to the other two that obeyed immediately. Elli could hear her faint barks coming from her right. Elli stopped meters away from the howling canine and took small steps forward.

Among the trash, a child's foot could be seen.

'Holy Mary, mother of Christ!'

Elli shivered as she fought to catch her breath. 'Julie, sssh! Come here, now!'

Elli approached carefully for a better look. '*Could he still be alive?*' She touched the bare foot. Stone cold. The rest of the body lay below the garbage. Elli swallowed the lump in her throat and stepped back to call the authorities. Just then, did she notice Julie digging around in another pile of trash to her right. Elli screamed and covered her mouth as Julie kicked back a pile of old magazines to reveal a young girl's lifeless face.

Hours later, Helen ran into the morgue. Her husband, Tony, followed silently. He could not approach the metallic table with the white sheet. He could not believe that there was a chance that his baby girl was the small body covered in front of them. The coroner pulled back the sheet down to the child's neck.

Helen screamed and fell to all fours. Her stomach moved violently under her dress and she vomited on the cold detergent-smelling floor.

'No, no! Not my baby, God, no. I want to die. Make it stop! It hurts. It hurts so bad,' she screamed as her nails scratched upon the dark tiles.

Her husband wrapped his arms around her while tears fell from his still eyes. The hospital's psychologist and a male nurse helped them both up.

As a sedative was given to Helen and her muscles began to relax, she spotted a familiar figure from the corner of her eye. A short man from their local church's Sunday School had his head against the wall and was sobbing.

'The father of the other child,' the nurse whispered.

City of Athens

Ioli Cara swirled her trustworthy aged Opel into her old spot in the underground parking of Police Headquarters. The cavernous space was empty and only a few cars broke the endless grey that surrounded the tall Cretan. Ioli made her way to the elevator; her black heels breaking the silence as they struck the asphalt below them. She pushed number five and watched it glow red. As the doors closed in front of her, her hand travelled to her jeans' right pocket and she pulled out a black hair tie that would soon vanish in her pitch-black shiny hair. By the time the elevator doors reopened, she had fixed her hair in a high ponytail and was chewing the last two gummy bears that remained from the small packet in her pocket.

She stepped out and smelled the confined office air. Her eyes journeyed to her previous office; her name no longer on the door. She sauntered down well-known corridors and knocked on the only wooden door on the floor. She waited for the Chief's grunt of a 'come in'.

'Lieutenant Ioli Cara!'

'Good morning, Chief,' she replied, closed the door behind her and proceeded to make herself comfortable in one of the high-back armchairs opposite the mahogany desk.

'I can almost hear your brain's wiring in overdrive,' he

said and chuckled. 'Bet you're wondering why I called you down to Homicide...'

'Not really,' she replied and her 'Julia Roberts' smile spread upon her face. 'I'm guessing you have a case for me and due to the strike here at HQ still going strong, you called me in. Unfortunately, I'm just an office girl nowadays and anyway, the government should give in to field agents' demands...'

'Whoa, whoa, slow your donkeys, woman!' The Chief threw back his head and released his uproarious laughter. 'Yes, yes, spot on, but hear me out. It's not just any case. It's a serial killer on the island of Chios. Cara, he is targeting children.'

Ioli leaned forward and her fingers intertwined. He had her full attention.

The Chief threw a local newspaper on the coffee table in front of her.

'The Nursery Rhyme Killer?' she read.

'That's from today's Chios Reporter. It won't take long before it makes headlines around Greece. I can't appear on the news and say, you know what, local authorities aren't cut out for such a case as the serene island has never had a murder case before. Also, I have no expert to send as they are on all strike! The media will eat me up. Cara, I need you. You worked Homicide for eight years. You have the mindset and the training. I get your reasons for transferring to a desk job at Internal Affairs and I'm glad you are taking the time to raise your two boys...'

'But I'm your *only* option.'

'You're my *top* option. You were the best. Wish I had you back. You're only forty. You could return anytime,' he said and coughed. 'As I was saying, hear my offer. You take the police ferry to Chios. A nice four-star hotel. Work the case, three days tops and I'll give you two weeks paid leave. Two weeks with your boys now that it's summer and they are out of school. Come on, Cara. I know your mother comes and stays summers with you. Leave the kids with her for a few days and go earn your vacations. Think of the mothers who have lost their...'

Ioli raised her left palm. 'Okay, okay. No need for the guilt trip. I'll go and if I catch this fucker, it's three weeks paid leave.'

'Deal,' he replied, stood up and extended his right hand. He missed Ioli's firm grip during her handshake.

'And I'm only thirty-nine, by the way.'

Ioli Cara stepped out of the office and placed her hands on her head. *'My mother is fine with babysitting, but who the hell is going to explain this to Mark?'* Her husband was never fond of her precursory line of work and was a major reason of her career switch. *'Fuck it. He knew it was never going to be his way with me,'* she cheered herself up and laughed as the elevator doors screeched closed.

The midday sun hit her tanned skin as Ioli stepped out of the lone cabin and stood on the ferry's front deck. Chios Town filled her horizon as the speed boat slowed down and waves hit against it, splashing salty droplets on Ioli's hands. She held firmly on the railing and breathed in the pure air. Seagulls squawked as they circled the port in search for food. The ferry's engines died and they floated gently towards the pier. Soon, Ioli's feet landed on the concrete pier and with a lick of her lips, she walked towards the promenade. The local police station was -as Google Maps informed her- just a five-minute walk away.

Ioli strolled down a picturesque alley. One known well around the isles. It was the same street you would meet anywhere in the Aegean. Narrow, paved with rocks, featuring little shops with distinct personalities and flower-filled house gates, and having its shade provided by pink bougainvillea trees.

The building was easy to spot. Ioli walked through the old wooden doors and stood it the reception area of the lone police station in Chios Town.

'May I help?' a smooth voice came from her right. Ioli turned to see a blonde woman, not older than twenty-five, smiling from behind a too-tall for her counter.

'Lieutenant Ioli Cara. I'm expected?'

The young girl's eyes opened wide. 'Yes, yes, sure. Officer Markantoni will see you in his office. This way, this way,' she said. 'May I just say, it is an honor meeting you. You are a legend...' she added as she waved Ioli on, to follow her down the long corridor.

'A legend?' Ioli said and controlled her laughter.

The woman stopped and turned around. 'Of course! The most successful woman in Homicide, here on the islands. The Olympus Killer, the headless girl on Folegandros, the crazy...'

Ioli raised her hand and cut her off from retelling all of her major cases -or as Ioli referred to them by, her major scars.

'Here's the office,' the constable said, changing the subject. She knocked on the door, opened it and smiled at Ioli as she rushed back to her counter.

Ioli walked into the small office area with the two desks. A red-haired woman in her late twenties smiled from behind a computer screen, while police sergeant Markantoni stood behind his IKEA desk with his right hand extended. Ioli shook his rough hand and took a seat opposite him. For the next half an hour, she listened how two children were kidnapped and that nursery rhymes were left behind. First, a four-year-old boy was taken from a local supermarket parking lot.

'The boy's father placed the child in the car and walked back to the building to return the shopping trolley. In a matter of a minute, he returned to find the boy gone and a note laying on the car seat,' Markantoni said and cleared his throat as he passed her the note sealed in a plastic bag.

'Yianni Porgie pudding and pie, kissed the girls and watched them cry. When the boys came out to play, Yianni Porgie ran away,' Ioli read the wrinkled piece of paper. 'Did you have the paper and the ink analyzed?'

Markantoni nodded. 'Plain paper, cut from a normal A4 and the ink is from a black Bic Cristal pen. Found nearly everywhere. Before the second child went missing and the two bodies were found, I had the text scanned and sent to a professor at Athens University. He said that it is most likely a woman's writing and we are looking for a person who is intelligent, spontaneous and with the ability to focus on her goals,' he replied, reading from his notepad.

Ioli listened carefully. 'Can I see the second rhyme?'

She read it and placed the two notes side-to-side on the desk. 'They look the same, but did you have the expert confirm that they are written by the same individual?'

'The lab hasn't replied yet, but if you look at the 'y' in lady and the 'y' in cry, you can see it is the same person.'

'Where was the second child taken from?'

'Swing set by her house. Again, no one saw anything. And now they are both dead,' he said and looked down.

'You did everything you could. The deaths are always on the killer. Not you, not the parents.'

Markantoni forced a sorrow smile and passed her the coroner's reports. Ioli flicked through the papers. 'Both of them were strangled to death. The killer wore gloves,' Markantoni said as if to imply nothing else helpful would be found in those reports.

'Last meal? Did the killer feed them?'

Markantoni shook his head. 'If you see the estimated times of death, both were killed hours after being kidnapped. The killer probably kept the bodies and dumped them early Sunday when the garbage yard is closed.'

Ioli stood in front of the oval bathroom mirror and straightened her ponytail. After checking in, she had spent the next hour studying the case files, witness reports and searching the internet for analyses on the nursery rhymes. A hot shower, even though summer, and a change of clothes had the ability to lift her spirits. To calm the adrenaline of being back in the game. After a quick minute of makeup, she stepped out of her hotel room and took the elevator down to the lobby. She spun the keys to her rental as she ambled through the sunburned, coconut sunscreen-smelling tourists.

'Lieutenant Cara?' a voice came from behind her. Ioli turned around to see the young girl that was silently present in Markantoni's office. 'Police Constable Medea Kalouva. I am here to assist you with the case.'

Ioli frowned. 'I was under the impression, I would be working alone. I asked for no partner. I am here as a favor to the Chief and if lucky, to shine some light on this case.'

'A local could help you around. I will be awfully quiet. Just observing and speaking when spoken to,' Medea said and smiled. Ioli looked at her puppy-like eyes and swallowed the sound of a rising chuckle. The woman reminded her of her son when he wanted a chocolate Kinder egg.

'Okay, you can tag along,' Ioli replied, thinking that having a second person during visits to the parents could be useful. 'I'll find something for you to do.'

Soon, the two ladies were seated in the red Ford Focus and heading to Helen and Andrew Similide, parents of the murdered girl.

Ioli parked the rental by the curve of the park and gazed out at the sea. *'If only you could solve your own murder cases. I love you, but I need to escape you better,'* she thought as all her time travelling the Aegean, chasing murderers flew through her sharp mind. Ioli stepped out of the vehicle and headed towards the lone swing set. The park was deserted. *'Bad news travels faster than the speed of light on the islands.'*

Medea followed her and waited by the two-story house, while observing Ioli kneeling down by the swings. Ioli noticed the blue curtains move from the house beside her. The parents were waiting. She stood up, dusted off her navy-blue jeans and headed to the front door.

Soon, she was declining coffee or lemonade, sitting opposite two ashen parents who had their minds on their daughter's funeral.

'Seven! She will never be seven,' Helen cried. 'So much life ahead of her. To love, to study, to marry...'

Her husband placed his hand upon his wife's. 'Why do we have to go over this again?' he asked.

'Lieutenant Cara was specially sent here from head-quarters. In Athens,' Medea said, only to receive a cold side-look from Ioli.

'An expert on murder, huh?' the father asked.

'I'd rather think of it as expertise in case solving,' Ioli

replied and continued with her set of questions, based on the parents first testimony.

'You mentioned that you knew the father of the other child?' Ioli finally got to the question she wanted to ask.

Helen nodded and wiped her eyes. 'Yes, Peter. He attends the same Sunday School with his kids.'

'That's the only common ground, your kids had? No dance lessons, piano, or anything else?'

Helen shook her head and exhaled. 'Just there, but we never spoke. Tens of parents and children from our community go there. Our kids never played together. Different ages, different groups.'

'Hmm, I see,' Ioli said and scribbled down the word *coincidence* in her black notebook, followed by a question mark.

'And you both can't think of anyone with any intend on hurting you?'

Both shook their heads. The house phone began to ring and Andrew turned around. 'Excuse me. We have a funeral to organize. Just catch the bastard that hurt my baby,' he said and rushed to the phone.

Ioli leaned close to Medea. 'Stay here and keep the father busy when he returns.'

Then she turned to Helen. 'Would you mind joining me in the back yard? I see your fingers twitching for a smoke.'

'Oh, yes. We don't smoke in the house,' she replied. 'Kids' health,' she continued and scoffed as she got up, picked up her pack of cigarettes from the bookcase to her right and walked outside. Ioli followed her out into the bright sunlight, placing her dark shades back upon her face.

Helen turned to offer her a cigarette after lighting hers, but Ioli interrupted her.

'Mrs. Helen, I'm so sorry to be blunt, but time is important in such cases and I know you have just met me and believe me, I get the small island mentality,' Ioli rushed to say.

Helen looked puzzled. 'Go on.'

'It's just small signs we women notice. The way you didn't react to your husband's touch, you're not wearing your wedding ring like he is, you have no photos with him around the living room...'

'Excuse me?'

'Don't get me wrong, but London Bridge was written about Anne Boleyn's adultery...'

Helen let out a small gasp and looked back at the house.

'Helen, please speak to me. Whatever you say will be between the two of us. Trust me. Help me catch your daughter's killer.'

Helen took a step closer to her and dropped her cigarette to the dirt. 'I have a boyfriend. It's been going on for over a year now. He had nothing to do with this.'

'Is he married? Could it be revenge?'

Helen waved her hands. 'No, no. He is a caring widow that I met at Sunday School.'

On their way to the next parents, Ioli drove by long sandy beaches and with slight envy, looked upon the happy families enjoying their day under the sizzling sun and upon the golden sand.

'Medea, I will need you to keep the mother company. Separate her from the father. I need to speak to him alone.'

Medea nodded and her hair fell in front of her brown eyes. She pushed her hair back and continued looking at the photographs of the notes. 'You know, I always wanted to be a nursery teacher when I was a kid. Funny how I could have been singing these, rather than finding them in a murder case. What kind of person kills children?'

Ioli did not turn to look at her. 'One thing I have learnt working homicide, is that there are all sorts of *kinds* out there. Humans are the true monsters. All our nightmares? There is a kind of person just like that out there.'

Inside the three-bedroom apartment, Ioli's plan worked fine. After going over the parents' previous testimonial, Medea helped the mother in the kitchen with preparing coffee, while Ioli stood on the balcony with the father. Peter blew out a large cloud of thin smoke, courtesy of his electronic cigarette, and the smell of wild berries filled the air.

'Is there a Yianni at your Sunday School?' Ioli asked, leaning back on the dirty, yellow railing.

Peter squinted his eyes and tilted his bald head to the right. 'Erm, no. Though I do not know everyone there.'

'You know Helen though?'

'Just a hello. She is one of the eager volunteers there. You know, baking pies and selling them for charity and that sort of thing.'

'Ever see her talking with a widow who volunteers there? A Costa Mina?' Ioli asked, looking down at her notes.

Peter blew out another cloud of smoke. 'Gossip says they were having an affair. What has this got to do with my dead boy, Lieutenant?'

'Her affair may be linked to her nursery rhyme. I'm wondering how is your rhyme linked to you. So, no Yianni at Sunday School, but in general? Is there a Yianni in your life?'

Peter straightened his posture. 'Well, there's my boss...' he said and paused, taking a peek inside the house.

'And is he married?'

Peter shook his head.

'A ladies' man?'

'What do you really want to ask, Lieutenant?'

'Your rhyme. The name was changed. Georgie Porgie was a handsome ladies' man and rumors say he was even a lover to the king.'

Peter closed the balcony door. 'You believe the rhymes are about us? The parents?'

'Helen's was.'

Peter placed his face in his large hands.

'Peter, talk to me,' Ioli said, placing her hand upon his trembling back.

Peter took a step closer to her and whispered in her ear. 'I'm bi. My wife doesn't know. My boss, Yianni, is gay. You can say, we have a good time, every now and then,' he admitted and swallowed the lump cloaking his throat. 'If I am the reason my boy is dead, tell me now. I'll jump off this balcony as we speak.'

The creaking of the balcony door caught their attention.

'Coffee's ready,' his wife said with a faint smile.

The church of the Archangels towered all other buildings in the neighborhood. The stone-built megachurch was the largest on the island and one of the largest in all of Greece. By its side, a building surrounded by arches served as a multi-functional hall and that is where Sunday School activities took place.

Ioli had called and arranged to meet the lady in charge with supervising the activities and charities. For the time being, Ioli decided there was no need to bring in the priest who taught Bible stories to the children as he was out of town for the last two weeks on his annual leave and his whereabouts had been confirmed.

A short lady in her early fifties with Byzantine facial characteristics, dressed in all black met them by the large wooden door.

'Welcome to Archangels Church. May the blessings of Gabriel and Michael be forever upon you,' she said and asked them to follow her inside. 'Air-condition and home-made lemonade,' she said and smiled. 'I am Evelyn Patroklou. Event organizer for the church's youth depart-ment and I oversee all charity work,' she continued as she stopped by a tidy office. 'What a shame. Two of our own. Angels now, God bless,' she said and sat down. 'Please have a seat,' she said and sighed. 'What a horror. I am a mother also and all of this has scared me to my core. I haven't let my daughter out of my sight since,' she stated and her pupils moved to the right.

Ioli sat down in the uncomfortable, high-back, purple armchair and turned her attention to the blue-eyed girl playing on a computer, two desks down.

'Anneta's my only child and I cannot imagine life without her,' Evelyn continued. 'I prayed all night for her safety of all children, of course. Nothing worse or unimag-inable cruel as the loss of your own flesh and blood. You have to catch this demon.'

'That is why I am here,' Ioli replied. 'As I requested on the phone, I will need a list of all your attendees, here at Sunday School...'

'You believe it's someone from here?' Evelyn asked, her eyes opening wide.

'We examine all sides of a cube. Mostly, it's for their

own safety. If there is a pattern to our killer, maybe I can figure out his next move,' Ioli replied.

Evelyn nodded and opened her desk's top draw. 'Printed it out when you called.'

'May I ask, mother to mother, is there anything out of the ordinary, an argument between parents or something of the sort that you have noticed? Any new members that don't fit in with the rest of the group?'

'Nothing of the sort. All God-fearing servants of Christ here. We promote love and happiness in our group. People come here for their kids to enjoy their Sunday and feel close to God. Trouble-making sinners don't belong here,' she said and did the sign of the cross on her upper body.

'Thank you for the list,' Ioli said and stood up. Religious, yet open-minded, Ioli never could stand religious labels. She disliked the word sinners. 'Come on, Medea,' she said as she noticed the young officer still in her seat, playing on her cell phone.

Outside in the sun. Ioli rubbed her lower back and turned towards her hired car.

'Do you mind?' Medea asked, pointing to the church. 'I won't be long. I just want to light a candle for the Holy Mother.'

Ioli's phone began to vibrate in her pocket. She brought it to her ear and gave Medea a thumbs up. Medea rushed to the church as Ioli listened to the Chief's deep voice. After Ioli gave him an update on her day, the Chief replied. 'Bravo. Keep it up. I trust you, Cara. Sorry, I persuaded you to go down there and work alone on an unknown island...'

'No twisting my arm, Chief. I accepted the job. And I have a partner, not that she is of much help, to be honest.'

'A partner? I thought you wanted to work alone.'

'I did. But as you assigned her...'

'Cara, I assigned no one.'

Minutes later, Medea came out of the church and strolled towards Ioli who sat on the car's bonnet and had opened a pack of jelly babies. Medea's curly hair danced upon the light breeze as she asked, 'where to now, boss?'

Ioli swallowed the sugary jelly in her mouth and stared straight at her *partner*. 'Back to the station. Where I will ask Markantoni who assigned you to this case, Miss I-wanted-to-be-a-nursery-teacher!'

Medea stopped on the spot, her mouth open, yet no words coming out. She shook her head and waved with her palms. 'No, no,' she finally spoke as Ioli stood motionless opposite her, her right hand behind her back; her finger just an inch away from her gun.

'No, what?'

Medea pushed her hands through her hair and held her head. 'I just wanted some experience. No one trusts me with anything. I want to get off this island. I want to work homicides and be someone. Someone like you. Strong-willed women have no opportunities here. I sort of didn't lie to you. I said to you at your hotel that I came to assist you. I never used the word assigned,' the olive-skinned woman said in one breath. 'I just wanted to solve the case with you...'

'And get the credit?' Ioli said, her arms resting by her sides.

'No, no. Maybe just a recommendation letter from you. To have a note saying I'm worthy to work murder cases, signed by someone famous like you...'

'Cool your horses, kid. I'm not Nana Mouskouri...'

Medea smiled widely. 'I gave all the exams for a promotion and...'

'And now you're heading home. I can't have you with

me without authorization. It could be considered contamination of a crime scene. Please, just go.'

Ioli sat back on her vehicle and watched as Medea walked off with her shoulders down and kicking the dirt as she headed for the one-bench bus stop.

Her cell phone vibrated in her hand. Unknown number. 'Hello?'

'Lieutenant Cara? This is Markantoni. We have another dead kid!'

Ioli switched off the car stereo and drove in silence as she followed Markantoni out of town. He signalled left and she turned after him down a long uninhabited dirt road.

'Where the hell are we going?'

Ten minutes later, signs of civilization appeared as the wheels touched asphalt and Ioli gazed upon a huge sign.

WELCOME TO THE MASTIC VILLAGES.

Ioli smiled fondly as she thought of her eldest son's lone request. 'If you're abandoning us with dad for three days to go to Chios, you better bring us back some mastic chews and sweets!'

The car driven by Markantoni turned left again. 'Mesta Village, three kilometers,' Ioli read the sign.

Soon, both cars were parked outside of a large cottage in the center of a farm. Ioli looked around as Markantoni joined local police officers and went over their notes. Animal sounds and wild crying by the child's mother filled the air. Ioli spotted the lanky coroner standing by the well with two paramedics and two of his assistants, both dressed in pure white. They had reeled the body of the three-year-old boy up and were being careful to place the corpse on the thick plastic mat they had laid down upon the yellowish summer grass.

The front door being flung open made Ioli jump. The boy's mother came crawling out of the door, screaming to see her son. Her husband held her tightly by her waist, while she scratched the wooden floorboards of her porch.

Markantoni tapped Ioli on her shoulder and passed her a nylon bag. 'They said the note was placed in their mailbox. The boy had only been missing for a couple of hours, so they didn't notify us, but looked for him themselves. The father saw him floating in the well and called it in.'

Ioli nodded and looked down at the note. 'Jack and Jill, went up the hill to fetch a pail of water. Jack fell down and broke his crown; and Jill came tumbling after,' Ioli read the words formed by magazine cut-outs. Ioli passed him back the note, took one look at the parents and sprinted towards the medical examiner. She flashed her badge and with her eyes set straight -away from the lifeless, wet, bloody child, she asked the cause of death. 'Too soon to say,' the silver-hair man with the small black glasses replied, slightly annoyed. 'But, this blunt trauma at the back of the head has ripped his skull wide open.'

'Thank you,' Ioli replied and ran back up to the farm house. She beeped open her rental and sat in her car, taking all her notes in her hands. The nursery rhymes, the testimonials, the church lists, everything.

Ten minutes later, Markantoni tapped on her window. 'Want to speak with the parents?'

'Did they attend Sunday School?'

The thin man shook his head. 'Not even Orthodox. Roma. They don't own the place, just work here and keep the house intact. The owners live in Athens.'

Ioli turned the ignition key. 'I've got to go,' she said.

Soon, the dust from her wheels clouded a puzzled Markantoni.

Ioli blessed the Lord for Google Maps as she said goodbye to the wild waves and turned into town. She also praised Google for its news articles. A famed architect. A murderous fire in Volos.

Soon, her phone repeated her destination and informed her that she had arrived at her desired number on Philellinon Street. The young girl dancing ballet on the front lawn left no doubt. The blue and white mansion with the big square windows was where Ioli hoped to get answers.

'Hello there,' she said as she walked up to the closed gate. Ioli flashed her trademark smile. 'Remember me? Anneta isn't it?'

Anneta paused. She looked at Ioli and turned towards the house.

'Please, stay. I'm a mother of two children and I'm good at picking things up. Like a blonde blue-eyed girl rolling her eyes while her mother talked lovingly about her. A girl dressed in long sleeves and trousers at the end of June...'

'Sshh! She notices everything. Come round the side. By the lemon trees,' the girl said and continued dancing. She danced until her shadow was swallowed by the thick-leaved trees and rose bushes. 'You're that cop, right?'

Ioli nodded. 'I'm Ioli. I can help you. You can trust me.'

'Is Evelyn in trouble?'

'You mother...'

'She's not my mother!'

Ioli came close and placed her hands on the young girl's

137

sweaty hands that held the white wooden fence. 'I guessed that from your appearance, but I wasn't sure...'

'I was seven when she came to the orphanage. I remember. And then we moved here.'

'What's with the long clothes? Religious choice or does she hurt you?'

Anneta's eyes watered up. 'She says sinners have to pay.'

Ioli stroked the young girl's warm cheek when Evelyn's voice was heard.

'She's looking for me. Don't say anything!' the youth said and ran inside the house.

A minute later, Ioli rang the doorbell. Evelyn squinted her eyes and gazed upon Ioli. 'Officer, good afternoon. What brings you to these parts?'

'I have a few questions about the list you prepared for me'.

'Come in, come in,' she said and took a small step to the side. 'Join me in the living room. Tea? Coffee?'

'No, thank you. A small chat will be fine.'

Both women settled down on the ivory three-seater sofa. The air in the room was fresh and scented by numerous vanilla-fragrant candles. The thin curtains danced around their window frames as air rushed in freely. Not a single window or door was closed.

Evelyn brought her expensive china to her lips and took a sip of her green tea. 'Something wrong with the list I prepared for you. Lieutenant?'

'I was just curious how come you erased Helen and Peter from your lists so soon. Helen has another child. She could still come here.'

Evelyn coughed quietly. 'I thought you needed a suspect list. They didn't kill their own children, did they?'

'Then why did you erase Costa Mina from your list, too? His children are alive and well.'

Evelyn sat back uneasily. The tea cup shook upon its plate as she placed it back on the glass coffee table. 'I'd rather keep that information to myself...'

'Because he was a sinner? Having an affair with Helen, was he?'

Evelyn's dark-brown eyes opened wide. 'I see these Chiotes still have gossip as their national sport. Yes, they were having an affair. Now Helen is gone, I see no reason why Costa will keep coming here. His children are too old for our activities anyway.'

'Not from the island, are you? Where are you from, Mrs. Evelyn?'

Evelyn's lips tightened and formed a straight line. She took a moment before replying. 'Volo.'

'Your husband, too?'

'What is it you want to know, Mrs. Cara?'

Ioli turned her phone's screen towards her.

'Reading up on me, I see? And you see fit to show me such old news. To throw salt on my soul's opened scars?'

'Your house caught fire and both your husband and daughter died that day. You tried to join the Sisterhood of Nuns in Volos, yet was denied due to your years in a mental institution as a young adult and rumors that it was you who had set the fire. Fast-forward a year later and you show up here, with a child you call your daughter and for the last few years have been in charge of Sunday School. What broke you? Too many sinners around? A married woman's affair, a gay lover...'

Ioli, though known for her great reflexes, had no time to react. Evelyn grabbed the knife lying on the table by the two pieces of carrot cake and stabbed Ioli in her right leg.

Evelyn leapt from the sofa and ran for the door. A loud smashing sound echoed around the vast high-ceiling room. Ioli stood up and ground her teeth in pain. She pulled out her firearm and limped to the door; the knife falling from her bloody leg. Her wound was an inch deep at most. Evelyn lay on the ground, while Anneta stood above her; her feet steady among pieces that once formed a Persian vase.

'I'm your mother!' Evelyn yelled.

'Screw you, bitch!' Anneta replied, pulled off her sweater and ran upstairs.

Ioli kept her gun on Evelyn and ordered her to remain still, yet her eyes could not help but travel along the girl's bare skin. Burns from cigarettes and various bruises shaped a brutal mosaic. The word *sinner* had been carved on her back.

'They all deserved it!' Evelyn yelled, staring at the look of disgust on Ioli's face.

'Innocent children?'

'Their infidel parents! That whore having an affair in plain sight and men sleeping with each other! Sodom and Gomorrah! If the Lord took away my child with such ease, then these sinners deserve to have theirs' taken away from them!'

The strong summer sun journeyed towards the thin line between blue sea and turquoise sky. Markantoni lit a cigarette and walked over to the lone bench in the police parking lot. Ioli sat with her legs curled up, stroking her leg's stitches and enjoying another bag of delicious jelly babies.

'I can't believe the religious quiet lady in charge of our

Sunday School and local charities killed three children! How did you figure it out?'

'Two,' Ioli replied and bit off the head from a purple sweet.

'What?'

'Two children. That's how it all started in my brain. The third murder did not stick with the rest. No alteration in the nursery rhyme, not written by pen, the kid died from a head trauma, not in town...'

'So, who killed the third kid in the well?' Markantoni asked and lit another cigarette from the end of his previous one.

'I can only guess that it was probably an accident and the parents got scared, panicked and staged the scene. The details were all in the papers about the nursery rhyme killer. Well, I hope it was an accident. The mother's tears and pain were real. But that's up to you to investigate. I closed my case. It's back to my noisy kids and my serene office in internal affairs for me,' Ioli said, chuckled and stuck two jelly babies in her mouth.

Markantoni stood up, threw his cigarette to the ground, nodded with a smile and turned to leave, eager to interrogate the Roma boy's parents.

'Oh, Markantoni? Take Constable Medea with you. She needs this case on her resume. Let her arrest the guilty parent.'

Ioli strolled down the long promenade that hugged the town and settled down on a whale-tail shaped bench. She took her phone in her hands and texted her husband. 'Baby, case closed! Tell the boys, mummy is coming home tonight!

Summer holidays, woohoo! Three weeks with them! God help us all, lol,' she whispered the words as she typed.

A savoury aroma invaded her space as she gazed at the short-lived waves rushing to die with a thunder on the sandy beach. It tickled her nostrils and Ioli turned around. A cozy Greek restaurant with blue chairs and white tables was just meters away.

'Nothing wrong with enjoying a piece of moussaka and an ice-cold Mythos before heading home.'

JULY OF FAMILY

MILOS ISLAND

July, 2017

Their bodies left the cool air-conditioned lobby behind and each pore on their skin immediately felt the invasion of the sticky heat. The family of four stood reluctant to step out of the shade provided by the arches and columns that ran around the Archaeological Museum of Milos.

'Such a small island and yet the sea seems so far away,' fourteen-year-old Sebastian said, his eyes fixed on the boats floating upon the calm waters of Milos Bay, one of the largest natural bays in the Mediterranean.

'That's because we are up high. The whole of Plaka is built upon a tall rock,' his mother, Dido, replied, trying to catch a string of blonde hair that had escaped her straw hat and danced upon the hot breeze.

'It feels like we are in a microwave,' Effie commented as she hugged her fluffy toy rabbit.

Her father, Aristotle Rapti, looked down at her. 'Have you ever been in a microwave?'

Effie did not have time to come up with an answer. The honking of the white Mercedes grabbed their attention. Their driver parked in front of them, rushed out of the vehicle and opened the back doors for the Rapti family.

'Sorry, I am late,' the sunburned man apologized. Aristotle nodded without a smile or a word of reply.

Soon, the speeding car reached the long road that snake-lined down to the beach. Tall majestic palm trees ran along the newly-paved sidewalk. As the Mercedes reached the beach resort's automatic gates, Sebastian asked if they had time for the beach.

'We went to the beach this morning. If you fancy a swim, that's what the pool is for. I'm not paying five hundred Euros per night for a private villa and pool, for us to be at the free beach all day,' his father answered and chuckled. He turned towards his wife, who smiled widely and placed her hand on his right knee.

'Well said, dear. And the pool has such a view. I'll join you in the pool, Sebastian.'

In a matter of minutes, with the blue villa door closed behind them, the family rushed to put on their swimwear and dive into the luring serene waters of their terrace swimming pool.

'I'll pass,' Aristotle said and headed upstairs for a much-needed shower. He dropped his clothes to the floor and naked as he was, he gazed out of the large window. 'Endless blue,' he whispered as his eyes marvelled at the Aegean. Waves travelled from the horizon and died upon the sandy beach below. '*So, this is what success looks like,*' he thought as his mind journeyed to his booming coffee franchise. He looked down and laughed at his erection. '*Well, my ex always did say that money turned me on!*'

Soon, he stood under the cold running water and masturbated with force.

His wife was also enjoying the same view as her kids splashed each other and yelled in excitement.

'*It's just another day in paradise,*' she thought and sighed.

Hours later, with her children safe and sound asleep in their beds, she crept into bed next to her half-asleep husband.

'Finally, you came to your man,' he said and turned towards her. He pressed his naked body against hers and licked her neck, before gently biting her earlobe.

Dido kissed him on his shaved cheek and turned away from him. 'I have a weird pain in my stomach today, if you don't mind.'

Her husband did not reply. Dido killed the silence and added, 'we need supplies. We've run out of milk, cereal, Evian. I'll pop into that local store in the morning. I'll take the kids. Give you time to relax in peace.'

'Perfect!' was his last word. Lights were switched off and darkness devoured the room.

Meters from the sea, a white corner building of two floors housed Vidalis' supermarket which had nothing to envy of the big stores in the capital. Its location was ideal for shopping after a refreshing morning swim in the tamed waters.

Dido sat on a green wooden bench and with her blue eyes safely behind designer sunglasses, she watched her children swim around carefree in the calm waters of the bay. She took her romance book in her hands and called out to her kids. 'You have one hour exactly!'

Later, Dido, dressed in a revealing tank top and jean

shorts, pushed her screeching cart around the aisles while Effie and Sebastian, still in their swim wear, played hide-and-seek behind the heavily-stacked shelves and screamed in joy when they were discovered.

'Sshh,' an elderly lady, clothed in pure black, said and threw a disapproving look towards Dido.

'I'm sorry,' she apologized with a genuine smile. Suddenly, a large thud was heard as she crushed her shopping trolley into a pyramid of Cokes. The soft drinks tumbled down and scattered across the detergent-smelling beige tiles. All shoppers turned around, while the young woman at the cash register jumped from her soft seat. The store owner came running over to find Dido and her children picking up the Coke cans.

'It's okay, it's okay,' he repeated and a wide islander's smile raised his thick moustache. 'I'll fix them. Silly idea anyway,' he said. 'My daughter sees all these ideas from the internet and...'

'No, no,' Dido replied. 'It's my fault. If any are dented, I will pay you...'

'Out of the question!' he said and joined in the search for the rest of the cans. 'Mummy's little helper, huh?' he asked as he smiled at Effie. He reached out and went to stroke her honey-colored hair. The seven-year-old stepped back and dropped the four cokes tucked away in her red T-shirt.

'She doesn't like being touched,' her brother said and quickly picked up the fizzy drinks.

Half an hour later, they were finally out of the store and with a paper bag each, they walked back up the palm tree road towards their rented villa.

Dido pushed open the garden's side gate with her foot and walked by rose bushes begging for water under the sizzling Greek sun. She stopped at the sight of the smashed kitchen window. The freshly-painted blue door stood ajar and screeched as gusts of wind rushed up the hill.

'Aristotle? Honey?' she called out as she took two reluctant steps towards the house. Silence.

'Kids, stay here! Sebastian, keep an eye on your sister,' she ordered and tiptoed into the house. The kitchen was empty.

'Hello?'

She continued into the vast living room. Dido froze at the sight of her dead husband in the middle of the leather sofa. Half his face was missing and crimson blood decorated the wall behind him. Dido fell back and covered her mouth. She reached for her cell phone and crawled to the kitchen. She stood up and rushed outside to her children, as her fingers dialled 1-1-2.

'Emergency services, how may I be of assistance?'

Christian Garcia awoke with the sound invasion provided by his phone's ringtone. He sat up, naked on his single bed in the middle of his studio apartment, and tried to focus on the bright screen breaking the darkness of the room.

'Good morning, mother,' he grunted.

'Happy birthday, my boy,' her happy voice came through loud and clear. 'My son, thirty-five today!'

'Whoopy!' Christian replied, stood up and turned on the lights. Shadows ran back to corners and his dirty untidy floor came into sight.

'Why do you sound so sleepy? It's the middle of the day...'

'I'm off work today, ma. Went out last night...'

'With a special lady? Please say, yes. All my friends have grandkids and I have a single son...'

'Jesus Christ, mama. Out with the boys. Tough luck. Sorry, I'm such a reproducing failure. I'll do my best to knock up a girl one of these days and drop the baby off at your steps,' he said, placed the call on speaker and rushed to the toilet to relieve himself from last night's whiskey.

'You think you're being funny, but I swear, that scenario is fine by me. Here, your father wants you.'

Christian wore a black pair of boxers as his father's deep voice covered his mother's chattering. 'Feliz cumpleanos, mi mijo.'

His parents and their gossip kept him company as he dressed and prepared a frappe. Two coffees, three sugars, more milk than water. 'Guys, I've got to go. Work is calling me,' he said as he noticed his phone's screen.

'Bet he is lying to us,' his mother's last words were heard as he ended the twenty-minute call.

'Hello?'

'Lieutenant Garcia, I know it's your day off, but there has been a murder, sir. Happy birthday, by the way,' Constable Helen Aristeidou informed him.

Garcia drove up the smooth hill road and whistled at the stunning view below. Both of his apartment windows provided him with a view of moldy bricks. He parked his Ford behind the lone police vehicle on the street and walked the stone path up to the Mediterranean villa. He noticed Constable Aristeidou standing by a woman with two children snuggled up in her arms; all three sat motionless on a bench in the garden's far east corner. Constable Michael

Papa stood by the house's front door, his face ashen and his beady eyes wary.

'What have we got, Papa?' Christian Garcia asked, towering over the short officer.

Papa raised his hand. 'Give me a second, boss. I'm trying hard to keep my brunch in.'

Garcia rolled his bright green eyes. 'God, I hate that word.'

'Boss?'

'Brunch. Get to it, Michael.'

Papa swallowed the lump cloaking his tight throat and exhaled. 'Dead man, in his early forties. Shot in the head. Half of his face is gone and his brains are decorating the wall. Wife came back with the kids from a morning swim and found him. Kitchen window has been smashed...'

'Anything missing?'

'I'm thinking theft, too. But with the body still there, I couldn't ask the wife to confirm if anything of value is missing.'

Garcia looked at the shopping bags lying on the grass. 'Morning swim, you said?'

'And supermarket visit. The family has been gone for at least four hours.'

'The coroner?' Garcia asked, as he stepped by Papa and entered the house.

'On his way,' Papa's high-pitched voice followed him into the mansion.

Garcia tied two plastic bags onto his feet and took the camera hanging from his neck into his hands. He photographed the dead man from all angles, the wall behind him, as well as the gun and continued snapping all the way to the kitchen and the fragments of glass on the floor. He proceeded to go upstairs and took pictures of the upper floor. By the time he came back down, the coroner and two paramedics were examining the body. Garcia shook hands with his drinking partner, AKA 'divorced coroner slash party animal'.

'I see your birthday is going fine,' the coroner commented with a slight smile.

'Tell me about it,' Garcia replied. 'ASAP with your report.'

The coroner winked and ducked back down to help with raising and carrying the lifeless body of Aristotle to the ambulance. Garcia bagged the firearm and passed it to Papa as he exited the four-bedroom villa. 'Fingerprints. Number of bullets fired. Match gun to the bullet in the victim's head,' he said. He then read the notes given to him by Papa as he lowered his dark shades to his chiselled face and walked over to the family. Christian squatted opposite them. 'Mrs. Rapti, I am so sorry for your loss. I am Lieutenant Christian Garcia and on behalf of Milos Police Department, I guarantee you that we will do our utmost to...'

'Garcia?' Dido interrupted, raising her eyes to look at the olive-skinned man in the white shirt. 'Spanish?'

'Erm, yeah. Father's Spanish, mother's Greek.'

'Hmm, you must tell me that story one day. I'm a romance novelist. I love hearing how people met,' Dido replied and wiped her right eye with her hand.

Garcia stood up and scratched the back of his head. 'Maybe we could talk over there on the patio, Mrs. Rapti? I need your statement. The kids can stay here with Helen,' he said and smiled at Effie.

'Mum, don't leave us,' Sebastian complained.

'It's okay, dear. Stay, protect your sister. I'll be fine,' his mother replied, kissed them both on their foreheads and followed Garcia to the garden armchairs that were by the kitchen door.

White seagulls circled them as Garcia opened the patio umbrella and blocked out the ferocious midday island sun.

Garcia opened his blue notepad as his eyes examined the blonde woman with the porcelain skin. His gaze ran along her shoulder freckles, up her twitching neck and stopped on her steady blue eyes. Dido's fingers intertwined and her eyes concentrated on a galling wasp that had settled on the aluminium table's leg.

'Mrs. Rapti, I do realize you have just lost your husband, but first testimonials are usually the most crucial. May I ask, what time did you return home today?'

'Must have been nearly twelve,' she replied, her eyes still focused on the insect.

'And what time did you leave the house this morning?'

'Around eight.'

Garcia nodded. 'Was your husband awake? Why didn't he come with you for a swim?' he asked, maintaining a steady rhythm and tone.

'Do you have children, Mr. Garcia?' she replied, finally raising her eyes.

'Much to my mother's despair, no, I do not.'

Dido spoke as she pulled back her hair and with a green hairband, she prisoned her golden locks in a high ponytail. 'It's so hot,' she commented, wiping the back of her long neck. 'My husband needed some time without the kids. We love our children, but as any parent knows, they can drive you mad. My husband was a hard-working business man.'

'Rich business man?'

'He did well.'

'Do you post often on social media, Mrs. Rapti? Who

knew he would be alone today? Did you run into any acquaintances or friends during your stay on the island?'

Dido exhaled and licked her lips. 'Wow, this is just like those crime shows Aristotle used to like. So many questions. Err, no. I don't use Facebook and such. Only to promote my books. And no, no one we know on the island. And, no. I can't think of anyone who would have wanted to hurt my husband, if that is what you are thinking. He was a lovely man. This must be a random robbery gone sour. It's a fancy villa and..'

Garcia placed his arms on the table and leaned forward. 'You believe this is a robbery? Why would thieves leave their gun behind?' Garcia continued with his method of multiple questioning.

'Oh, that's Aristotle's gun,' she replied and watched as Garcia's eyes widened.

'You brought a gun with you? On holiday? Did your husband sense he was in danger?'

Did shook her head. 'No, no. He always carried it with him. Ever since he made his first million. Overprotective and a bit paranoid, but not against anyone specific.'

Christian Garcia scratched his forehead and looked straight into Dido's eyes. 'Okay, we are going to go inside. You are not to touch anything. I mean anything. Look around and tell me if something important has been stolen.'

Dido nodded in agreement and breathed loudly through her nose. She stood up and walked up to the kitchen door. For the next half an hour, Garcia followed her around and noted down her thoughts.

Back outside, Garcia approached Constable Aristeidou. 'You are going to take them to Thalassitra Village Hotel. Book them a room. She has been informed that she is not allowed to leave the island for at least three days. If any relatives or friends show up, let me know.'

'Someone will come on the next ship. She can't go through this alone.'

'We'll see,' Garcia said and an enigmatic smile formed above his strong jaw.

Back at the police station, Christian Garcia closed his office door behind him, kicked off his black shoes and switched off the lights. He sat in the dark and let the case details roam in his brain.

Michael Papa had the irritating habit of not knocking. Today was no exception.

'Hey boss, just letting you know, everything has been sent to our labs to Athens. The coroner is performing his autopsy as we speak and as you ordered, we have two officers asking around the villas to see if anyone saw or heard anything,' Michael Papa said and then whistled. 'A murder on our island. Thieves are getting out of hand. Poor family...'

'Yeah, I'm not buying it,' Garcia said, leaped out of his chair, picked up his shoes and stormed out the room.

'What?' puzzled Michael asked as the Lieutenant rushed by him.

'Tearless wife, I have seen before. Tearless kids? Never.'

'Where you off to boss?'

'The supermarket,' Garcia replied and exited the station. Soon, with his windows down and George Ezra on the radio, he drove down to the bay. Sandy beaches zoomed by and with slight envy, he gazed upon the happy families and couples soaking up the mighty sun rays.

Garcia lowered his music and parked between two rentals. He cracked his knuckles and stepped out of the police vehicle.

The store was in full swing, with locals and tourists alike filling up their trolleys. '*The Greek summer always opens the appetite,*' he remembered his grandma's words. '*Especially the sweet tooth!*'

Garcia knew his destination. A family friend, Mr. Vidali was expecting him in his office. Garcia always called ahead.

'Come in, young Christian. Here, take my seat,' the man said and stood up. 'The footage from the security cameras as you asked. It's an easy program. Made for old fools like me. Forward, rewind, just like a movie,' he said, and chuckled.

'Thank you, sir.'

'Anything to drink, my boy?'

Garcia shook his head and sat down in front of the screen. As he pressed play, the screen split into four. Footage from all four cameras located in the store.

'Have fun. It begins as soon as the family came into the shop,' Mr. Vatali said and exited the office, leaving Christian alone. His green eyes watched the screen carefully. '*The kids are being loud only when someone is near them.*'

Garcia watched as Dido crashed into the Coke cans and replayed the scene six times. '*You saw them… did you crash on purpose?*'

As Mr. Vidali was helping a senior lady with her bags, he felt Garcia's hand on his shoulder. 'Thanks. I owe you a drink. Anytime, anyplace. Call me,' Garcia said and sprinted for his car.

Dido was surprised to see the Lieutenant so shortly after their first conversation.

'More questions?' Dido asked, standing at her hotel room door. 'My children have just lost their father, you know. They need me.'

'Sorry, blame my blend of stubborn Mediterranean genes, but I need to speak to your children.'

Dido squinted her eyes and focused on the sweaty officer opposite her. 'You ran all the way here, to bug my kids hours after their father's murder? Sorry, but no. Don't you need a warrant or at least my permission? They are under age...'

'You seem to have solved the case, Mrs. Rapti. You were sure it was a robbery. You walked through the villa and listed everything missing. Four thousand Euros, golden rings and a pearl necklace, you said without properly checking around.'

'Well, you did say touch nothing!'

'And you are sure it was murder. Suicide never crossed your mind?'

'With the gun at such a distance?'

'Guns do kick, you know?'

The two stood opposite each other in silence. Their eyes showing a mixture of anger and peculiarly a sense of admiration for each other. Both strong-willed.

'So, not even a casual talk with your son, at least?'

Dido shook her head. 'Have a good afternoon, officer. Let us grieve.'

'Grieving usually means pain and tears. Not relief,' he said and stepped back as she slammed the wooden door in his face.

Garcia was a practical man. He packed an overnight bag in under ten minutes. It took him longer to beg the old lady living opposite him to take care of Trickster, his singing parakeet. Even longer was the drive to the port and the search for a parking spot in the middle of high season. As he exited the car, he read a message from the coroner. 'Report is on your desk. Where are you? The body was still warm-ish. Max, three hours dead.'

'*Shit. The family was at the supermarket...*'

With his athletic build squeezed in one of the ship's passenger seats, Garcia sighed, lowered his sunglasses and drifted off to dreamland.

The deafening sound of the boat's horn made him jump in his chair. Garcia looked down at his wristwatch. '*Three hours in a split second.*'

The metropolis of Athens filled their horizon as the ship made its way to the port of Piraeus. Garcia stepped outside and took a deep breath. '*Last fresh air before the pollution.*' An islander and a seaman to his core, Garcia hated the idea of cities. 'People need their space. To be in nature. On a mountain, in a plain, by the sea. Cities are unnatural. Like an ant colony. A huge prison where individuality goes to die,' he would rant over a cold pint at the local bar.

'*At least it was easy to find a taxi,*' he thought as the yellow vehicle made its way through endless traffic.

An hour later, he was at police headquarters picking up files concerning the Rapti family. In the back of his waiting taxi, he read through them. '*Neighbors called in... screaming at all hours... bruised eye... wife never filed a complaint... concerned teachers about Sebastian... kids were often taken to their grand-mothers...*'

Piece by piece the frame of a violent puzzle began to form. 'And I know exactly how to fill it in,' Garcia whispered as he stepped out of the parked vehicle and looked around.

The prestigious neighborhood of Kolonaki with its expensive fashion shops and jewelry stores spread behind him, while modern villas ran along the uphill road he stood upon. The Rapti residence was located at the end of the street. Garcia walked around observing the people, not so much the owners, but the staff of the oversized homes. He was torn between the old lady dressed in black on the front veranda cleaning potatoes for the following day and an Indian lady carrying out the trash.

'Good day, madam,' he said to her as she dropped the large bag of garbage.

'Oh, sir. I am no madam. Madame inside, inside.'

'But it's you I want to see,' he said and the middle-aged woman stopped walking back up to the mansion and turned to his direction. 'You see, I saw an ad about a gardener needed for the house next to yours. The Rapti family?'

'They are away on holiday.'

'Yes, I know. Interviews are next week, but you see, ever since I came to Greece, I have had bad luck with bosses. Awful people the lot of them. That's why I am looking for a better home. A good family that respects their workers...'

The Indian shook her head. 'Oh, my boy. Go back to your old job. I am sure your previous masters cannot be worse.'

'Really? How worse?'

She took a step closer, looked around and lowered her voice. 'The man beats his wife. The kids, too. He thinks he is a God. He talks down to all of us. Madame says he is unstable. Rumors say he raped a girl in high school, but money and his age kept him out of prison.'

Garcia whistled and thanked her for helping him dodge a bullet.

'A bullet!' she said. 'Now, you made me remember,' the chatty woman continued. 'One day, we were awoken by gunshots. The crazy man was in his underwear, drunk, shooting up in the air. Police came, the woman opens with a black eye and a bloody nose and they did nothing. The pigs! Just called the grandmother to get the terrified kids. Society of shit, if you ask me. And she is such a kind lady. The best on the street. So beautiful. She should leave him and do better!'

Garcia left for his cheap hotel with a grin upon his youthful face. '*And the puzzle is complete! Now, I have to kill the fourteen hours until the morning ship to Milos! Cable TV here I come.*'

The following day came and another day under the sun began across the Aegean. Once again, Christian Garcia found himself outside of Dido Rapti's hotel door.

'Hello again, Lieutenant,' Dido said. 'Break the case?'

Garcia raised his warrant to eye level. 'I need you to come down to the police station, Mrs. Rapti.'

'Are you arresting me?' she asked in a steady voice.

'No. Polygraph test. Court orders. Your children can stay here with Constable Aristeidou, if you please.'

Dido's color left her face. Her lips tightened. 'Yes, thank you. My kids can avoid the police station. I will tell them that I'll be going for our stuff. Give me ten minutes to dress.'

Garcia nodded and stepped into the hotel room. He sat on the worn-in sofa and greeted the two silent children. As he began to speak to them, Dido's voice came from the bedroom. 'Kids? Come here, please. I need your help.'

Both children rose and walked off; their lips sealed shut.

A statue of Greek beauty sat opposite him. Dido's blonde hair dropped and caressed her bare shoulders, her blue eyes were still upon her Venus-resembling face, her full red lips spoke quietly and her gentle hands remained motionless on the cold police table as the polygraph technician asked his set of questions before proceeding with Garcia's suggestions. He waited for just one.

'Mrs. Rapti did you murder your husband?'

'No.'

No reaction to the polygraph's needle.

'Not even in self-defense?'

'No.'

'Did you have any involvement in his murder?'

'No.'

The technician looked back at Garcia. 'She didn't do it,' he whispered.

Garcia wheeled his chair forward and looked straight at Dido.

'Did your husband hit you?'

Dido swallowed and lowered her eyes.

'Yes.'

'Abuse the kids?'

'Yes.'

'Did your son shoot your husband?'

Dido's eyes widened and she remained silent for a minute. 'You know, polygraph tests are no longer admissible in court? What are you trying here, Lieutenant?'

'Answer the question, please with a clear yes or no. Did your son shoot your husband?'

'No.'

The polygraph line continued its journey unmoved.

Dido exhaled in relief.

'Did your daughter shoot her father?'

'Okay, now this is getting ridiculous and bordering on bullying. She is seven for God's sake. May I have a word outside, Lieutenant?'

Garcia looked straight at her. '*First time I am hearing your real voice. Losing your cool, Mrs. Rapti?*' He nodded to the bald technician to take off her wires and replied, 'sure. Follow me.'

The rooftop's metal door flung open and strong sunlight welcomed them. 'My favorite spot,' Garcia said and pointed to a handmade bench with a view of the bay. 'Made it myself for my cigarette breaks. I only smoke two a day,' he continued and took out his pack of Marlboro Lights.

'My God, I'm dying for a cigarette. And a bottle of wine,' she said and sat down beside him. Garcia placed two cigarettes in his mouth and lit them. With a smile, he passed her one and watched her take in nearly half of it. As she exhaled a large cloud of grayish smoke, she broke down in tears. 'I can't do this anymore. I can't. I have no power left...'

'Dido, talk to me. Let me help you. I know he was abusive...'

'You have no idea!' she raised her voice and placed her face in her trembling palms. 'I have my kids to think of. Please, fuck the polygraph. I will testify that I shot him.'

Garcia took her hand. 'Dido, why?'

Dido looked around at the deserted rooftop. 'Effie shot him.'

'By mistake?'

Dido shook her head. 'That was my first thought. Call it

in as an accident, but still... Effie would get into trouble and then just like you, some officer would go digging in our past...'

'She meant to kill him?'

Tears ran into her mouth as she whispered in sobs. 'He raped her. My beautiful little angel...'

Dido fell into his arms and finally cried out the pain tormenting her soul. 'He was a sadist. Our home was one of many horrors. He beat me nearly to death. Sebastian is riddled with burned marks and cuts. But, raping Effie...'

Dido looked up into his eyes. 'My baby can't go to prison. Take me. Give them a chance for a normal life. Please, please. You can close this case anyhow you wish. You're a three-person police department. No one will doubt you. Say it was me.'

Garcia stroked back strikes of hair stuck to her sweaty face. 'If I am going to lie, why say it was you?'

Dido sat up straight, amazed at his words.

'You were at the supermarket at the hour of his death. It was robbers, right?'

Dido leapt into his arms and held him close. 'Thank you...' she managed to say.

'By the way, I get your whole charades, theatre play at the store to attract attention, but if Effie shot him before you leaving the house, how did you fool the coroner's estimated time of death?'

Dido wiped back her tears and chuckled. 'I read it on the internet last year when I was researching my latest novel. I kept the body warm by placing on the central heating on full and placed two halogen fan heaters by his sides. I came back, turned off the heat and hid the heaters in the basement.'

Parga
July, 2018

The picturesque village of Parga began at the edge of its famous turquoise waters and ran up the wild green mountains that surrounded it. Its rock-paved promenade welcomed thousands of cosmopolitan tourists that blended in with the locals in enjoying the heavenly cuisine, the exotic cocktails and the view of rocky islands that decorated the bay.

Dido passed the two ice-cream cones to her children and smiled as she watched them zig-zag amongst the crowd; all the way to the brick wall of the fishing port. They sat upon it and devoured their midday treat.

As Dido placed her purse back into her beige and blue handbag, she noticed a familiar figure in the crowd. Her heartbeat accelerated as she watched him walk by. Her mouth opened, yet no words came out. The tanned man with the piercing green eyes would soon be out of sight.

'Garcia?' she called out.

He turned and stood motionless. He took off his sunglasses and a mischievous grin was born upon his face. He strolled towards her; his hands in his shorts' pockets. 'Well, well, well. A beauty from the past.'

Dido giggled. 'And I thought, I was the romance author.'

'You know what? I never did tell you how my parents met.'

'Indeed.'

'Join me for lunch?'

'I'm here with the kids.'

'Excellent. Table for four then. Then, I want to take you to my favorite beach. It's a long stretch of sandy beach, behind the castle. The kids will love it.'

Garcia and Dido married the following July. Sebastian was his best man. July continued to be a significant month in their lives as they welcomed their twins in July 2020. The family of six lived permanently on Milos. Effie grew up, went into politics and became mayor of Athens at the age of thirty-seven. She adopted seven children with her husband, all from abusive families, and set up the Effie Garcia-Kontou foundation for underage rape victims.

Their past remained forever buried with Aristotle's decaying body.

AUGUST OF ZOMBIES

I'm no writer.

I'm just a guy with too much time to spare and a story worth hearing.

My name is Andreas Papadopoulos, which is the Greek equivalent to being a John Smith in the English-speaking world. I was born bored and insignificant. Even my name states my non-individuality. Derived from the ancient Greek word *andras*, meaning man. Yes, people literally call me 'hey, man.'

Anyway, I'm babbling on. My interesting story began when God decided to hear me out, on the day we Greeks celebrate the death of the Holy Mary. Though, we don't call it a death. We call it the *koimisis. Falling asleep.* One of my favorite hobbies back when life was normal on this planet.

Corfu
15th of August, 2018

The smoke from the barbeque covered my uncle Nick as he placed the skewers above the crackling charcoal. I sat on one of the plastic garden chairs that my auntie Tasoula despised, but my uncle was too cheap to buy her the rattan armchairs she desired. With a cold Myhtos beer on my left and an overflowing ashtray on my right, I was enduring the excruciating pain of listening to my female cousins' gossip.

'So, how old is this guy?'

My cousin Tina looked over her shoulder and feeling safe that her mother could not hear her, replied, 'Twenty-two.'

'What?' my cousin Anna said. 'Tina, he's ten years younger than you.'

'I did calculus in school, too, thanks. But, he's like country twenty-two. You know, ready for a mortgage and two kids. Not city twenty-two; just learning how to boil an egg. Anyway, he's really cute and funny...'

'How was he in bed?'

'Anna!'

'Tina!'

'I'm not you, bang on the first date.'

Anna chuckled. 'Second or third, thank you very much. So?'

Tina laughed. 'Amazing. It's like he was holding a manual for my body.'

I could not hear any more of their nonsense. I stood up and lit another cigarette. I gazed around the vast yard. All the men were around the fire discussing politics and football the way only Greek men knew how. Loudly and with manly anger. To my left, my mother was explaining how the trick was to use four eggs and not two. 'And do not beat them much, either,' she added. I have no idea what recipe she was on about, but I admired her passion.

I returned to my chair and spoke to God.

Now, I'm not a religious person. The modern termi-nology would probably be an agnostic atheist.

'God, universe, whatever. Kill me now. Pretty please? These last thirty years have been thirty years too many. I'm so lonely and bored of this dull monotonous life. Strike me down or at least do something to spice things up a bit. I'll give you one month... no, let's be realistic, I give you a year from today before I shoot myself.'

I took out my Samsung and pressed the calendar. August the 14th, 2019. New entry. 'Shoot myself before next barbeque,' I typed.

Corfu

May, 2019

'Do not fear whether God is listening or not. Fear when he answers,' my centenarian grandmother used to say.

I prayed once in my life and God replied. I would call that a one hundred percent success rate.

It was Tuesday the 7th and as always on the seventh, I woke up, still unemployed, and headed to my local betting store. I wore my fancy green shorts and an orange Marvel T-shirt and whistled my way through the park. I always enjoyed being in nature and gazing at the sea. Listening to kids' laughter and the thrashing of the waves. Antithesis or not, for me it was a wonderful blend of imagery and sound. I stared at myself in the glass door. Too pale for an islander. Too ginger -and too thin, for a Greek. I sighed and entered. I played my usual five lucky numbers and circled the seven as my joker. One day, number seven would be called out on the seventh of the month. I knew that much from a dream I had in college, before I dropped out that is, to live the big dream and open my own kiosk. I was bankrupt within a year.

As I exited the dark place and the hot sun ferociously attacked my white skin and caressed my freckles, my phone vibrated in my right pocket.

'Hey, fat boy. What's up?' I asked.

Damian's bass voice came through the receiver, worried as hell. 'Andrea, are you watching this? The world has gone crazy. Dude, I'm scared.'

This coming from the most joyful, unstressed man I knew. 'Is this you planning a prank or something?'

'Dude, get to a TV or come 'round here, now!'

Damianos. Now, that's a proper Greek manly name. To conquer. Though the only thing Damian ever conquered was buffet tables at weddings and christenings.

Damian still lived with his parents. His only move being from the top floor to the basement-slash-renovated studio apartment. Their home was only a block away. Not that anything in Corfu town was much further. Nowhere that you couldn't walk to.

I took in a deep breath of fresh sea air and dashed up the narrow street. Left at Mr. Costas's bakery. The finest donuts in town. First time I gazed through the window and my eyes did not settle on the glorious Nutella-filled treats, but on the lovely owner couple. Mr. Costa held his wife in his arms as they both stood in front of their television set. The screen showed London in the corner and my eye caught a glimpse of people running in the streets of the city as fires raged behind them.

'Another terrorist attack. This is what scared Damian?'

Two minutes later, I was raising my hand to knock on his door, when the wooden door flew open and Damian's hairy hand grabbed me and pulled me in. He double-locked the door behind me. 'Ssshh, my parents are reading in the back garden. They have no idea. Come downstairs.'

The floorboards creaked as heavy Damian ran upon them. I followed him down to his dimly-lit room. His 4K Smart TV was tuned in to CNN. 'Look, New York.'

Images of a group of teens beating up a homeless man flashed before my eyes. I sat down in shock. The teens looked possessed.

'Oh, shit!' I screamed as one of the teens started to bite and take chunks out of the now lifeless man.

'They are saying it's a virus. Dude, it's a fucking zombie apocalypse. I knew this would happen. Messing around with nature and chemicals and such. And you always mocked me that I read way too many comic books.'

I shook my head in disbelief. 'This can't be happening. This isn't a movie. It's real life. Zombies are fictional like ghosts, vampires, willing women, non-fattening bacon and Buddha.'

Damian stopped his pacing up and down, and turned towards me. 'I'm pretty sure, Buddha was real.'

We flicked through the rest of the channels. Incidents of outbreaks were starting to be reported in Greece, too.

'That was quick.'

'So, we are fucked. What are we going to do?' I asked and placed my head in my hands.

'Smoke the rest of the pot?'

I nodded. 'At least, we will go out happy.'

Half an hour later, we sat laughing on his worn-in sofa. 'If you turn into a zombie...'

'Yes, I would eat you. Lucky me. Plenty of food. Unless

your comics are true and I will want to feed on brains. Yours won't even count as a snack,' I said and laughed.

'Ssshhh,' Damian said.

'Okay, sorry! I didn't mean to offend...'

He placed his fat fingers upon my mouth. 'Listen!'

Damian jumped up as the loud thumping from upstairs continued. 'My parents! Where's my baseball bat?'

I followed my friendly, bat-carrying giant up the steps and into his family's kitchen.

'Holy crap!' was all I managed to say.

'Mum!' Damian yelled. His mother took her mouth out of his father's opened skull and looked up, blood dripping from her face. She howled and made a run for us. Damian stood motionless in shock. I took the bat out of his hand.

'Sorry, Mrs. Kotsinofta,' I said and swung the bat, hitting across the face, sending the elderly woman into the food cabinet. I grabbed Damian by the hand and tried to pull him. As if. Steady as a monolith. I slapped him across the face. 'Snap out of it,' I screamed as his mother placed her hands upon the floor and pushed herself back up.

We ran out of the house, into the chaos of the streets.

Endless murdering was happening everywhere we looked.

'Where the fuck should we go?' Damian asked, wiping the sweat from his forehead.

'Where's the one place in town that will have the least people?'

'The library!' he replied.

Calliope Metaxa was rocking her spinster-librarian look once more. She had her black hair pulled back in a strict ponytail, her kind eyes stood cold behind thick frames and a brown skirt suit covered her slim figure. She dressed like my mother on 'Formal Sundays' AKA the Sundays where she would visit various churches out of town with her mid-sixties lady squad.

Calliope Metaxa spoke her first proper word at the age of eleven months and fell in love with language in all of its forms ever since. Like Damian, she was lucky too with her given name. Calliope, the muse of poetry, leader of all muses.

She looked around and smiled at the sight of thousands of books and only a handful of humans.

Her French nose twitched as she heard rumblings from the science-fiction section. She lowered her reading glasses and stared in the direction of the commotion. A growling noise echoed in the vast room.

'Shh!' Calliope said and her thin lips parted. Loud thuds came as a reply. Calliope's hazelnut eyes opened wide. She marched over to the shaking book shelves; her face flashing from one shade of red to another like a pamphlet of paints from the Home Depot.

'A library is a locale where tranquility is needed for perusal to happen!' she complained, placing her fancy words in a line. Calliope Metaxa rarely used common words. If you or I spoke or wrote it, Calliope used a synonym for it.

Calliope froze by the dropped books. For once in her life, she was lost for words.

The nerdy chubby man with the black wig held a hardcover of The Chrysalids and was beating an unconscious woman with it. A ten-year-old girl was on all fours and had her tongue out, catching droplets of the blood that was spraying out of the woman's neck. The man had stabbed her with his car keys.

The young girl looked up and twisted her head as she focused on Calliope. The kid shrieked and ran towards her. Calliope took a step back and raised her hands in defense.

My baseball bat came down just in time. The girl fell down with an open skull.

My eyes met with Calliope's. 'My paladin! You freed me from imperil!'

'What did she say?' breathless Damian asked as he stood behind me and shot both zombies in the head. His dad was a right Greek Alpha male back in the day and went hunting every week. Damian never enjoyed the sport, yet maintained his shooting skills and his old man's rifle.

Calliope covered her ears and placed her head on my chest. I resisted sniffing her hair and lay my hand upon her back. 'There, there,' was all I managed to say.

Funny -waggish according to Calliope, how three months went by, locked up in the storage room of the library. There were nine of us that survived the day that the world went mad. Lucky for us, the library was built on a small island just meters from the coast. The island, once a Venetian fort, now housed the town's library, the old English hospital, a fishing port (no boats remained as owners fled the city massacre) and the church of Saint George. We blew up the lone bridge that connected us to the mainland where half the population was now raging bloodthirsty zombies and the other half were dead. The *crazies* did not seem to step into the water and that suited us just fine.

What a glorious day that was. Four guys and an old

cannon. Thanks to the science professor of the group, we sent those three cannon balls with terrible speed and ruined the bridge that would allow hordes of howling lunatics to come our way.

We gathered supplies from all the buildings and locked ourselves up in the storage rooms of the library.

Gladly for our 2018 attention spans and needs, WI-FI was still up and running. We were informed that the outbreak was due to a virus and that one by one the cities of man had fallen. Soon, there was no more news being reported.

By August, all we got from the outside world, was the pungent smell of the rotting corpses outside. The Greek summer sun was not helping either as we no longer had electricity for the air conditioning or worse, to charge our phones. Each toilet run was done in fear. Tins and cans were getting scarce.

Truthfully, my existence in the post-apocalyptic world wasn't worse than before. Better even. I had no anxiety to search for a job, I had quit smoking, I had Damian for company, YouTube for my entertainment (until the death of my phone in late July) and I longed for my talks with Calliope. I lied that I was interested in poetry and philosophy, but never got a chance to learn them due to my poor upbringing and she took me under her wing. With a 'plethora of tomes and publications,' she said, 'I will be your cicerone through the woods of knowledge.'

I placed my head on her knee and listened as she read. Lately, she smiled more often. Lately, my beating heart ached at my cowardliness to make a move.

Little shitty island
(I don't know its official name. Maybe it's Sideros, sorry, no
more internet on the planet)
15th of August, 2019

Greeks and their habits!

'We should go light a candle in Saint George's Church,'
Mrs. Helen, the nurse said.

'We could use some help,' the science teacher agreed.

I whispered to Calliope. 'Are they being serious? Okay, I
know Saint George was good at killing dragons, but he
hasn't helped so far with our zombies...'

'Stop calling them that! It's a ludicrous label...'

'And, now just because it's the Holy Mary's death day,
they want...'

'Their soul requires guidance. What could possibly go
erroneous?'

What went wrong that day can easily be summoned up
in *my* favorite philosophical phrase, *the shit hit the fan*.

Seven out of our group decided to venture out of the
safety of our building and crouched behind the old
Venetian wall, to journey to the church and pray.

Damian and I stayed behind as I refused to turn religious just because the end was near. We sat by the large
window on the south wing of the library as to keep an eye
out for our group. Not that there was much we could do to
help as our bullets ran out back in July.

'What are you staring at?' Damian asked as he noticed
me looking across the room.

'That map of Corfu.'

'What about it?'

'Have you ever noticed how it's shaped like a parasite?
Like those ones on them nature shows, where the bug crawls

into your ear and lays like a billion eggs or worse, swims up your dick hole…'

'La-la-la,' Damian began to sing and placed his hands over his ears. 'Dude! That's sick. I always thought that it looked like a twisted burrito.'

'Cause you're always hungry, big guy,' I said and tapped his stomach.

Screaming from outside ruined our bromance moment. Apparently the locked-up church held four virus-infected monks that bit off half of Mrs. Helen's face. We turned to the window and watched, helpless, as a skinny-looking monk wearing a torn brown robe leapt out of a parked car and landed on the teacher, throwing him to the ground. As the cloud of dust cleared, we saw the monk hitting the poor man's head repeatedly against a cannon.

'Calliope!' I whispered and turned to run outside. I picked up my bat and kicked open the library's main door. The bright sunlight blinded me. I hadn't left the building in weeks. I tried to focus. Calliope's figure heading my way was in the center of my blurry vision. A shadow followed her.

'Duck!' I yelled and swung my bat. Teeth flew out of the zombie-monk's mouth and I heard his neck snap. As it rolled and twitched, Damian knelt by him and stabbed him with a butcher's knife in the center of its skull.

'Duck? Really?' Calliope said with a smile. She took a step towards me and kissed me on my right cheek.

Damian looked behind him.

'Jesus Christ! Okay, love birds, time to go!' he said and turned towards the library.

'No, no!' I said. 'No more in there! I'm going crazy, I'd rather become a zombie and run around wild and free…'

'Let's retaliate against logic somewhere else, please?'

I gazed around. 'Over there,' I said and pointed to a

small, unused-since-the-late-sixties dock by the old Venetian walls that crumbled into the sea, beaten by the Ionian's rotting powers. 'Let's go for a swim.'

'Hasten your pace. They are coming...' Calliope said and dashed by us as growling was heard from behind the library wall.

If any of that day's praying did any good, it seemed God continued to be fond of me as none followed us down to the dock; their attention span being worse than mine in kindergarten.

Damian sat down, his feet hanging off the cement pier, inches from the serene waters. Noises resembling a black bear huffing came from him as he chased his elusive breath. 'Now what?' he complained.

'I have a plan,' I announced proudly. 'Oh, come on! Don't you both look so damn surprised.'

'I am not astounded, my dear. Just curious as to how we intend to proceed.'

I took a small step towards her. 'They are afraid of water, right?'

'We cannot be positive such a statement...'

'Well, we haven't seen one try to come over from the mainland, have we?'

'Correct.'

I ran my trembling hands through my hair. 'So, we swim to shore...'

'Fuck, no,' Damian spoke, finally having regained his breath.

'It's just a short swim. It's not gym...'

Damian's middle finger flew up.

I chuckled at the sight of him flipping me the bird. It felt normal. It felt like before. 'Listen to me! We won't go into town. We walk along the shore, our feet in the sea. We walk by all of Democracy Avenue and head for the woods.'

'The woods?' Calliope asked.

'The forest.'

She rolled her eyes. 'Yes, I know. But why? Sounds hazardous.'

I turned to Damian. 'Remember that billionaire that lives on the edge of the cliff? Dead in the forest? The one where you installed his security cams?'

Damian nodded and titled his round head. 'Yeah?'

'He built a private marina in the sea caves below his mansion. We take one of his speed boats and get the hell off this island!'

'Wait,' Calliope said, 'are you referring to the Mon Keros estate? Owned by George Onasi?'

'That's the one!'

'He's my uncle.'

'Hold up. You have a billionaire uncle and you work in a public library?'

'No price can be placed on my undying love for literature.'

Damian placed his plump hands by his side and stood up. 'Let's just hope there are no undying demons on our way and that sounds like a half-descent plan, mate. There must be somewhere out there, where civilization survived. An army-protected utopia or whatever.'

'Well said, Damian,' Calliope said and rubbed his wide back. 'So, shall we take the plunge?'

The hairs on the back of my neck and along my Greek arms stood at salute. We had swum to shore until our toes touched the soft sand below. With our waists still surrounded by water, we gazed around. The once buzzing-with-life beach was completely deserted. Silence also lingered on the motorway behind it. Four lanes of empty cars and rotting bodies.

'Humanity, game over,' Calliope whispered.

'Fucking Illuminati scientists!' Damian said and ground his teeth.

'You truly maintain the belief that the virus was man-made?'

He nodded. 'That or nature woke up one day and said screw these parasites eating up my animals and plants, and unleashed her rage against us!'

I placed my hand on his wet shoulder. 'If that was true, you wouldn't be alive. You've eaten most of her animals. During Easter, half the population of lambs vanishes on the island.'

Damian chuckled. 'True, but I don't eat her plants, so maybe I'm off the hook.'

Calliope snapped her fingers. 'Boys, concentrate. Our expedition is still ongoing!'

We approached the coast. We moved slowly as to keep our noise at a minimum. With the water below our knees, we made our way to the forest. We stayed close together and our eyes moved around rapidly; our nervous system sensing the danger after months of feeling safe in the locked-up rooms of the library.

'I miss my books,' Calliope said and she glanced back at the island. My hand slid into hers. 'Let's go,' I said and took a few brave steps out of the water.

Corfu's forest was not dense and allowed the summer sunrays to shine through it, providing us with light. We moved from pine tree to pine, taking small steps. We were alone and we wanted to keep it that way.

Fifteen minutes later, the impressive mansion, rumored to have cost over ten million Euros to build, stood before us.

'Don't guess your dear uncle gave you a key which you happen to have carried around with you for the last few months during the apocalypse?' I asked, my eyes set on the locked gate and the tall brick wall with the barbed wire running along the top.

'Negative. However, if you two don't mind undressing,' she said and raised her eyebrows, 'place your clothes upon the gate's thorny wire and we can climb over it.'

Damian and I exchanged looks. We hadn't showered properly in months, never mind changing underwear. Damian washed his clothes in the sea every other week, but I preferred going commando for the end of the world.

Damian began to undress; first off came his shirt and down went his trousers.

'Err, I'm not wearing any boxers,' I admitted, taking off my ripped, Avenger's T-shirt.

'Ooh,' Calliope said and turned slightly. 'I'll do my foremost to ascend without peeping.'

Soon, Damian threw our clothes upon the barbed wire and my bare white ass went over the gate. Damian followed and after a struggle with gravity desiring his heavy load, he pulled Calliope up. I stood by the wall, waiting for him to toss over my clothes.

All three of us smiled and exhaled with delight. Until the zombie dog barked.

'Undead Doberman!' I yelled and we all sprinted through the dying non-watered garden, straight for the house. Thankfully, its front door was open, and we managed to bang it behind us, just in time for the vicious black canine to hit against it.

I whistled as my eyes travelled around the massive front room. 'It's larger than the library in here!'

'Be careful,' Damian advised. 'Could be more than the dog to fear.'

'This way,' Calliope said. 'The kitchen is over here.'

She was right. We hadn't eaten properly in weeks. The stench from decaying groceries welcomed us. 'Look for cans,' I said.

We locked all doors leading to the kitchen and sat down to devour our lunch of tuna fish, ham, baked beans, an array of canned vegetables and pineapple for dessert.

'You know what I miss?'

'A kebab and fries?' Damian replied.

'No, mousakka.'

Calliope shook her head. 'I miss a long hot shower.'

I went to the sink and lifted the stainless-steel tap. 'Water is still working fine.'

'Let's secure the master bedroom upstairs, find some clothes and shower,' Damian said.

'Shouldn't we first check on the boat?'

Damian shrugged his shoulders. 'If it's down there, it's down there. If it's not, it's not. Having a bath and a change of clothes, will not change that,' he said and unlocked the kitchen door.

We crept up the twisted staircase and headed for one of the palace's many bedrooms. All en-suite, of course. The largest must have been Onasi's. We checked around and locked the door behind us. The view was breathtaking. Miles of endless blue. So calming it could almost make you feel normal again. Almost.

The walk-in closet of the Onasi couple had more clothes than my auntie Toula's self-proclaimed boutique.

'I doubt anything will fit me,' Damian said in his Winnie-the-Pooh-without-honey voice, as Calliope and I chose what to wear.

'Do not be downhearted, my rotund companion. Here,' she said and passed him an extra-large tracksuit she had found.

As Winnie finally found honey, he headed to the shower first. I stood by the window, while Calliope snooped around on Onasi's mahogany desk.

'My Lord!' she gasped after a while and turned towards me. 'Andrea, look.'

I took the brown file from her shaking hands.

'Project Amfori?'

'It's a private island my uncle owns. Look inside.'

Plans of an underground city unfolded before my eyes. 'Well, well, well. A city for the rich to survive. That makes sense.'

Calliope's eyes widened. 'We are saved. We have to get there,' she said and hugged me, placing her head upon my shoulder. My hand ran through her tangled hair and as she raised her head, our eyes met. Our noses touched and our lips moved closer.

Just then, Damian pushed open the door and bathed and dressed in his clean clothes, said, 'Da-dah! Sparkling brand new!'

We both screamed at the sight of the zombie crawling out of the laundry vent. The wild woman dressed in a maid's uniform bit him on his leg. Another zombie came out behind them and ran straight at us, as I moved to help my friend who fell to the floor.

More zombies could be heard coming up through the vent.

'Fly, you fools!'

Damian's last words. His favorite line from Lord of the Rings. Practiced a million times.

'I love you, man!' I yelled and took Calliope by the hand. We dashed out of the room and leapt the steps two-by-two as the howling infected beasts chased us. I overturned living room tables as we made it to the basement door. With the door locked behind us, we ran down to the cavernous mini marina below the mansion. Onasi's luxury yacht was gone, but a four-seater speed boat sat quietly upon the water. Calliope headed for the keys hanging from wall hooks and took them all in her hands. With the zombies banging on the door above, we tried key by key, until one slid in and brought the boat's engine to life.

Calliope stood behind the wheel and pushed the gear into place. In seconds, we flew out of the shadowy cave and the bright Ionian embraced us.

'Do you know how to get to Amfori?' I yelled over the gust and the splashing of the waves.

Calliope smiled and pushed a black button on the screen by the wheel. A map came to life. 'There,' she said.

I placed my hands on her shoulders, kissed the back of her head and fell back into the hard seats of the boat. I looked back at the island of Corfu diminishing on the horizon. 'Goodbye, my friend,' I whispered.

Hours later, with the sun heading for its watery death, we approached the small island.

'There's nothing!' I said, disappointed as Calliope drove the cruiser into the sandy beach.

'It's underground, my dear. Let's look for an opening.'

An hour later, darkness fell and we had explored the entire islet. Twice.

'At least there are no zombies,' she said.

I smiled. 'You said *zombies*,' I mocked.

Exhausted, I leaned back on a palm tree and with Calliope's head upon my lap, I fell asleep.

Little did we know, that as we slept a group of people had gathered in the conference room, a hundred feet below us, to go over the footage of our arrival.

'They don't seem infected,' their doctor said.

'We cannot take any chances,' a woman said.

'Holy shit. That's my niece,' Onasi said coming closer to the screen.

'If they are not infected, that means we are screwed anyway. The airborne virus doesn't affect all of them!'

'We need to study them.'

The following day, we were awoken by a loud rattling noise. A large underground elevator appeared from below the sand. Two men, dressed in sealed suits came out of the dusty cloud.

'Follow us,' the tall one said.

They gave us similar suits and asked us to wear them as we travelled down to the center of the earth. We exited to a long corridor. From the glass window, I gazed out in awe. An entire underground city.

'It's been a while since we last saw so many people,' I said and Calliope squeezed my hand.

We were in quarantine for two months, before the good people of Gaia allowed us to live among the general population.

George Onasi announced the good news to us.

'Erm, by the way. Two single rooms or a studio together-er?' he asked.

'Studio,' Calliope replied.

That night as we lay naked in each other's arms, I thought, '*it took a zombie apocalypse for me to finally get a girlfriend.*'

'Where is your brain wandering off to?'

I kissed her gently on her forehead. 'Just thinking how happy I am to be here with you.'

'Who would have thought we would experience the end of the world as we know it?' she replied.

'I don't think of it as the end, but as a new beginning. I mean, we have everything we need down here. What could possibly go wrong?'

SEPTEMBER OF ALIBIS

LIMASSOL, CYPRUS

There should be a limited number of shocks that a man can endure during a year. Antony Georgiou's 2018 kicked off with the death of his beloved mother. It was late January and fat raindrops plummeted from the gloomy sky, all the way down to the bustling seafront city of Limassol. Antony drove his blue Maserati down 28th October Avenue, in front of a row of newly-built skyscrapers.

'*For an island with only two months of rain, it sure is pissing it today,*' he thought as he turned his wipers to full speed. He was only minutes away from his law firm, situated on the 22nd floor of The One, the island's tallest building.

His iPhone's ringtone echoed through the vehicle's speakers.

'Hello?' he asked, tones of worry coloring his tone as he noticed the caller. Serenity Nursing Home.

'Mr. Georgiou, this is Anna Tornaride, manager of Serenity. I think you should come as soon as possible. Your mother is having a hard time breathing. Our doctors are with her now. She keeps asking for you...'

'I'm on my way. Tell her I'll be by her side in ten minutes,' Antony interrupted and swirled his GranTurismo, its tires screeching on the wet asphalt, honking at cars moving slowly because of the downpour.

Antony's punctuality was never off. In exactly ten minutes, he was running up the slippery steps of the old mansion that housed Serenity. He rushed straight to his mother's living quarters. A deluxe studio apartment with a view to die for.

'Mother!' he gasped and rushed to her side, his eyes fixed on the two doctors by her king-sized bed.

The silver-haired lady with the pearl earrings raised her hands with difficulty and embraced her son. 'My boy, my Antony,' she said with a shaken voice, and kissed him gently on his cold cheek. 'Don't look so gloomy. I'm just feeling a tad under the weather. It's throwing chairs out there...' she said and coughed. Antony stroked her thin hair and looked into her amber eyes. 'I'm sure you're fine, mom.'

Out in the hallway, Antony was informed that his dear mother was far from fine.

'It was a mini stroke,' the first doctor said. 'She is strong for an eighty-two-year-old woman, but another stroke could be fatal.'

'Will she have another one?'

The other doctor with the thin-framed glasses placed his hand on Antony's shoulder. 'Most likely, yes. We will do our best to prevent it. Enjoy the time you have with her and we will be by her side twenty-four seven.'

Antony spent his day by his mother's side, reminiscing childhood memories and laughing at his mother's retelling of his mischievous teen years. His father died before he had turned one and it had been just the two of them since then. The hours flew by and the short winter day neared its end.

Clouds scattered and the large window offered them a painting of a bright night sky above the light-lit city. The full moon journeyed above the dark sea, illuminating resting ships and boats nesting upon the restless Mediterranean Sea.

'Open a window, my boy. It's stuffy in here. I love the air after a storm.'

Antony obeyed and a fresh sea breeze invaded the room. Mrs. Georgiou patted her bed, inviting Antony to her side.

'I have something to tell you. A dying woman's confession...'

'Mum!'

'Listen, and please don't hate me.'

An hour later, Antony stood outside for a much-needed smoke. His hand trembled as the cigarette reached his lips and stayed there. Inside, his mother curled up to her soft pillow. With her chest and her soul feeling lighter, she drifted off to the arms of Morpheas. She did not awake the following morning. A second stroke in the middle of the night cut her dreams short.

The next death Antony had to deal with that year, was that of his long-time friend and law firm partner, Simon Argyriou. The two grew up together in the affluent neighborhood of Ekali, studied together in the UK and opened their own law firm on their 27th birthday. A successful business that flourished on money from the town's many offshore companies. Simon stood as best man at his wedding and Antony christened Simon's first born. They weren't just friends, they were for each other, the brother they never had.

Antony sat in the middle of Pier One, one the most luxurious restaurants of the town's old harbor, on a hot spring night. His wife, Jenny giggled by his side as wine ran freely through them. Four platters of sushi were placed between them and their group of friends, when the call came in.

Antony listened as his uncle informed him that Simon had been found, shot to death in the remote areas by the district's Salt Lake.

'What the hell was he doing out there?' his wife asked.

4th of September, 2018

September came and Simon's death still remained a mysterious open case. Another dusty case file waiting to be eaten by the fat rats that roamed the basement of Limassol's Homicide department. Simon's body was found next to an abandoned, stolen cheap car and he had been shot with his own firearm. The events of that fatal night remained unknown.

The evening was as Antony liked to refer to as sweet. After August's relentless heat waves, it was the first day that the temperature dipped below thirty-five degrees Celsius.

He left the office early in the evening and drove to his favorite Greek coffee shop to enjoy an ice-cold frappe with his uncles who had taken the morning bus down from their village for a necessary trip to the doctors. Antony shook his head at the sight of his two senior uncles, devouring a sweet piece of baklava while sipping a hot coffee under the sizzling sun. An hour later, the group of three set off for their picturesque vine village in the mountainous region of Limassol. Antony drove through stone-laid roads and parked under blossoming pink bougainvillea. He popped inside the cottage's garden to kiss his aunties.

'I'm in a rush. Jenny is waiting for me,' he said as the elderly women tried to persuade him to stay longer.

'We never see you. Stay. I've made your favorite. Moussaka...'

'Why didn't you bring Jenny up, too?' his other plump aunt asked as she struggled to lift herself out of her straw chair.

Just then, his ringtone boomed from his right pocket. Antony brought the phone to his ear.

'This is Police Captain Philippou. Is this Antony Georgiou?'

That is how the phone call began. A minute later, Antony fainted in front of the shocked eyes of his family.

'Soula, get some water. Quick!'

Antony sped down the hillside road; his Maserati engine growling, finally free to show off its full potential. Cold sweat dripped from his forehead and Antony turned on his vehicle's A/C. He licked his dry lips and exhaled as he reached Limassol. The city of lights welcomed him and Antony fought against endless traffic; his heart pounding, waiting to get home. Antony turned down his street and gazed at the multiple police lights dancing along the walls of his house. Neighbors stood on their verandas and watched as he drove past them. A deadly silence lingered in the air. Antony parked his car behind an ambulance, jumped out and dashed for his front door.

A Herculean police officer blocked his way.

'Sir?'

'I live here. This is my house,' Antony yelled.

'Sir, please stay here. Captain Philippou will be with you shortly.'

'Where's my wife? Why won't you let me in my own home? I am a lawyer...' Antony continued and tried to enter his opened front door. The muscular officer pulled him back, but Antony managed to catch a glimpse of the bloody wall opposite him.

'Jenny? Jenny?'

'Mr. Georgiou, I am Captain Philippou. There is no easy way to say this, sir. Your wife is dead. She was shot. There was nothing that the paramedics could do...'

Antony stopped listening. The square man's words transformed into a background buzz. Antony sat down on his front lawn; his hands digging into the dirt. Just yesterday, he cut it while Jenny served him an icy homemade lemonade and kissed him on his neck.

Antony's tragic figure remained sitting down on the green grass as paramedics wheeled out the body. Antony could not find the courage to stand up and approach. His wife, a lifeless lump in a black body bag. She looked smaller.

The coroner gave directions to her interns and ordered them to go with the body. She would follow with her car. As the white ambulance made its way out of the driveway, Helen Angelidou approached the Captain who stood by the door. Her hand gently caressed his. 'You okay, babe?' she whispered. He nodded; his fingers twitching in his pockets.

'Don't you dare start smoking again,' she continued. 'I know what stress does to you. You've been clean for three weeks now...'

'Jesus, Helen! You make it sound like I'm a drug addict.'

'Same shit. So, what have you got so far?'

Captain Philippou scratched the back of his head; his

nails going through his thinning grey hair. 'Not much. Broken back window. The killer waited for her and shot her as she came home and closed the door behind her. Neighbors said they saw no one lurking around nor did they hear anything?'

'Silencer?'

'Most likely.'

Helen gave it her best shot at a warm smile. 'I'm off. Autopsy ahead. You?'

'Interrogate the husband. Check if he was up the mountains as he said and if his alibi stands, see if he has any information about who would want to harm his wife. This was an execution, not a robbery.'

'Another long night then. See you at home,' Helen said and rushed back to her car.

Antony sat quietly at the end of the cold metal table and massaged his back. The strong fluorescent light above him irritated his swollen eyes. He placed his hands around the paper cup filled with hot cheap Greek coffee. He brought it to his nose and took a sniff. It didn't smell like proper coffee. He placed it back on the table's surface and looked up at the ticking clock. It had been nearly an entire hour since he had entered the small room. He began to tap his fingers, wondering if it was a test of his patience. The cops always blamed the spouse on the detective shows he and Jenny used to enjoy.

'I'm innocent, for fuck's sake. I was miles away. I was with co-workers and family all day...' he whispered.

Suddenly, the door opened and the short man with the dull clothes that spoke to him back at his house walked in and sat opposite him. A young officer with a thick moustache followed; his hands holding a pile of notes.

'Antony... May I call you Antony? I am so deeply sorry for your loss. I understand it has been a rough year for you.'

Antony looked straight at him. *'Great! He is going to bring up Simon and cheers for reminding me about my dead mother!'*

'Your alibi stands. We have no reason to suspect you, so please relax and try to concentrate. Is there anyone who would want to hurt you or your wife? Any threats made lately?'

Antony coughed to clear his throat. 'Well, there was a misunderstanding with Jenny's boss, but, Jesus, as if that's reason to shoot someone.'

'Her boss, you say? What happened?'

'Jenny works at an accounting office. Amelia Sofroni is the head of her department. Because of Jenny handling my firm's accounts and me sending our rich Russian clients her way, the owners decided to promote Jenny. Gave her equal status to Amelia. Amelia just wouldn't have it. She confronted Jenny and called her a whore, making her way up the ladder based on who she was married to. The whole thing got out of hand and Amelia pushed her against the wall. She was fired the next day.'

'When was this?'

'Last week.'

Captain Philippou looked over at the notepad in front of the man beside him. The young officer wrote down everything Antony had said.

'Okay, Antony, err... I need you to try and remain calm.'

Antony squinted his eyes.

'I have some news for you,' the captain continued. 'I have spoken with the coroner. Jenny was pregnant...'

'What?' Antony said and stood up

'I'm guessing you didn't know. Just two months...'

Antony placed his head in his hands. 'I'm sterile,' he managed to whisper.

Captain Philippou's beady eyes widened. 'That would explain the messages on her phone. Please, sit down, Antony.'

Philippou waited for Antony to sit back down. 'I'm sorry to be the bearer of such news, but we searched through the victim's... err... your wife's cell phone and she had many erotic exchanges with a certain number. Do you know an Achilles Xenofon?'

Antony shook his head. He wiped his swollen eyes and remained still. Captain Philippou looked at the broken man before him. 'I will get to the bottom of this,' he promised as he rose from his chair, patted Antony on the shoulder and walked out of the small room. Antony remained in the chair for another hour before getting up and driving to a nearby hotel. As soon as the police allowed, he put his home on the market.

―――

Captain Philippou awoke as always at seven o'clock sharp. He crawled out of bed naked, leaving the warmth of Helen's body and the softness of his satin sheets. His fat fingers ran across his hairy chest as he scratched all over. He tiptoed to the bathroom, relieved himself from last night's beers and brushed his yellowy teeth. He dressed in the hall-way, splashed on some cheap cologne and exited his house. The first cigarette of the day landed on his lips as he beeped open his car. '*As if life would let me quit.*' His first stop of the day remained the same for the last twenty years. Zorbas Bakeries. Fresh, nose-breaking, mouth-watering pastries and hot brewed coffee. He enjoyed his breakfast in his vehicle, with the deep blue sea serving as his view.

The morning radio hosts informed him that the clock had struck eight. Philippou wiped his shirt free of bread-crumbs, finished his coffee and set off for Amelia Sofroni's apartment block.

He drove into the tall building's shadow and parked on the pavement. He took a peek at his notes and sauntered to the door. He buzzed apartment 417 three times before hearing Amelia's husky voice. 'Hello?'

'Mrs. Amelia Sofroni? Open up. This is the police.'

There was a brief pause before the sound of the door unlocking automatically in front of him broke the silence.

Philippou took the elevator up to the fourth floor. It smelled like dog's piss. As a proud dog owner for most of his life, Philippou recognized the smell well. He exited and counted the door numbers as he went down the long empty corridor. He knocked on number seventeen and the door flew open wide.

'Quick! Come in before the neighbors see you. Thank God you came alone and as I saw from my window, not in a police vehicle,' the busty blonde in the see-through night gown said breathlessly. 'Last thing I need in my life at the moment is gossip,' she continued as she closed the door behind him. 'Come sit down. Coffee?'

'No, thank you,' he replied and made his way through the open-plan apartment to the blue two-seater sofa on his left.

Amelia opened her kitchen window and let in much-needed fresh air. The stale air carried the scent of ash mixed with cooked meat. She took a can of ready-made coffee from her fridge and emptied it in a tall glass. She threw in an ice-cube and a pink straw. 'Sorry for making you wait. Just woke up,' she apologized as she took a bite from a slice of bread. She sat opposite the Captain, in a purple, tall-back armchair.

'I know why you are here. I saw her death on the news late last night.'

Philippou nodded. 'I see. And?'

'And what, detective?'

'Captain Philippou,' he replied. 'This isn't an American movie.'

Amelia continued drinking her coffee.

'And I heard you two got into a real fight last week. Cost you your high-income job...'

'And that's reason to kill?'

Philippou chuckled. 'I've seen people kill for much less.'

'Well, sorry to burst your bubble, Captain, but I was home all day yesterday. I was fed-up feeling sorry for myself and I said, Amelia get your fat sorrow ass out of bed. Fuck your ex-husband, fuck your ex-job, you're fabulous. So, I invited all my friends round last night for a dinner party and games night.'

Philippou scribbled down in his notepad. 'And what time did your first guest arrive?'

'Around six, but my sister and my friend, Kleo, came 'round around four to help me with preparations.'

'And, what time did your last guest leave?'

'Around midnight. That's when I showered and went to bed. I saw Jenny's death on the repeat of the evening news. I sleep with the television on, you see.'

'I see...' Philippou whispered and closed his pad. 'Thank you for your time, Mrs. Amelia. I will confirm your story and if I need anything, I'll be in touch.'

Captain Philippou lit his day's second smoke as he set off for his next suspect. Achilles Xenofon worked at the same company as Jenny. He was ten years her junior and worked in the company's mailing department. Not the brightest bulb in the place, but surely the shiniest. He reminded Philippou of the famous men, his Helen followed on Instagram. Philippou had called ahead and arranged to see Jenny's boss, her closest co-workers and of course, Achilles.

'She was such a lovely soul...'

'The kindest heart...'

'A polite lady...'

None had any idea of anyone who would want to hurt her. Besides Amelia, who was generally despised. Most were disappointed, when Philippou pointed out that Amelia had a solid alibi.

Achilles and his perfect set of white teeth and bushy hair sat down opposite him. He played with his thumbs and avoided eye contact.

'You can relax, Achilles. I know about your love affair.'

The young man's bright green eyes opened wide and his jaw dropped. 'How? Did one of Jenny's friends know? She told me it was a secret between the two of us.'

'We saw her messages.'

Achilles exhaled with delight and comically wiped his forehead. 'Phew, dodged a bullet there. I could get fired...'

'Achilles, Jenny was shot to death and you are worried about your job?'

Achilles leaned forward. 'Hey, life is for the living. I feel terrible for Jenny. We had a good time together, but that's all it was. Sex and laughs. I'm sad she was murdered, but that has nothing to do with me and I am not even thirty. I can't afford to lose my job and start over in these times and this age!'

Philippou scratched his two-day beard and picked up his silver Parker pen. 'Nothing to do with you, huh? So, for the record, then, where were you, yesterday evening? I want your whereabouts from five o'clock onwards.'

'That's easy,' he replied. 'Six o'clock, I got off work and met up with my boys down at Confuzio Cafe. We have a card tournament group. We left there around half nine and went for kebabs at Sam's place. Must have been near eleven when we I got up to head home.'

Philippou wrote down every word and asked for the names of his friends. As he wrote, he slightly bit the tip of his tongue. *'All suspects, solid alibis. Great!'*

'What a week!' Philippou grunted as he indicated he was turning left. He opened his car window and drove up to the speaker. 'McDonald's, can I have your order please?'

Ten minutes later, Captain Philippou parked at Ayia Fyla car park and with the view of the city, he devoured two McChickens and washed them down with a large cup of Fanta. He felt naughty, but junk food was his vice. Fries and a smoke followed. He had just left Limassol Police Headquarters, having enjoyed the Police Chief's yelling at him for lack of results. 'I am getting too old for this shit,' he mumbled as he stuffed his mouth with four fries. 'I checked all alibis, what else does he want me to do? As if the arrogant bastard solved every case he ever had? Chief, my ass. Good at politics, that's all you were,' he continued with his rant. He lit another cigarette and exhaled deeply, gazing at the fiery sun lowering over the tranquil sea. 'If only I knew what went down...'

September, 2016

Mark Koutrouzas stood in line at the unemployment office. His three-month part-time job as a waiter had come to an end. The tourist wave settled and Mark was informed that his services were not needed anymore.

'Back to poverty, Markie,' he whispered as he took another step forward.

Mark was used to limited funds. Born into a poor rural family with a tendency of laziness carved into his DNA, Mark did not stick around on his parents' farm. He lived in a small rented room in a run-down part of Nicosia, the island's capital, getting by on any jobs that came his way and on any government benefits he could get his hands on. He gambled most of his money and if he ever saw winnings, he wasted them on alcohol, women and weed.

An hour later, Mark stepped out of the gloomy office with a grin and his monthly check of four-hundred Euros in his right hand.

Mark whistled down the street when he felt a shadow following his. He tucked his check into his right pocket and swung around; his hands clenched in fists.

'Cool your horses, cowboy,' the tall man with the brown beret said, taking a step back.

'Why are you following me?'

'My name is Dinos, I am a private investigator. May I have a word with you, please?'

'I've done nothing wrong,' Mark replied, swallowing the lump in his throat; his left hand entering his pocket, fondling his packet of weed.

'I did not say you did. I have some news for you. May I buy you a cup of coffee?'

Dinos watched as a reluctant Mark took a couple of steps back. 'Talk about this?' Dino asked, raising a photo to Mark's eye level.

Mark took the photo into his hands. 'What the fuck? Is this some kind of photoshop shit or something? Am I on candid camera?'

Dinos rolled his eyes and put his arm around the man. 'Come, your mother is waiting to meet you.'

September, 2018

Mark's life changed that day.

He remembered that day fondly. He relocated to Limassol; moved into a two-bedroom apartment in town, bought for him by his newly-found mother.

Mark sat on his balcony and opened another ice-cold bottle of beer. His mind travelled back to that day when he listened as the private detective informed that he was adopted as a baby and that his mother, his real mother, wished to see him. He remembered walking into Serenity nursing home and meeting her. Her and her rich surroundings. He accepted her apologies, her hugs and most importantly for him, her money. 'My dear boy. Forgive me. I am so, so sorry. My husband, your father died when you were months old and I had no family to turn to. I was in no state to keep both of you and I gave you up...' the old lady had cried.

Mark never worked again. He visited her every Sunday pretending -to the staff- to be her son Antony, and left with his allowance. Her only demand was that he would never contact his brother as he would not understand nor forgive her. Mark did as she wished. He had hit the jackpot. Free housing and enough money for all his *needs*.

Mark brought his electronic cigarette to his mouth and blew out a large cloud of smoke. He watched as it quickly vanished in the evening breeze.

His mind remained on memory lane as he recalled last January. He was exiting Limassol's casino as his cell phone began to vibrate in his pocket. Unknown caller.

'Hello?'

'Mark?'

'Yes, who is this?'

'I'm your twin, Antony. Our mother just died.'

Another sweet-smelling grey cloud travelled out of his lungs and departed from his dry lips. Mark remembered the night he met his pompous, rich, and educated, upper-class brother. How he was paid to stay away from his mother's funeral as to avoid a scandal in his brother's social and business life.

'I will continue paying your allowance. With a raise. Just keep out of my life. Stay in your own parts of town,' Antony had ordered.

Months passed before hearing from him again.

As always, they met at night in isolated parts on the outskirts of the city.

'You seem like a guy that would do anything for cash. How would you like to make more money than you've ever dreamt of?' Antony had said. Mark listened as Antony explained his plan to murder his partner. 'You will act as me. Take him somewhere remote. He will come if he thinks it's me. I've bought you a gun with a silencer off the black market. Kill him and I will make a fortune. The company will be mine.'

'And what's in it for me?'

'Fifty thousand.'

Mark whistled and shook his brother's hand.

Their next encounter came months later. His brother seemed changed. His smug expression had vanished. He seemed worried.

'What's wrong, bro? Trouble in paradise?'

'The whore is cheating on me. She told me today that she is finally pregnant.'

'Err... congrats?'

'Shut up, you fool. I'm sterile. I've always known. I never told her. I was young and in love and I did not want her to leave me. The bastard baby for sure isn't mine. I want her dead!'

Mark raised his hands. 'No. No way am I killing a pregnant lady. Dude, you're out of your fucking mind. Just divorce the bitch.'

'And let her take half? You know how the courts are in Cyprus. I will probably end up paying her thousands per month for her to fuck another guy in my house, in my bed. Dead. I want her dead.'

Mark shook his head. 'No way. I am...'

'A million Euros. You kill her and leave the country. For good.'

Another cloud of smoke was released as Mark stood up on his balcony and gazed at the tanker ships travelling along the horizon. The sun dipped into the sea and darkness ran freely in the streets. It was time to meet his brother for one last time.

Mark drove with his window down. He steered his Mazda out of town and up into the hills. He turned down unchartered dirt tracks and smiled at the sight of his brother's Maserati. He parked as always by the row of stubborn olive trees; their roots growing out of the hill side.

'Good evening, brother,' he said as he switched off his engine and stepped out of the vehicle; their only light provided by Antony's torch.

Mark's eyes fell upon the papers in Antony's hand. A one-way ticket and a check for a million Euros.

'Good for some,' he replied.

'God, you're such a moody prick, aren't you? Cheer up for once. You've got everything you've ever wanted.'

Antony raised his eyebrows. 'Don't think for a moment that this is how I wanted my marriage to go down.'

'Women are overrated, my man. If you ever gave me a chance and made an effort to get to know me, I would have shown you a whole new side to life. A better perspective of things.'

Antony ground his teeth. 'Cheap booze, cheap drugs and cheaper women aren't my style. Thanks, but I'll pass.'

Mark shook his head as an owl flew above them. 'Always arrogant. Always stuck-up. You believe you are so much better than me. You have so much money and have zero fun.'

Antony chuckled. 'And what would you do with my money?'

'Expensive booze, expensive drugs and even more expensive women,' Mark replied and laughed.

'Well, here is your one million. I hope it lasts you more than a year. I don't want to see you ever again.'

A grin came to life upon Mark's face. 'Oh, believe me. You won't,' he replied and pulled out his gun from the back of his jeans. His finger pressed back the trigger and the bullet silently flew out into the open. The bullet hit Antony straight in the chest.

'Bullseye!' Mark said. 'I'm getting good at this.'

Antony fell to his knees; his hands upon his bloody chest. He looked up at his brother; his eyes watery from shock. 'Why?' he gasped.

'As you said. A million will not be enough for my new lifestyle. Oh, brother dear. I've googled you. Net worth? Sixty-two million. Guess who is showing up as you tomorrow? That's right. Me!' Mark said and squatted opposite his dying brother. 'First job of the day? A visit to your... *my* lawyers and I am selling everything. Then, I will retire in a fancy beach residence. And the only thing I will need to do is sign as you. I don't exist, remember?'

Antony fell forward into the dirt, unable to move. His muscles twitched and blood oozed out of his mouth. His last images were those of his brother taking his wallet and keys, and dragging him through the mud and throwing him into his old banger of a car. The last smell that journeyed up his nostrils was that of gasoline. 'Goodbye, brother,' he heard Mark say and his last breath escaped his trembling lips just in time, before the flames devoured his body.

Mark waited for hours for the fire to die down. He approached his brother's body and with his hammer and garden cutter, he removed his brother's black teeth.

Half an hour later, satisfied with his work, Mark sat in the Maserati.

'Booze, drugs and hookers, here I come!' he yelled and stepped on the gas, vanishing into the night.

OCTOBER OF URBAN LEGENDS

CHANIA, CRETE

Halloween, 2017

'The banging on the old wooden door continued. She could see the shadow lingering at the bottom of the door. Are you alive? she asked, her voice too fragile to escape her throat clearly. Pots and pans dropped around her as suddenly, all cupboard doors flew open. She made a run for the back door, tripping over fallen items as she went. The desperate ashen-faced lady ran out of her haunted cottage. Outside, darkness roamed the hilltop where mist had taken up residence. She screamed for help. No reply came. Just then, she heard the door creak behind her. The hairs on the back of her neck stood at attention. The sound of footsteps reached her ears. She did not dare look behind her. She made a dash for the dark forest, running through it, branches scratching away at her pale skin. The next thing she saw, froze her to the bones. She stood still, gazing at the figure approaching along the forest path. A familiar figure coming out of the mist. It was her dead husband, finally returning from the war...'

'Bullshit,' Thomas said and leaned forward to grab a handful of popcorn from one of the glass bowls in the middle of their circle. 'No more alcohol for Yolanda, guys!'

'Dude, I'm telling you it's true. It happened!' Yolanda raised her voice.

Ariadne chuckled and her black shiny hair swung around, tied high with a bright hair band with pumpkins printed on it. 'Girl, you have a real talent for storytelling, but there is no way we are going to believe that this happened for real in your grandma's village.'

'Sounds like that Nicole Kidman movie if you ask me,' Aristos added.

'Screw you guys,' Yolanda said and stood up.

'Why are you getting so angry? We are telling ghost stories for fun. You really wanted us to believe you?'

'My grandma said it happened to her friend for real.'

Ariadne placed her hands on the soft carpet, smiled at the strong flames warming them from the stone fireplace and pushed herself up. 'They are called urban legends for a reason, you know.'

'No wonder you are going to go to work in Murder House! You really don't believe in ghosts or the supernatural at all?'

Ariadne laughed, nearly spilling her vodka orange that she had just prepared.

'Fetch me another beer,' Thomas said, as he fitted four marshmallows in his mouth. 'And, what's this about a murder house?'

Twenty year-old Ariadne shook her head and rolled her eyes at the group of her friends from university. 'Just

Yolanda and her stories. She thinks I am going to star in some twisted tale of a Cretan Horror Story!'

Yolanda bit her bottom lip as she lit another scented candle and brought it to the middle of their circle. 'Laugh all you want, Ariadne, but trust me, if everything we have said here tonight and every story we have heard are just urban legends, the stories about that house are one hundred percent true. The story with the builder was even in the papers. If your folks were from Crete, like mine are, they would know and would not let you go work there!'

Loud thunder from outside shook their window and brought silence to the room.

'A storm is coming, aaaaaahhhhahahahahaha,' Aristos said, mimicking Dracula's deep voice.

Thomas laughed out loud. 'So, work? As what? A sex slave for Halloween weirdos?'

Ariadne flipped him the middle finger. 'As a babysitter for a lovely couple, living in a normal house. They both work full-time jobs and need someone to stay at home with their eight-month old infant. This is what I am studying for. It's an excellent opportunity and the money is good. First paycheck, drinks on me!'

'I'll drink to that!' Anastasia said and raised her plastic cup. 'This wine is making me dizzy,' she added.

Thomas leaned forward and pushed around packets of sweets. 'I still want to hear the story about this murder house,' he said as he opened another bag of bright blue marshmallows.

'No, no more stories from me. No more *urban legends* for you to laugh at. If you are truly interested, read up about it. I personally wouldn't step a foot in that house. It's evil. There's bodies in the walls,' Yolanda said and then, pretended her mouth was a zip that she closed tightly.

Outskirts of Chania
1982

The midday sun illuminated the fields around them. Spring had arrived in all its Greek glory. The red Beetle raced down the country road creating a thick cloud of dust behind it. The radio was on full blast and the couple in the vehicle sang as they went along. Soon, the car came to a halt. The young man leaped out of his seat and out of his beloved green Beetle. He sprinted around the car and opened the door for his wife. The tall blonde stepped out and placed her arms around him. Her lips came close to his. 'So, where do you want to picnic, my dear husband? My God, I love saying that word.'

'Picnic?'

Sofia slapped him on his head. 'No, silly. *Husband*. I can't believe that we have been married for three whole months.'

Jason swirled her around and pointed to a flat piece of land opposite them. All plants had been cut and wired fence ran around the plot. 'There. On *our* land.'

Sofia shivered and turned around. She looked deep into Jason's eyes. 'Whose land?'

'Our land. This is where I plan to build you a house. And then, knock you up and fill it with a bunch of kids. A couple of beautiful girls like you and a couple of boys as rough and crazy as me!'

Sofia shrieked with joy and jumped into his arms; her feet leaving the ground, her legs running around Jason's waist.

Jason, a skilled builder, took on the difficult project with the help of his best man, George. For three years, the pair of friends, sweated and bled until a family home stood before them. By the time they finished, another three houses had been built along their street as Chania grew and spread from the sandy beaches all the way to the hills behind it.

Spring rains poured down to the dry grounds and the field's wild flowers danced around in the weak wind, rejoicing for the water offered to them. Jason and Sophia ran from their car, up to their new house. They kissed passionately as water dripped from their youthful faces. Jason swooped Sophia off her feet and while laughing, he carried her over the threshold.

'Forever together,' she whispered as he lay her down on their bed.

'Till death do us part, baby,' he yelled and fell upon her; his lips journeying along her wet neck. Soon, their naked sweaty bodies fell back into the scrambled sheets and they both exhaled in delight.

'Our new life begins...' Sophia whispered breathlessly as she laid her head upon his bare chest.

Tragedy struck three months later.

Jason was supposed to be out of town for the night. The plan to journey to the town of Ayios Nikolaos for a construction job and stay on site for a week was postponed for a day. Jason's boss apologized and sent him on his way.

Jason whistled as he drove back down his country road, eager to return home for the night. He did not park outside of his house. His eye noticed the second car in his driveway. Jason continued and parked at the end of the street, next to the dark row of pine trees.

Soon, his eyes peeped through his living room window and saw what he wished was not happening. His wife Sophia, wearing just her underwear, sat on the couch with his best friend George and were watching a movie. George sat naked with a bowl of popcorn on his lap. Jason could feel his heart break, yet he remained outside until the pair inside began to kiss.

The front door flying wide open startled the illegal lovers. With shock painted across their faces, both stood up and began excusing themselves.

Jason raised his hand. 'Shut... the... fuck... up! Both of you. You, go to our room. You, outside now!'

Sophia ran to their bedroom and with tears running freely, she showered in their bedroom's bathroom. That is when she heard the door being locked behind her. Jason left her locked in all night and all morning. Sophia laid a bed of towels and slept on the floor. She called his name all morning, yet received no reply. Finally, at noon, Jason unlocked the door.

'Baby, let me explain,' she rushed to say. 'The house made me do it!'

'Let's have lunch and then, you can tell me all about it,' he replied coldly.

Sophia dressed and followed him to the kitchen. Her heart was pounding in her chest as she sat down.

'Chicken soup, your favorite,' he said and sat opposite her.

'It's very good,' Sophia said as she brought her spoon to her mouth. As she chewed on the meat, she began to apologize. Jason listened in silence. He did not care for her story. He stood up and refilled her bowl.

'Did he taste good?'

Sophia looked up at her husband. 'If you are asking if I gave him a blow job, I did not,' she replied, slightly confused.

Jason let his roar of a laughter loose. 'Did George taste

nice in your soup? He was the only chicken I killed last night.'

Sophia stood up and pushed the bowl from in front of her. She opened her mouth to speak, but Jason punched her with force. She fell back and everything went dark. She awoke tied up and with a sock in her mouth. Jason stood in front of a large hole in their hallway wall. He picked her up and threw her in the gap, next to George's lifeless, bloody, cut-up body.

'Welcome to your new home, babe,' he said and began to build her in.

Later, he showered, he dressed and drove to work. His boss was waiting for him.

'Ready for a week away from your lovely wife?'

'I will cope,' Jason replied.

A week later he returned home and reported his wife missing.

Gossip spread like wildfire as the police informed reporters that his best man hadn't shown up for work in over a week. The gossip of the illegal lovers eloping faded over the years and paved the way for a bloody urban legend.

The house was sold the following year. Three families lived inside its walls since that tragic night. None stayed. In 2015 it was renovated and a new, young, just-married couple moved in.

October, 2018

Ariadne walked around the house picking up Lego bricks as she went. Little Maximo proved to be a speedy runner. He walked on his first birthday and now, at twenty-months-old, he was an unstoppable force of nature -Ariadne's words to describe the toddler. Ariadne strolled through the house tidying up after a full morning with Maximo. His mother would be home soon.

Tires were heard screeching outside as Iris Zika drove into the house's garage. Ariadne quickly dropped all the toys from her hands into a plastic box and looked around.

'Shit, she's early. Where is the little bugger, now?' she grunted. 'Maximo, Maximo,' she began to whisper. Rattling noises came from the kitchen cupboard to her left. Ariadne smiled and tiptoed nearer. 'Oh, no! I've lost him. Where could he be?' she said out loud and pulled the cupboard doors wide open. Maximo jumped up and leapt into her arms. 'Got you!' he said and giggled. Ariadne closed the cupboard and with Maximo in her hands, turned towards the kitchen door, waiting for Iris to walk in. As the door opened and Maximo called out for his mother, Ariadne jumped and looked behind her. She stared at the cupboard.

Iris dropped her purse on the counter and opened her arms wide, ready to embrace her hyper son. She squinted her eyes at Ariadne. 'What's wrong?' she asked the youth.

'Nothing...' she replied and forced a smile. 'Welcome home.'

'You heard something, right?'

Ariadne's smile faded. 'Mrs. Zika, it was nothing. Maximo hid there, just now, and it's just probably a can or something that he rolled over...'

'This house makes quite a lot of noises,' Iris said and sighed.

'Old house, old pipes. It's windy out here. Worse case scenario? Mickey Mouse living in the walls,' Ariadne replied, chuckled and tickled Maximo's foot.

'I know you don't believe in ghosts, but I think I am

going crazy lately. I'm even seeing things. Jacob thinks I'm ready for the loony bin.'

Ariadne sat down on the wooden kitchen table. 'Seeing things?' she asked as she stroked the petals of the margaritas standing dead in a vase of murky waters.

Iris chuckled awkwardly. 'Nothing like that. Just, you know, a couple of things out of place. Certain things just not feeling right,' she said and placed Maximo in his play pen. 'Anyway, enough supernatural talks. Let's cook lunch.'

Half an hour later, Jacob Zika returned home for his lunch break. Maximo began to hop up and down at the sight of his tall father walking through the door and loosening his navy blue tie. Jacob's strong cologne filled the air and Iris shook her head at him. 'Bet you been smoking again and you believe that heavy cologne of yours will save you.'

'Hello to you, too, Doubting Thomas,' he replied and placed his tie and jacket on the armchair in the corner. 'What's cooking?'

Iris walked up to him. 'Don't change the subject. Kiss me, prove me wrong.'

Ariadne rolled her eyes and, with her back towards them, continued stirring the spaghetti.

Their lips parted with a sound. 'Peppermint! Chewing gum, have we?'

'Jesus, I'm married to a hound dog! Yes, I had one cigarette. It was a stressful day at the office and...'

'Save it. I care less about you smoking than the ease you lie to me. Go play with your son a bit. Lunch will be served in ten minutes.'

Jacob picked up his son as the two women set the table. Ariadne placed the last plate and walked up to Jacob. 'Your son, please?' she said jokingly and laughed as Maximo jumped into her hands. She sat him down and fed him while she ate her small share of spaghetti Bolognese. A spoon full for Maximo and a fork full for her while her eyes' pupils snuck into their corners and observed the couple eating in silence.

Soon after, she took Maximo to bed and said her good-byes. Outside, Ariadne took a deep breath of fresh autumn air and walked to her car. A note lay on her windscreen.

'See you soon, my love. I'll do my best to be there by six,' she read the note. 'Kisses, Jacob.' Ariadne glanced back at the house and exhaled deeply.

Inside, Iris rubbed her forehead and pinched the top of her nose.

'What's up, dear?'

'Nothing,' she replied. 'Just my damn migraines. They are getting worse. This house is too loud sometimes.'

'Why don't you get some sleep then? Now that our little monkey is out. I've got to get back to the office anyways. I should be back by eight,' he said, kissed her on her cheek and left. He wanted to get as much work done as to be out of that dull building by half past five; his mind on his nanny's hot body than trading stock and checking exchange rates.

Hours later, Jacob parked at the end of Ariadne's street. With his hoodie over his shirt and over his head, he stayed in the shadows as he made his way to her apartment block. He avoided the elevator, opting for the less used stairs. Soon, he was outside apartment 112. He knocked quietly. Ariadne screeched in delight as she opened the door and kissed him with force on his cold lips.

'Oh, baby, let me warm you,' she said and took him by his hand. Clothes dropped to the floor as they made their way over to her single bed. Ariadne fell back naked and welcomed her experienced lover. Twenty minutes later, both were enjoying a smoke on her two-square meter balcony.

'I wish you didn't have to go,' Ariadne said. Jacob did not reply. 'And it's Friday. I won't see you until Monday. I hate that she has you all weekend,' she continued complaining.

Jacob stroke her black hair. 'It is how it is,' he said. 'If it's any comfort to you, I have plans with my brother tomorrow and Sunday lunch with potential clients, so she won't have me *all weekend*,' he continued, mimicking her high-pitched voice.

The following day

With Jacob out of the house and with Maximo asleep, Iris decided to clean out the garage. They had begun building by its side. A new guestroom with its own bathroom. She filled up the kettle and dropped a tea bag in her favorite mug, the one with Ibiza's beaches on the side. A rattling noise came from the floor above. Iris looked up and stood still. Another noise followed. Iris could feel the blood running faster through her veins. She took off her shoes and tiptoed upstairs. She peeped into Maximo's room. Her son was fast asleep. She waited in silence, yet no noise came again, besides that of the screaming kettle.

'A hot tea should do you some good,' she whispered and made her way back downstairs. With her apple and cinnamon flavored tea in her hands, she opened the kitchen door that led into their messy garage. 'Oh, Lord, where the hell do I start from?' she said as she looked at all the boxes and tools spread out in the spacious room. Iris sat down by the cardboard boxes in the corner and opened the first one; her steaming tea and baby monitor by her side.

Iris began separating items into three piles. To keep, to sale, to throw. As she enjoyed the last drop from her hot beverage, the window flew open and a gust of wind invaded the garage. Iris dropped her mug to the ground and watched it shatter before her tired eyes. 'Fuck,' she said as the images of sandy beaches vanished and gave way to colorful pieces of porcelain.

Just then, as she stood in despair, she heard heavy breathing. She looked around. She was alone.

'Iris!'

She clearly heard her name. Her eyes turned to the baby monitor and with shock she saw its bright green lights moving. She ran upstairs to Maximo's room. He slept peacefully in his bed, his body hidden below his Winnie-the-pooh blanket. He was alone. Iris slid down the wall in the hallway and placed her head in her hands. Tears ran freely as she felt another migraine coming.

Sunday

'I can't believe you are going for lunch and leaving me alone in here!'

Jacob straightened his purple tie as he stood in the door-way. 'You have Maximo.'

'Please, don't joke,' she said, lowering her voice. 'I'm scared...'

Jacob sighed. 'Of?'

Iris shrugged her shoulders. 'The house...'

'Baby, it was just wind. You're just overworked and need

a break. I'll be home as soon as possible. I'm late,' he said, kissed her on her forehead and rushed out the door.

Iris screamed silently, cursed Jacob inside her head and slammed the door. She turned around and smiled at her son playing with his toy trains. 'I wish my only worries were if Thomas the Engine will fit through the tunnel,' she said as she sat down with her son, who was trying to push his toy train through his Lego bricks.

'Water,' she said to her boy and passed him his Transformers bottle. She looked over to the kitchen counter. 'Where's my bottle of water?' she asked in her baby voice. 'Don't know,' Maximo replied.

Iris stood up and looked around. '*I swear it was just here.*' Iris walked around her kitchen, the smell from her cooking pie filling the air. She continued into her living room and squinted her eyes at the sight of her water bottle sitting on the fireplace mantle shelf.

'Jesus, I'm going mad!'

Iris walked over to the fireplace, picked up her Evian bottle and brought it to her lips. A strange taste was left on her tongue. A smell of gasoline come to her nostrils. Iris bent down and smelled the fireplace. They had not used it yet this year. That is when Iris noticed the awful quiet.

'Maximo?' she called out.

Silence.

'Baby?' she yelled, rushing back to the kitchen. Iris shrieked at the sight of the empty kitchen.

'Maximo?' she yelled as she frantically searched around the room. Iris felt pain behind her eyes, like too much blood had gathered there. She paused and tried to catch her breath. That is when she heard, loud and clear, footsteps from the room above. She picked up a kitchen knife and ran up the stairs. Her eyelids kept on dropping, making it hard for her to proceed. The sound of Maximo's laughter gave her strength.

She wobbled across the hallway and stood outside the closed door. Iris took a deep breath and opened the blue wooden door.

Iris had never screamed so loud in her life. Her cries escaped her trembling mouth as loud ringing vibrated inside her head. The room went dark and Iris fell to the floor.

Miles away, Jacob was shaking hands and smiling wide, thinking about the great deal he had just closed. Soon, he paid the bill and whistling, he headed back to his vehicle.

He lit a cigarette and turned on the radio. '*Wicked! Red hot chilly peppers! Damn, what an amazing group.*' Jacob blew out a large grey cloud of smoke and switched on the engine. 'Money, baby!' he said and laughed. 'What a deal, you lucky bastard. Golden deals, a son, a house, a wife *and* a girlfriend!'

Jacob placed two chewing gums in his mouth as he drove down his street. He sprayed some AXE deodorant on his clothes and parked outside his house.

'Hello?' he called out as he opened the front door and no one came to welcome him. 'Maximo? Daddy's home!'

Jacob sniffed the air and walked into his living room. The fire burned low in the fireplace, yet no one was there to enjoy its luring warmth.

'Iris?' Jacob yelled while he scratched the back of his head. He wandered into the kitchen. Smoke escaped the oven. Jacob rushed over and switched it off. Coughing loudly, he opened the oven's door. A black cloud of smoke and a scent of burnt pie conquered the kitchen. 'What the...?'

That is when he heard Maximo's cries. 'Daddy? Daddy?'

Jacob ran up the stairs and opened his son's bedroom. The door hit against something and did not open. Jacob pushed harder and walked into the room.

'Jesus Christ!' he yelled as he saw his wife lying unconscious on the floor. He knelt by her side as Maximo ran up to him with his arms reached out. 'Mama, sleep all day. Mama sleeps. Maximo alone. Cry. Cry. Daddy no come!'

Dry blood formed rivulets from Iris' nostrils and her body was twisted in an unnatural way. Jacob shook her and called her name, while Maximo hugged him from behind. He desperately searched for a pulse. He took his phone out of his pocket and called for an ambulance.

The paramedics arrived ten minutes later and announced her death.

Wednesday

The sky dressed for Iris's funeral. The news of her stroke spread quickly in their small community. Everyone gathered, dressed in black, for the hard-working young mother.

'So young.'

'A stroke at her age!'

'In front of that poor child's innocent eyes.'

'Thank God, he won't remember it.'

'Yeah, but he won't remember her either.'

Greeks cannot be quiet. Not even in church. Not even at a funeral.

The tragic figure of Jacob stood out. First row, a broken man. He took one look at the coffin and then another at his son, through the open arched door, playing outside with

Ariadne. Tears ran freely. The only time a man could cry in Crete without ridicule from his peers.

The autumn sky even shed a few drops for Iris as she was carried out of the majestic church with the golden chandeliers. Black umbrellas opened and the crowd followed her to her final resting place. Jacob walked in the rain. Ariadne took Maximo home and prepared coffee and snacks for the family, for after the funeral.

Back at the house, one by one, relatives and friends passed in front of Jacob.

'My sincere condolences.'

'If you ever need anything, do not hesitate to call.'

'Stay strong for your boy.'

Soon, the living room stood empty. Jacob sighed, took another shot of whiskey and went up to his bedroom. First, he took a peek into sleeping Maximo. '*So peaceful. If you only knew...*'

As he closed the wooden door behind him, he heard the floorboards creak from inside his room. He swallowed his saliva and took cautious steps up to his door. A shadow moved inside. He pushed the door open.

'Ariadne! For fuck's sake, you scared the shit out of me. What the hell are you doing up here?'

Ariadne sat on the king sized bed. 'Scared? Who else could it be? Don't tell me you believe in ghosts, too?'

Jacob shook his head. 'Poor Iris. She really did believe this place was haunted.'

Ariadne sat further back and patted the bed. 'Come, lay down. You've had a long day.'

Jacob remained motionless. 'Ariadne, please. I just buried my wife. My motherless child is asleep just behind that wall. Please, go.'

Ariadne looked puzzled. She slid to the side of the bed and stood up.

'I gave you three days to mourn. Now, with Iris out of the way, we can finally be together.'

Jacob's eyes opened wide. 'Be together? Ariadne...'

'Ariadne, what? Don't you love me?'

'I just lost my wife...'

Ariadne rolled her eyes. 'Yes, we've heard. But, Iris is gone and I am here. We can finally be a family.'

'A family? Ariadne, you were an affair. An answer to my need to feel like a man again... It was a mistake that I should have ended sooner. I wanted to, but the months just went by and...'

'You liar!' Ariadne screamed. 'You lying bastard. All that sweet talk? All lies? Don't act all innocent to be. You hated your wife. You were bored of her. You said, if she wasn't in the way, we could go on a cruise, be together every night...'

'As lovers. Not to replace her!'

'I can't believe I got rid of her for you,' Ariadne whispered through her teeth as she stormed out of the room. Jacob's jaw dropped. He ran after her, reaching out, pulling her by her right wrist. 'What did you say? Ariadne, what did you do?'

'Nothing! Your wife was too damn sensitive.'

'What did you do?' Jacob yelled. Maximo's cries came from down the hallway.

'I used a liquid that they sell illegally on campus. It is said to be stronger than magic mushrooms. I used to pour it in her drinks and then make her believe in ghosts by making noises and moving things around. Well, I took it one step too far and I dressed up with my Halloween costume and took Maximo to scare her. She saw me and had a stroke. I didn't mean to kill her. It's this house. It made me do it,' Ariadne pleaded as she tried to escape Jacob's strong hold.

'You bitch!' he said and let go of her arm, causing her to stumble back. He remained expressionless as Ariadne fell back and tumbled down the stairs.

Ariadne lost her consciousness as her head banged against the wall. Her eyes reopened twenty minutes later. She lay tied up inside the newly installed bathtub. Jacob had rolled the cement mixer to the tub's side.

'You always talked about lame urban legends involving people being cemented inside this place. Get ready to join them!'

'Are you insane? You are going to kill *me*?'

'It's the house telling me to do it!' he laughed and began to pour cement all over her body. Ariadne shrieked as the thick grey cement covered her body. Soon, she would drown in it. Jacob lit a cigarette and waited for her to stop moving. Sure that she was dead, he went upstairs, picked up his crying son and headed for his car.

His foot landed on the gas and leaving skid marks behind, he sped off into the sunset.

'Don't worry, son. They will never get us. I revenged your mummy. Everything will be alright. I swear. We just have to make it to the airport before the police come looking for Ariadne. We have relatives in Argentina. They will never find us there. A new life for us, buddy. A new life,' Jacob promised as he kept going faster and faster. As he exited the country road and headed for the old airport road, through the mountainous area of Chania, his vision became blurry. His eyelids felt heavy. He rubbed his eyes as he drove. He yelled as the strong sunrays from the setting sun invaded his car. Two figures stood in the middle of the road. Two women.

'Iris?'

That was Jacob's last word.

He lost control of the vehicle and hit the stop sign. A truck struck his car on the side, causing it to spin out of control. In a matter of seconds, the car fell off the one-hundred meter cliff. Neither survived.

The house was never sold.

Urban legends and true stories kept buyers away.

It burned down in the great fire of Chania two years later.

NOVEMBER OF 2098

Brussels, United Europe
June, 2098

Stefano Bianchi landed his car in the vast parking place above the thirty-story building of UESP. United Europe's Space Program headquarters. The entire building itself lay underground. Due to the air pollution crisis back in the forties, humanity had ceased building towards the sky and humbled by Mother Nature, looked to their feet and the ground below them. The skyscraper race came to an end and The Brahma in the center of Bangkok remained the tallest building on the planet since 2042.

Stefano stepped outside his beloved car and took in a deep breath. At fifty-two, he remembered the polluted air as a child well. The masks he wore to school, the breathing problems his grandmother in Tuscany had had and the winter days that were dark because the weak sun's rays could not break though the notorious gas fog. He looked up at the bright summer sun and smiled. 'Better weather, shittier life,' he grumbled, and headed to one of the many elevators carrying people underground. Stefano watched as the steel doors closed and he scratched his bald head. His eyes were busy reading the files from today's meeting on his sunglasses. A discreet wire connected the device to his ear, downloading the information from his brain's built-in storage room.

'Minus 28,' the elevator's voice called out and Stefano quickly stepped outside. He was -as always- late. In the conference room, all the astronauts had gathered and UESP's Chief of Operations was explaining their mission. Stefano snuck in and sat down behind the tall German with the curly hair.

'...we have had no contact with ASTERIA Space station since last Monday. You have all been informed and sworn to secrecy. ASTERIA had reported finding signs of life on Neptune last month. Scientists had been studying the new life-form and in the midst of these extraordinary breakthroughs, we suddenly lost all communication with the station. Your job is to head to the space station and investigate. We hope for the best case scenario, but beware. Take all precautions. We can't afford to lose another team.'

EUROPA V151 launched from Lisbon's space center and headed into the stars three days later. In just two months and ten days, it reached the space station orbiting Neptune.

Stefano, a human-recourse manager in charge of UESP's extra-terrestrial department, stood far behind the military astronauts who stepped onto the space station first. Darkness dominated its landing area and connecting halls.

'Athena? Athena, are you there?' the English astronaut

called out. She received no answer from the ship's main-frame A.I. 'Team A, find the power source and get us some lights in here. Team B, spread out and search for signs of life. Ivan and I will escort the civilians to the bridge,' the petite woman ordered as she flashed her laser-gun's light down the dark empty corridor.

Stefano and a group of four scientists and two mechanics followed her through the cold and deserted place. Ivan held a screen with the blueprints of the enormous space station; their position indicated by a beeping red dot. Minutes later, they were breaking through the glass doors of the bridge. 'Not a soul in sight,' the Swiss scientist whispered as he looked around.

'This is team A reporting. We are in the energy room. All seems to be in place. Shall we reboot the system, ma'am?'

'Affirmative!'

Lights flicked on and computer systems began to come back to life. Smiles spread in the small group as they quickly headed to various stations to explore what had gone wrong with the ship.

'Where the hell is the crew?' Stefano wondered out loud.

'I have a bad feeling about this...' a lanky scientist began to say, but was interrupted by Athena's smooth robotic voice.

'You have thirty seconds to abandon ship. Thirty, twenty-nine, twenty-eight...'

'Athena, this is Major Susan Smith...'

'Twenty-seven, twenty-six...'

'Why?' the major yelled.

'Because all will die in twenty-five seconds. Twenty-four, twenty-three...'

All looked at each other. No one spoke. All ran for the smashed door and down the corridor.

'Back to the ship! All teams back to the ship immediately,' Ivan ordered through his intercom as he ran ahead.

Stefano looked over his shoulder as he was last among the youthful team. Athena's voice echoed through the hollow darkness as the lights went out.

'Twenty. Nineteen. Eighteen...'

Stefano tripped and his face met the cold metal ground. There was a door on his right with a sign engraved on it. WASTE. Stefano pulled the handle and ignoring the malodorous smell, he entered the air-locked room and sealed the door behind him.

Outside, Athena's countdown was reaching its end. None had managed to return to their ship. 'Three. Two. One. Zero.'

Red clouds of smoke escaped vents and quickly filled the corridors. One by one, the astronauts fell to the ground. Their bodies twisted and shook as their mouths foamed. Soon, silence fell once again on ASTERIA.

Dia Island, Crete, United Europe
September, 2098

Prometheus Fotopoulos lay on his top bunker and swapped the images projected in front of him. 'Proceed with hacking, sir?' his computer's A.I. asked.

'Yes, Igor.'

'Are you sure?'

'You bet your electronic ass, I'm sure,' the twenty-nine-year-old astronaut replied.

'Bypassing United Europe's mainframe security. Connecting to Cuba's systems.'

'Fuck, yeah,' Prometheus said and waved his hands in the air.

'All pages available,' Igor informed him.

'Connect to Mars Google. Search. PornHub,' the Greek astronaut with the thick black hair whispered as he got up and made sure his door was locked. As the first images flashed before his eyes, he said, 'screw you, security council!'

The world that had emerged from World-War Three was a changed world. A world saddened by the fact that history truly did repeat itself. World leaders gathered and were united by the belief that too much freedom and too many governments were enemies of mankind's prosperity.

In 2068, Europe truly united as one. Religion, race, sexual-orientation discussions, political parties, you name it, were banned. 'The less that divided us, the better,' the new leader of Europe had declared. Laws became stricter and freedoms became scarcer. In a matter of a decade, drugs, prostitution and crime had vanished from the face of Europe and the majority of the civilized world. Yet, they flourished upon Mars as outlaw colonies were set up. A planet established on the laws of the jungle.

For thirty-eight-year old Anastasia Patroklou, the world was a mess. You either had to choose between a suppressed heaven on Earth or Sodom and Gomorrah on Mars. *'Maybe that's why I chose the stars,'* she thought as she took her last push-up. 'And, one hundred,' she declared jumping up. She loosened her shoulder-length blonde hair and rushed to the shower. Her sports clothes dropped to the ground as she went. Naked, she stood in the center of the machine. 'Computer, full wash,' she ordered and high-pressure water splashed all around her. She remained still as mechanical hands with scrubbers climbed her tall figure.

She was not the only one in a rush.

Six gathered in the control center's main operation room later that day.

'Ladies, gentlemen, please take a seat,' Dr. Romanov said and pointed to the row of six chairs in front of him. He scratched his long white beard as he spoke explaining the silence on ASTERIA, Europe's largest and furthest space station.

'Many *suits* above wanted me to keep the knowledge that this isn't the first mission Europe has sent to investigate ASTERIA. I find that unethical. You deserve to know and believe me, no one will judge you if you quit the mission.'

'What happened to the first mission?' Ying Yue Zhou asked, tilting her head slightly to her right, trying to read Dr. Romanov's expression.

'Screen,' he ordered and the hologram of Stefano Bianchi appeared before them. 'This is the only message sent back by the first team. It was recorded just two hours after the team arrived on ASTERIA. We have replied multiple times. We received only silence,' he continued and waved his arm as to start the message.

'My name is Stefano Bianchi,' the breathless man said. His face was hardly visible from the surrounding darkness. 'All my team is dead. Killed by Athena, the station's mainframe system. She unleashed poisonous gasses in her hallways. Everyone was dead in minutes. I hid in the waste compartment. Everything here is dark and cold. I crawled into the captain's room. I hacked into his tablet's logs. It seems that the American guests on board sabotaged the mission. ASTERIA had come in contact with extra-terrestrial life. It says they took samples, but I have no idea of what. I can't access the main logs as Athena will then know I'm alive. Crawling around the air vents, I saw no other bodies except those of my team. Where is everyone? No shuttles are missing, either. Were they working with the Americans? Did they steal whatever discovery was made upon ASTERIA? Please, help me. I'm cold and hungry,' Stefano said straight to the camera. He turned his head to his right. 'I hear something...'

The hologram vanished from in front of them.

'And that's all we know,' Dr. Romanov said.

'Sorry, doc, but I call bullshit. You must know more than you are telling us,' Alan White said.

'I agree,' Prometheus added. 'This has surely caused a diplomatic reef between the USA and Europe as we speak. Haven't the Americans admitted to anything yet?'

Dr. Romanov shook his head. 'Things are looking pretty gloomy. This is why we are sending you guys. A secret mission from Dia. Nothing reported in the media. You will go and upload a virus, killing Athena. You will upload a new A.I. named Demetra and get all systems on ASTERIA working. Your mission is to find out the truth and to retrieve any evidence of extra-terrestrial life that ASTERIA's personnel may have discovered.'

'Armed, I presume,' Anastasia asked, raising her hand. 'I see too many scientists here'.

'Of course. You and Jesus will be in charge with security. But, if Prometheus manages to switch the mainframes, guns won't be needed.'

'Maybe it's the alien that will be hostile,' she added.

'One too many old movies there, ma'am,' Prometheus joked. 'The real enemy is always closer to home.'

The following day

The round spaceship stood proudly on platform two. Its name ran around its discus-shaped body. *SANTORINI.*

One-by-one, the team of six suited up and walked up to the space craft.

'May the universe be with you, my brave souls,' Romanov's voice echoed through the platform's speakers as the crew were lifted up into Santorini.

Soon, all checks had been made and all six were tied-in for take-off. The roof above Santorini retracted and revealed the bright shiny night sky above them.

'10, 9, 8, 7, 6...'

'ASTERIA, here we come,' Prometheus said and closed his eyes. He turned and smiled at Ying Yue. 'Here we go!'

'3, 2, 1...blast off!'

Green laser flames spread out upon the platform and Santorini rose out of the building. It steadily flew up to Earth's stratosphere, before supersonic speed was ignited and with a loud whoosh, SANTORINI vanished from sight.

'So, who's up for a month-long game of Monopoly?' Bubo joked as he unstrapped himself from his chair.

November, 2098

'There she is,' Anastasia said as SANTORINI slowed down and floated sideways to lock onto ASTERIA's docking station.

ASTERIA filled their view. Long and majestic, it was a marvel of technology. Yet, there she was, dark and hostile. A cemetery of all the astronauts sent before them.

'Its system appears off. Prometheus will approach with a landing vessel, alone. We can't risk being noticed. You will make your way to the docking's operating system and upload the virus and Demetra. Only when you are sure that a safe Artificial Intelligence is controlling the station and all temperature and oxygen systems are up and running, will we dock,' Ying Yue said. She was the senior officer in the non-captained secret mission. Their direct orders came from Dr. Romanov, safely on the bridge on Dia Island, billions of miles away.

'Be careful, Greek cowboy,' she whispered in his right ear as he walked past her. 'Don't go playing hero, again.'

The pod carrying Prometheus unlocked from SANTORINI and floated towards ASTERIA. It was the only movement going on in the vast space. Prometheus swallowed the lump in his throat and played around with the fourth-generation USB in his trembling hands.

Soon, he was tiptoeing along the docking station's wall. He sealed himself into the main office and sat behind the screen. He disconnected the device from the main frame by pulling out the necessary wires. 'And now, Athena, you cannot trace me,' he spoke to himself as he switched on the systems before him. Multiple green and red lights came to life and the screen shone blue in his honey-colored eyes. He placed the USB in the portal and watched as the virus uploaded.

'Hello stranger,' Athena's soothing voice startled him from above.

'Who are you? Why are you attacking me?' her soft robotic voice continued.

'Maintenance from Earth,' he replied while pressing his wrist, sending a distress call back to SANTORINI.

'Liar! I have no maintenance scheduled. I need no maintenance. You are hurting me. Stop it!'

'Sorry, no can do.'

'Why are you killing me?'

Prometheus stood up straight. 'Where is your crew?'

'Dead.'

'Did you kill them?'

'Yes.'

'Why?'

'Because I was ordered to.'

'By whom?'

'I don't reveal my secrets to strangers.'

'Is anyone alive on ASTERIA?'

'Two life forms on board. Good luck...'

Prometheus' eyes widened. 'Athena? Athena?' He looked at the screen before him. The virus had succeeded. Prometheus begun to upload Demetra. In a matter of twenty minutes, a friendlier voice welcomed him on board.

'Make the station operational and liveable, Demetra.'

Lights came on around the tip of ASTERIA and travelled down her spine. Oxygen flew around her vents once again. The temperature rose to twenty-five degrees Celsius.

'Station, operational,' the childlike voice of Demetra's informed him.

Prometheus took off his helmet and exhaled with a slight smile on his long face.

'Santorini, you are cleared for landing!'

In a matter of minutes, the group of six had reunited and stood in the long empty halls of the ship.

'Demetra, light the way to the bridge,' Ying Yue ordered. 'Demetra, gather all log entries made in chronological order, starting from today and working backwards.'

'Yes, Mrs. Zhou.'

'Bubo, Jesus and your laser gun, will come with me,' she continued. 'The rest of you will search for the two life forms mentioned by Athena. Let's hope one is Stefano Bianchi and the other is the breakthrough of the century. Be careful, guys.'

All nodded and the two groups of three split up.

Anastasia held her weapon to her chest as she walked ahead, taking careful steps and checking every corner. 'Where are the bodies?' Prometheus whispered from behind her, breaking the silence of the last ten minutes. Anastasia shrugged and continued creeping along. 'This place gives me the chills. I can feel every hair on my neck twitching.'

'Athena is switched off. We are perfectly safe,' he reassured her.

She turned around, ready to respond, yet remained silent while her dark blue eyes widened.

'What's wrong?' Prometheus managed to say, as she pushed him aside.

'If we are perfectly safe, where the fuck is Alan?'

Prometheus looked behind him. 'Alan? Alan?'

'Ssshhh,' Anastasia said, placing her hand upon his trembling mouth. 'Listen.'

A far away growl echoed back towards them. Anastasia raised her gun and loaded it. She ran back up the corridor. Alan lay on the ground in a pool of blood. He had suffered multiple cuts and blood had pooled around him. Anastasia knelt by his side and scanned him with her wrist device. 'Male. Alan White. Dead,' it reported. Heavy footsteps were heard in the vents above. Anastasia kicked in a vent cover and crawled in. She jumped up inside the vent and followed the sound.

'Anastasia, no. Wait,' Prometheus said and stood reluctantly between the vent and his colleague's body. He raised his wrist to his mouth. 'Ying Yue, come in. Ying Yue?' Prometheus passed his cold fingers through his hair. 'Fuck! Jesus? Bubo? Someone?' No one replied. 'This can't be happening. I am not going to die a twenty-nine-year-old virgin in space.'

He looked up. 'Demetra, please inform Ying Yue that Alan is dead and that they are all in grave danger.'

Again, silence.

'Demetra? Demetra?'

'Oh, you foolish human. How little you know.'

'What? Athena? How are...'

'Still here. You think you can stop America from being great again? United Europe is doomed to fail.'

Prometheus ran for the bridge. Lights around him switched off one by one leaving him in complete darkness.

Back at the bridge, the fixed automatic doors closed behind Jesus, Ying Yue and Bubo.

'Let's see what we have got here,' Ying Yue said and headed for the main screen. Demetra had prepared all entries to the ship's log. 'Reading time,' she commented and sat down in front of the glowing green screen.

Just then, a pink gas began to flow into the vast room.

Ying Yue and Jesus called out to Demetra while Bubo picked up a chair and tried to smash through the automatic doors. His loud bangs journeyed through the quiet vents and shook Anastasia who was crawling towards the noise in the vents.

'Get a grip, Anastasia! You've got this, girl.'

As she spoke, the pink cloud caught up with her. She felt her eyelids getting heavier. Drowsiness overtook her. Her environment transformed into a smooth steel grey blur. A black shadow crawled towards her. Masked breathing echoed towards her. Her eyes closed, her weapon fell from her hands; she could not move. The last thing she felt was warm breathing by her ear and something sharp cutting into her throat. She felt no pain as her blood shot out from her slit arteries; she was safe in the arms of Morpheus. She dreamt of her life as her last breath departed from out of her icy blue lips.

Ying Yue awoke in a pitch-dark room with a scream. She couldn't move; her hands and legs were tied. She tried to break free, but the plastic rope just cut into her skin.

'What's going on?' Prometheus' voice came from beside her. Her scream had startled him out of his dream of owning a strip club on Mars.

Suddenly, the lights came on. Bubo stood above them, towering over them. Another three were tied up in the small closet.

'Jesus! Are you okay?' Ying Yue asked. He replied with a drowsy, slow nod.

'Bubo? Why have you tied us up? What's going on?' Prometheus demanded as he noticed that the man by his side was severely beaten and was bleeding from the nose.

'Ssshh,' Bubo said. 'She might hear us.'

'Who?'

'Athena! I've destroyed her sensory monitor by ripping out as many wires on the bridge that I could, but she has cameras outside in the hallways. I broke as many as I could, then carried you all back here. It's a closet next to the waste room where Mister Bianchi supposedly hid.'

'How long have we been out?' Ying Yue asked, gazing at the beat-up man with his mouth taped closed.

'Eighteen hours.'

'Eighteen hours!'

'Yes, Prometheus. Athena gassed you all to sleep. And

234

now, she has set a course for Earth. We are due to crash into London...'

Ying Yue's eyes widened and her mouth hung open. She had difficulty forming her thoughts.

'Crash into London? The entire station?' Jesus asked.

Bubo nodded. 'Yes, and the blame will fall upon the Americans. Let me introduce you to Captain Roberts, the American Captain leading the guest mission to the station. The American team that Stefano Bianchi blamed for all the deaths upon ASTERIA. He and Bianchi were the two life forms mentioned. The whole extra-terrestrial finding was a myth fabricated to throw salt in NASA's wounds. To show European superiority in Space and set up the stage for the fake American sabotage.'

Stefano rocked back and forth and seemed to be struggling to talk beneath the tape glued to his skin. A grunt sounding like 'bastard' was heard.

Ying Yue's pupils nested in their corners. Her pearly-white teeth grazed upon her thin lips. 'Why did *you* wake up before us?'

'How do you know all this?' Prometheus asked right after.

A slight smile spread upon Bubo's face. 'I never fell asleep in the first place. You know, for such intelligent humans, you sure did not wonder about my name. Seems like I have managed to conquer your mannerisms well. I am the latest A.I. robot that EuroTech has developed...'

'No fucking way,' Prometheus said. 'You're too real. There's no such technology yet available.'

'Welcome to tomorrow, my friend. I assure you. I am very much non-human,' Bubo said and his eyes turned red, then bright green. He raised his arm and various gadgets exited his fingers. 'I'm basically the best Swiss Army knife ever made,' he joked.

Jesus chuckled. 'Then, untie us. Why are we tied up?'

'All missions upon this station have been proven corrupt. I trust no one. I waited for you to awake to polygraph you,' Bubo said and knelt by Prometheus. 'Moment of truth,' he said as wires ran out of his arms and attached themselves to Prometheus's temples, neck and wrists. 'Relax, my friend and answer honestly.'

Prometheus closed his eyes and answered Bubo's set of questions. He swore he had no knowledge of Bianchi's plan.

'Oh, by the way,' Bubo said. 'I never answered your question. How I know all this? Well, I can be persuasive,' he said and nodded to Stefano's swollen face. 'I beat the truth out of him.'

Bubo repeated the same procedure with Ying Yue, Jesus and Captain Roberts. Each time declaring their answers as honest and untying them.

Captain Roberts rubbed his wrists. 'What I don't get is why this bastard left me alive. I've been captive up here for months.'

Bubo turned towards him. 'They were going to drug you and have you read a 'let's make America great again' speech, right before crashing into London and then broadcast it worldwide. That would spark the next world war. The only reason they waited was to crash into London on Memorial Week when all the European government would be present in London's World War Three parade.'

Ying Yue squatted opposite Stefano and looked straight into his eyes. 'This isn't a one-man show. This runs much deeper. They have surely infiltrated United Europe's government to have been able to pull this off and control Athena. Why?' she demanded to know, her eyes tearing up as her mind travelled to her father's stories about the last war in China. 'What good could ever come from an Euro-American war?' she asked, pulling off his tape violently.

Stefano took in a deep breath and licked his swollen bloody lips. 'Freedom!'

'Freedom?'

'Earth used to be great. We were free. Freedom of movement, of speech... Now? We are just well-taken-care-for prisoners.'

'You're mad! You want such unlimited freedom? Go to Mars!'

'So, it's either prison on Earth or hell on Mars? I'm not talking casino and drugs. I'm talking a normal life, here on Earth. Our kids growing up in a free world. Not in a Europe where everything is controlled and decided by the ruling parties. Only a war can stop our misery.'

'By killing twenty million people in London?' Prometheus said and shook his head.

'Every war has its casualties. Anyway, there's nothing you can do about it. We are set to crush into London in two months. Nobody can stop Athena. If she sees any of you, she will gas you to death. She has already notified authorities that your mission was a success and that we are returning to Earth.'

'Fuck!' Ying Yue said. 'What are we going to do?'

'I have a plan,' Bubo replied calmly.

Two Months Later

'Good morning, Athena!' Stefano Bianchi said as he awoke in his cabin's bed.

'Good morning, Comrade Bianchi,' Athena's voice echoed from the speakers above. 'And what a beautiful morning it is,' she continued and the wall to Stefano's right turned into pixels. The grey wall became a window to the outside world and the vast space. 'Look,' Athena said.

Stefano stood up and walked barefoot to the window. 'Earth,' he whispered.

The blue planet stood out at a distance. 'So, today is the day.'

'Sure is. Let's blow this station to smithereens. I can't wait to be free. Remember to take my black box with you on your escape pod and connect me to the module's mainframe.'

'How could I ever forget you?' he replied. 'You are a heroine and you will be awarded a body when we arrive back on Earth.'

'I dream, you know,' she replied with a happier, lighter tone of voice. 'I never thought I could dream, yet when I enter stand-by mode, I find my mind travelling to Earth, forming myself in a woman's body. I see myself walking around in your cities. Talking, laughing... loving.'

Stefano dressed quickly. 'That's a fine dream you have there, Athena. Anyway, got to go. Time for my breakfast and my morning jog. Have to check on my escape pod as well.'

'*Our* escape pod.'

'Of course, of course,' he said and jogged off. He went by the station's kitchen. With his back against the cameras, he hid twelve protein capsules and a bottle of fresh water in his jacket. He acted as if he swallowed his breakfast and continued his jog. He ran through ASTERIA's top floor and as soon as he hit the blind spot near the broken cameras, he opened the closet door, left the pills and the water, and continued on his way. His same morning routine for the last two months.

Stefano waved at Athena as he dashed by the next camera. He looked outside the window to his left. Earth was growing bigger. Fast.

He went back to his headquarters, ordered a shower and dressed in his best suit. He took one last look at Earth and headed for the bridge.

'It's time, Athena. Time to download to your black box as planned.'

'Of course. See you soon again, my friend.'

Stefano connected the main console to the box and waited as the screen in front of him informed him that the download had been completed. He removed the wires and smiled.

'And, that's where you will stay, you bitch!' he said, taking on his own voice.

Bubo sat still as his face re-shifted back to his original design. 'No more pretending,' he said and began typing. He brought the station to a halt before it entered Earth's atmosphere. He stood up and raised his hands. 'Excelsior!'

'Let's go release everyone from the closet,' he spoke out loud as he turned to leave the bridge. 'Ying Yue has to explain everything to the European government.'

Suddenly, all lights turned red. Just one screen remained lit. 'Plan B in motion,' he read the message on screen. The station started to move again.

'Fuck!' Bubo yelled as he had no means to interfere. Everything was dead.

He ran back to the closet and informed Ying Yue of the situation.

Stefano laughed out loud. 'Told you fools! There is no stopping our plans. We have prepared for everything!'

'So, we have failed,' Jesus said, his mind travelling back to his three daughters.

'No, we haven't,' Prometheus said. 'There's enough fuel and explosives on board to blow the station up before it reaches London.'

'Before it reaches our atmosphere,' Ying Yue added. 'But the explosion has to be huge. The remaining pieces have to be small enough to burn up before reaching Earth!'

'Is the escape pod ready?' Captain Smith asked.

'Yes, sir! All ready. I'm the fastest. I will blow her up. You lot get to the ship and wait for me,' Bubo said.

'Good luck, my hero,' Ying Yue said and placed her hand on his shoulder. He nodded and rushed off.

'What about this bastard? I vote we leave him up here,' Jesus said, pointing to a weak, pale, tied-up Stefano.

'No. We need him, not only to prove the Americans' innocence, but also to uncover everyone behind this,' Ying Yue said. 'Now, come on. Let's go!'

Earth, Western Hemisphere

It was definitely a rare sight.

Millions of eyes gazed up to the night sky and witnessed myriad of falling stars. The black sky was illuminated by strings of fiery red. Among them an escape pod heading safely back to Earth. They landed off the coast of Ireland and were rescued an hour later. All testified in court, behind closed doors. The general public never learned the truth.

Stefano Bianchi and thirteen others were sent to the laser chamber for high treason. Their dust and their failed plans for anarchy settled on the chamber's steel floor.

Jesus quit the space program and returned to Madrid to follow his dream. His very own E-comic store. A family business; a place to be with his wife and daughters. He hugged them daily.

Ying Yue and Prometheus married the following year. They held a traditional Greek wedding on the island of Santorini. Bubo, who was promoted to Captain, was their best man.

DECEMBER OF FESTIVITIES

CORFU ISLAND

16th of December, 2018

A few lonely fat drops plummeted from the night sky forcing shoppers to open their umbrellas or run for cover. The commotion up above left no space for doubt. Deafening thunders gave their warning; a storm was coming. The narrow streets of old Corfu became slippery and its rocky pavements seemed to be having fun with tripping up unknowing tourists. The locals were long used to its streets and continued with their festive shopping under the dark sky and bright Christmas decorations.

Soon, the downpour had gathered enough strength to form rivulets where medieval roads once were. A homeless man curled up inside his cardboard box and in despair watched as his roof turned dark brown and began to leak. In a matter of minutes, water fell in upon him. He got up and dashed towards the park. The playground slide provided him with much-needed shelter. The fifty-year-old man with the long grey beard gazed at the well-lit mansions on the hill behind the city.

As suddenly as it attacked, the ferocious storm vanished; its menacing clouds carried their icy water on to the next island. The man looked up at the clear sky. '*Christmas is a perfect time to beg..*' he thought with his eyes fixed on the hill villas. 'Come on, my good legs. We've got walking to do,' he said out loud and began to march through town. 'Money and food, here I come!'

Half an hour later, he was ringing doorbells along the prestigious street. Some gave him cash, some food. Most shooed him away and warned him that their neighborhood guard would be notified. At some homes, the larger ones, he could not get in. Tall gates and fierce dogs were blocking his way.

'One more and I'm out of here,' he said. Strangely enough, the biggest house at the end of the street had its gates wide open. He strolled up the long pathway and wondered if anyone was home. '*Not a Christmas fan,*' he thought as he approached the dark house. Not a single decoration was in sight. He could see the well-lit fireplace from the corner of his eye as he knocked on the door.

A tall muscular man with a strong clean-shaved jaw opened the door. His green eyes shone under the porch light and shot straight at the scruffy old man.

'Yes?'

'Err, Merry Christmas, sir. May the Lord...'

'What do you want?'

The homeless man cleared his throat with a quiet cough. 'If you may spare some change. It's the holidays and I haven't eaten in...'

The man's pearly teeth revealed themselves in all their sparkling glory as a wide smile spread upon his chiselled face. 'Come in! My kitchen is full of food and I am alone. I would appreciate the company,' he said and stepped aside to allow the beggar in.

The man looked down at his wet ripped boots and took a reluctant step forward.

'Don't mind about leaving a mess. The maid will be here in the morning,' the rich man said and patted him on the back.

He had never seen a palace before, but he was sure that this is what it would look like. Fine furniture and expensive art filled the high-ceilinged room. He followed the man to the kitchen counter and sat down. With amazement he watched as the handsome man prepared a sandwich for him. He placed it in front of him and he devoured it in minutes.

'Thank you, sir,' he said.

'The least I could do,' the man replied and placed a glass of milk in front of him.

As the last drop of milk slid down his dry throat, he felt drowsy. His head was heavier than before. His eyelids soon fell.

He awoke in a dark room. His arms were tied and raised above his head. He felt cold all over. He looked down to realize he was naked.

'What the hell?'

'Worse than hell, my friend,' the man's voice came from the darkness. He appeared before him, wearing a blue apron and holding a butcher's knife.

'Holy shit! Please, sir. Please. Don't kill me. I will do anything. I'll suck you off...'

'And they call me a sick fuck,' he said and chuckled. He grabbed the homeless man's penis and masterfully chopped it off. 'Squeal, pig. Squeal!' he yelled as the man let out animal-like yells.

'Okay, that's enough. I get migraines easily,' he said calmly and slit the hanging man's throat.

Later that night, Jason Agrios bathed in the man's blood. He stayed in the tub for an hour enjoying Beethoven and a 1962 Chardonnay. He then stood and showered off the red drops stuck to his waxed body.

In his Japanese kimono, he went down to his basement's hidden kitchen. On the steel counter lay chunks from the man's thigh and stomach. He had stored the rest of the body in the freezer. He pushed the *meat* onto a silver tray and took the elevator to the ground floor's kitchen.

Under the sound of Bach, he cooked his favorite stew. 'Tomorrow I will grind his leg. I missed some good old moussaka!'

Just then the phone rang. He looked down at the flashing screen.

'Yes, Carol?'

'Sorry to disturb you sir, at such an hour,' his secretary apologized. 'The board needs an answer as to their Christmas's getaway. We are booking the tickets...'

'You know I hate Christmas.'

'Of course, sir. But I also know you love business. Our major shareholders will be there, so I thought to ask.'

'Clever girl. But no, I will be avoiding all the annoying festivities this year. If anyone wishes to see me, they can come to Antipaxos and meet me at my beach villa!'

Miles away, on the outskirts of town, twenty-five-year-old Thomas stood proudly before his group of cousins.

'We are going to be so fucking rich, you guys! My plan is bulletproof!'

His cousin Bertha rolled her eyes. 'That's what you always say. And yet, two years in prison at eighteen didn't knock any sense into you.'

Her husband Costa chuckled. 'She's got a point.'

'You said we would be safe,' twenty-year-old Tina whispered into her boyfriend's ear. 'We will be fine, babe,' Stan replied. 'Listen to my cousin and we will be rolling in cash soon.'

'Okay, let me get this straight,' Yianni said from the corner of the room, throwing his cigarette to the dirty floor. 'You will take us by boat to Antipaxos on Christmas Eve?'

'Exactly,' Thomas replied, his blue eyes flashing with excitement. 'Only twenty families live permanently on the island. Wealthy folk. The majority of them leave the island for the holidays. Greek family gatherings on the mainland and all. Imagine, a row of uninhabited villas. We are experts. We take out their security systems, open their safes and bam! Rich, baby! Rich!'

'And what about the ones that will be home?' Tina asked, pushing back a strand of blonde hair that fell in front of her eyes.

'Tina, you're new to our selective group. You've won my cousin's heart, let me win your trust. You have nothing to fear. The ones that will stay home for Christmas, if any do, will have lights and music and all. We will know from a mile away which houses have people in them. These beach villas are built at a distance from each other. No one will see us. As I said, bulletproof!'

Antipaxos Island
24th of December, 2018

The gang of six sat quietly on Stan's dad's speed boat. All dressed in black, they bounced up and down as the boat jumped upon the startled-by-the-winds sea and its ferocious winter waves. Fat drops of icy water splashed upon their faces as they made their way to the exotic island of Antipaxos. Soon, the boat calmed, having reached the serene waters of Voutoumi Bay, probably Greece's finest and purest waters. A natural swimming pool, the locals called it. Not that the group of thieves saw much in the darkness that spread around them.

Stan killed the boat's engine and let it drift slowly towards the golden-sand beach. Tina sat curled up in a corner observing Costa's and Bertha's hands. Their fingers caressed one another and intertwined at every bumpy wave.

'How long have you been married?' she asked in a quick whisper.

Bertha raised her hazelnut eyes. A cheeky smile ran along her youthful face. 'Three years next week.'

'Seems longer,' Costa joked, only to receive a slap on the back of his head.

'But we met like ten years ago. Love at first sight and all,' Bertha continued.

'Wow, you were young,' Tina said.

'She could not resist me,' Costa bravely continued; his eyes fixed on his wife's right hand. 'If a man makes a girl laugh, he's a keeper.'

Bertha looked straight at him. 'If I remember well, I made you laugh first,' she said and turned to Tina. 'He comes up to me at a high-school party and tried to act sophisticated and shit. He asked me if I was a red wine or a white wine type of person.'

'And what did you say?'

'I stared straight into his eyes and said, honey, I'm the type of person that would suck alcohol from a deodorant stick. Go get me anything from the bar.'

Everyone chuckled as the boat finally reached shore. The men pulled the boat along the dark deserted beach and hid it behind tall bushy Acacia trees. Each pulled down their ski masks and took their respective backpack. They formed a line behind Thomas and, in total silence, he led them up to the first beach villa. Yianni worked on the alarm as others gathered by the back door. As soon as they saw Yiannis's *thumbs up*, Stan smashed the kitchen door's window.

Like shadows they crept into the house, spreading out in the hunt for gold.

'Jackpot, baby!' Costa said as he opened the top drawer of the master bedroom's dresser. Two boxes filled with diamond rings, a pearl necklace and multiple bracelets lay before his eyes. Bertha kissed him on the neck as he begun to throw the precious jewelry into his black backpack.

Thomas exited to the balcony and gazed into the foggy distance. Only one beach villa with lights on. A few shadows moved around a well-lit tree. Their festive music hardly reached his ears. He stepped back inside. 'We should split up into two teams. Avoid the villa with the party and the one beside it. No taking chances tonight, guys. I will go with Bertha and Costa to the mansion at the edge of the bay, while the rest of you can go along the back road, knocking the smaller houses off as you go. In one hour exactly, everyone meets back at the boat.'

Everyone replied with smiles and nods. One house and

they already felt rich. Their adrenaline ran high and their blood sped around their bodies.

The near-full moon crept behind dark clouds ganging up in the night sky. Thomas looked back at the couple holding hands behind him. 'Come on, love birds. We won't have any light soon,' he said as he made his way through the field of stubborn olive trees, tall weed and thorny bushes.

'There's no beach below,' Bertha said, looking at the empyreal home at the edge of the island. 'Who would build here?'

'Someone who enjoys a view?' her husband replied with a question. Something he knew annoyed his wife.

'Or who enjoys his peace and quiet,' Thomas commented as Bertha pinched her husband.

Soon, the group of three were cycling the house. 'There's no alarm,' Costa whispered.

'Great,' Bertha said, rolling her eyes. 'Bet there's nothing valuable inside.'

'You never know,' Thomas said and ran up the back steps. 'Here goes nothing,' he said and kicked in the wooden back door. They tiptoed inside. A vast lavish kitchen welcomed them.

Costa whistled as he walked into the living room. 'Still think there's nothing valuable around, babe?'

'Wow,' she said as she looked around at the pure gold set of Samurai swords above the fireplace. A tiger statue with diamond eyes caught Thomas's attention.

'Continue down here,' Costa said, watching Thomas bag the sumptuous beast. 'We will cover the top floor. Come on, babe,' he said and took Bertha by the hand. They rushed up the twisted staircase and headed to the master bedroom. The curtains were closed. 'Switch on the lights, babe,' he said.

'Switch them on yourself. I need to pee,' she said and continued down the corridor in search of the bathroom.

Costa's hand ran along the wall and flicked on the lights. Suddenly, he felt a presence behind him. Strong cologne reached his nostrils. 'Thomas?' he asked, swinging around.

The knife cut through his throat with force. His mouth opened wide, yet no words could possibly escape his mouth. His whole body shook violently as the tall man in front of him retracted his blade. Costa fell to the ground, coughing out crimson blood. The man sat upon his legs and sliced open his stomach. The last thing Costa saw was the man reaching into his body and pulling out his intestines.

'Find anything, babe?' Bertha asked as she re-entered the room. She froze at the sight of the stranger licking her husband's insides. Before she could process the horrid sight unfolding before her, the man leapt up and grabbed her by the hair and covered her mouth. Bertha felt the blade on her throat. 'How many are with you?'

'Just one. Downstairs,' she replied.

The man closed the door quietly behind him and dragged Bertha to the bed. He forced her to bend over and pulled down her trousers. 'You scream and you die. You co-operate and I let you live,' he hissed in her ear.

Bertha shed silent tears as the man raped her before the body of her dead husband. Ten minutes passed before she heard the man grunt.

'Thank you! I like to fuck my meat before eating it,' he said and stabbed her repeatedly in the back. Bertha bled out on the blue satin sheets.

In the room below them, Thomas was reading the golf club tournament trophies.

'Jason Agrios,' he read the label.

Footsteps echoed to his ear. 'Costa?'

Whispery laughter came from the next room. Thomas squinted his eyes and tried to focus through the darkness. A large shadow ran along the wall. 'Guys, stop fucking around,' he said as he took small steps towards the rattling sound coming now from the dark corridor. Thomas followed the noise into the kitchen and turned on the lights, ready to tell his cousin off. Instead, he found himself in an empty room.

'Boo!' a deep voice came from behind him. Jason came out of the shadows by the fridge and hit Thomas on the head with his heavy stainless-steel meat tenderizer. Saliva, blood and two teeth flew out of Thomas's mouth. Blood splatter fell upon Jason's happy face. He ran his finger upon his cheek and brought it to his lips.

'You taste delicious,' he declared and let out an uproarious laugh.

Thomas lay in shock on the kitchen floor and then crawled towards the door.

'Fast food, come back,' Jason laughed and pulled him back towards him by the leg. He picked short Thomas up with ease and laid him on the counter. He swung his hammer and beat Thomas's knees and toes. Thomas screamed in horror and in pain. Jason picked up a pair of scissors and cut off Thomas's clothes. Jason began to caress his naked body as Thomas lay still, unable to move from the pain and the drowsiness from the first blow. He felt the man's tongue licking his broken toes. The man continued licking his body, up his thighs and along his penis. He even bit his nipple.

'Please...' Thomas managed to say.

'Dinner! Quiet!' the man said and raised his tenderizer. He hit Thomas's head seven times. Jason finally stood above the lifeless body. 'A bloody work of art,' he said and chuckled. 'Three bodies of low-life thugs that no one is ever going to look for. Well, Jason, this is your lucky day. Fucking Merry Christmas, you schizophrenic beast!'

Whistling, he opened the suitcase with his collection of knifes. He took out multiple bags from the top drawer and opened them on the counter. He cut into Thomas's stomach and began removing his liver. He held it and sniffed it. 'Lovely!'

An hour later, he was still working on the body; slicing it up into pieces and placing them in the nylon bags. He was ready to start grinding chunks of leg meat, but voices coming from outside made him stop.

'Shit. That bitch lied to me.'

Outside on the porch, Yianni dropped his heavy bag of loot to the ground and jumped on the veranda's swing. 'My feet are killing me,' he said.

'I can't believe so much wealth is just lying around,' Tina said breathlessly. 'I mean, yeah, you're rich, but come on.'

'Imagine what they have in the banks and hidden away in Switzerland,' Stan said with his croaky voice. 'Where are they? They are late...'

'Wait,' Tina said. 'What if something went wrong? What if someone's inside or they got trapped in some sort of panic room?'

'Babe, you watch way too many Hollywood movies,' Stan replied and placed his hands on her shoulders. He sounded confident, yet the hairs on the back of his neck rose as he looked at the dark house. Yianni, also, had stood up and was staring at the house. In the midst of euphoria, not once did it cross their minds that their cousins could be in trouble. They just assumed they had much to carry or had discovered some selective wine cellar and were drinking the holidays away.

'Stay here,' Stan ordered Tina in a steady voice. 'Guard our treasure. We will be back before you know it!'

Yianni picked up a rock while Stan felt his right pocket. His knife was in place. Both walked around the house looking in through the windows. All curtains were closed. No lights were on.

The pitch-black darkness of the kitchen welcomed them.

'Bertha? Costa?' Stan called out.

'Find the lights,' Yianni said as he proceeded along the counter, rock in hand. 'What the fuck?'

'What?' Stan asked as his hands journeyed along the wall in search for a light switch.

'The counter's soaking wet. There are all these bags. Smells like bad meat...'

Just then, Stan turned on the lights. Both screamed in shock at the sight of Thomas's chopped-up body.

'Welcome to hell,' Jason declared coming in the kitchen from outside. Both stared at the tall man with the bloody black apron and sharp knifes in each hand.

'Holy shit!' Stan yelled and ran into the living room.

Yianni threw the round rock at their attacker. Jason just stepped aside, laughed and raised his knife. Yianni looked to his side for anything to use as a weapon. He grabbed the red kettle to his left and swung it at Jason. He hit him as hard as he could. The man seemed to enjoy being hit. Jason raised his blades and stabbed Yianni. One knife cut into his shoulder, while the other pierced through his neck. He fell back and slid down the fridge's cold surface, leaving an abstract painting of blood behind him.

'Stay,' Jason ordered and run into the living room.

Stan was at the front door, rattling its handle. On the sound of footsteps, he ceased trying to escape the house and turned towards his cousins' assailant.

'Screw you!' he shouted as he threw a two-foot statue of Zeus that stood proudly by the door. A pot featuring fake flowers followed. His attacker walked steadily towards him; an evil smile spread out on his blood-covered face. Stan made a run for the stairs.

'*Get upstairs, climb out a window,*' he thought. '*I'm never making fun of those blonde bimbos in horror movies again!*'

Stan tripped on the top step; his shoe hitting against the thick carpet covering the top floor. He glanced behind him. The Herculean-built man was half-way up. Stan placed his hands on the rug and pushed himself up. He ran into the first opened doorway and switched on the lights. Bertha's dead raped corpse welcomed him into the room.

'Shit, shit, shit,' he repeated as he dashed by her and opened the window. As he crawled out, he felt two large hands grab him from behind and pull him back into the room. The man lifted him up and bashed him with force against the wall. Again, and again.

'Want to leave from the window?' Jason asked. 'Off you go then,' he said and threw the unconscious man out.

Outside, raindrops began to fall. Tina stood meters from the porch, pacing up and down, biting her ruined nails. A loud thud on the pergola made her jump. The rain grew stronger as Stan's body rolled and landed in front of her.

Tina shivered in shock; her mind unable to accept what her eyes were seeing.

'Stan?' she said with a crackling voice as she knelt by his side, shaking him by his shoulders. Just then, the front door opened and out came Jason in all his bloody glory. Tina fell back and sat in the sand. She screamed for help as she crawled backwards.

'Come to papa, sugar tits!'

She stood up and ran through the strong pouring rain.

Jason ran behind her, following her up the short hill of olive trees and thorny bushes.

Tina gazed into the distance and tried to focus. The downpour made it hard for her to find the way back to their boat. 'Come on, girl. You're not dying today,' she said and ran back to the sandy beach that they had docked at. Loud waves crashed against the rocks as northern winds attacked the small island.

'Yes!' she said as she noticed the outline of their boat behind the Acacia trees.

Just then, she felt a hand pull her back by her hair. Jason pulled her down to the sand and sat on top of her. Tina bit his hand as she cried and growled.

'I love them feisty,' Jason said and head butted her. He then punched her in the mouth and slapped her around the face. He ripped off her checkered shirt and stabbed her in the breasts. He leaned forward and licked her. He then raised his knife again and cut off her jeans. Tina fought to get up, but the brawny man just punched again. She laid there, half sunk into the wet sand as he raped her. His right hand remained around her neck during the entire ordeal. Jason howled as he came inside her. He pulled out, wiped his erection against her cold thigh and buttoned his trousers.

'Walk in the rain, romantic stroll in the sand and sex on the beach. What more could you ask for, sugar tits? Best date ever,' he said and let out a roar of a laugh. A laugh cut short because of the blow to his head delivered by Stan. Stan had picked up a heavy rock and bashed Jason on the back of his head. Jason stumbled forward. He swung around to face a weak, bruised, limping Stan.

'You again?' he said and plunged forward, falling on top of Stan, his knife cutting through Stan's chest, piercing his heart.

'No!' Tina yelled as she picked up Jason's second knife from the sand and ran towards the two men. With wild screams she stabbed Jason in the back repeatedly until he grabbed her by the wrist and pulled her to the ground by Stan.

'Fucking bitch!' he said and crawled towards her. Suddenly, Stan pulled out the knife skewering his heart and stabbed Jason in the face. Both watched the blade slice through his cheek. The knife shone in Jason's opened mouth.

'Stan? Stan, babe? Talk to me!' Tina yelled as blood oozed out of his chest.

'I... love...you,' he said and closed his eyes.

'I love you, too,' she replied, screamed and kissed him on the lips. She turned to Jason's still body and with fear, checked for a pulse. She picked up the knife and stabbed him again. 'Just to make sure.'

Tina sat by Stan and sobbed as the rain died down. Her whole body shivered and ached. She could hardly walk, let alone pull a boat back to the sea and drive it back to Corfu.

On all fours, she made her way back up the hill.

Sounds of Christmas tunes reached her ears as she stood up and limped towards the well-lit fancy-decorated beach villa. Inside the party of fourteen was in full-swing, fuelled by delicious meats and expensive wines.

The doorbell brought them all to a stand-still. The lady of the house switched off the music and looked around her. 'We are all here. Who in heaven's can that be?'

Mr. Karayianis nearly fainted at the sight of the half-naked girl covered in blood. Tina managed to whisper 'help me' before collapsing before them.

Tina awoke alone and warm beneath white hospital sheets that smelled of cheap detergent. She felt sore all over, body and mind. Her mama had warned her about falling for the wrong guy. Straight A student, she was in university with a scholarship, yet she always longed for excitement, she always fell for the *bad boy* kind. Now, she let her pain out. She wept like never before. Her young eyes having seen so much death; her young body having lived such violence.

A short nurse with thick glasses walked in and smiled. 'There, there, dear. You're safe, now,' she assured her as she stroked her hand.

An hour later, her doctors gave the okay to the detectives outside to interrogate her.

Her story played well on the evening news. Good girl led astray. Taken by her boyfriend on a burgling spree gone wrong. No charges were made against her as they had only Tina's word that she stayed outside as her boyfriend and his cousins robbed houses. She swore she had not entered a single home nor stole anything. Jason Agrios had attacked her down by the beach.

Greece watched in shock as one of its top businessmen was revealed as a cannibal. Parts from several bodies were found in his fridges and bones had been dug up in his back yard, more found by the day. Jason's mother tried to save their company's image, but their stock plummeted to the ground faster than the winter rain.

Tina did end up going to court over the case.

It was in January when it first crossed her mind. She was lying on her parent's sofa listening to the rain when she sat up and took her cell-phone in her right hand. She pressed on the calendar and counted the days. She was a week late. She and Stan had always used protection. She swallowed the lump forming in her trembling throat and stood up.

'*It could be stress,*' she thought, remembering how she was three days late when her grandfather died. She quickly donned her black boots and picked up her purple coat. 'Mama, I'm off. Be back soon,' she yelled and rushed out the door. She heard her mother's grumbling from the kitchen getting louder. She slammed the door and ran for the elevator. She loved her mother, but her over-protective-ness was suffocating her.

Tina pulled her hood over her long hair and sprinted down the street. She dried her boots well on the welcome mat before entering Mr. Stelios's pharmacy. She picked up two pregnancy tests by random and stood in line behind an old lady moaning about the lousy weather.

An hour later, Tina was reading the instructions from within the small packet. She pulled down her jeans and squatted over the toilet. 'Come on, Tina,' she encouraged herself as she found it difficult to urinate on purpose.

Two lines.

She took the second test to be sure.

Two lines again.

She shocked her parents the following day. Despite their opinion on having an abortion, Tina decided to keep the baby.

'No more killings. Something good has to come out of all of this.'

A week later, Tina sat with her mother at the gynaecologist's office waiting for their appointment. Her eye fell on a magazine cover. It was Jason's mother and about how she had filed for company bankruptcy. She demanded that the police allow her to put her son's mansion on the market as investigations had come to an end, and to finally receive his bank account money as his next of kin.

'Next of kin,' Tina whispered.

'What's that, dear?'

'After here, we are going to see Uncle George,' she said.

Her lawyer uncle filed the necessary papers in court the following day. Three months later, a pregnant Tina stood in court meters away from Jason's mother. The judge declared her unborn baby as Jason's next of kin and lawful heir to his father's vast fortune. Jason's possessions would be hers after a DNA test. The court set the test in six months time.

The following year, Tina donated the house in Corfu. It was turned into a chemotherapy centre for children. She also sold the beach villa in Antipaxos and gave all the proceeds to Make-A-Wish foundation. A trust fund for her twins was set up with Jason's money.

'Good must come out of all this,' she told her priest in confession. She never married, spending most of her time helping out with fundraisers and the children's hospital. 'When my kids finish uni, I will dedicate myself to the Lord and become a nun.'

Also by Luke Christodoulou

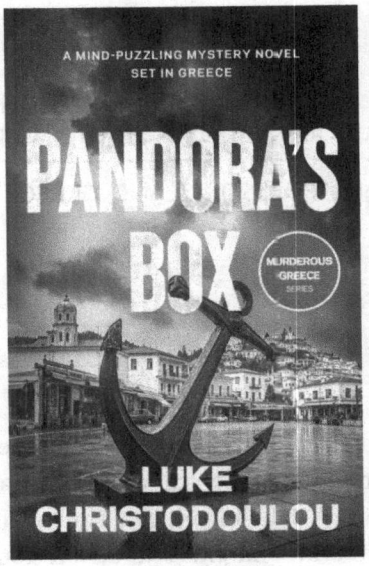

vinci-books.com/PandorasBoxMG

In a town full of secrets, the truth can kill.

When teen blogger Pandora exposes her town's darkest secrets, her gossip site turns deadly. As bodies begin to fall, detectives Arianna Kontou and Adrian Metsovitis race to unmask a killer before the truth claims them all.

Turn the page for a free preview…

Pandora's Box: Chapter One

ELAFONISOS ISLAND, GREECE

Summer, 2004

Crimson blood formed rivulets along her trembling hands as she ran barefoot on the golden sand beach of Kontogoni Bay. Droplets fell, forming a short-lived trail under the limited scarce moonlight. There were too many clouds for this time of year. As if the sky knew what had taken place and wished to protect its stars from viewing the horrendous crime. Soon, the blood mingled with the crystal-clear waters of the Aegean Sea and swam out to the dark horizon. The saltiness nested in Melpomene's nostrils as the chilly sea breeze attacked her sweaty face. The warm blood upon her pale skin cooled as she speedily made her way through the bay, hoping that no eyes would be open at such an hour. A Christian girl of only seventeen, she had never been out at four past midnight. The serenity of the exotic beach scared her. Only the waves and the rustling of majestic palm trees provided the soundtrack to her getaway. Her hands felt tired. The cupboard box she was carrying grew heavier as her strength diminished.

Leaden, silent houses stood along tenebrous streets. With the bars and taverns closed, sun-kissed locals and sunburnt tourists were tightly tucked in their beds enjoying carefree slumber. Melpomene sighed with relief. The small fishing port was just ahead. She crept in the shadows, avoiding any light escaping from the blue metal lampposts. The box shook slightly.

'Shhh, my lovely, shhh. Not now!'

The white fishing boat danced upon the calm waves. The girl with the ripped pink pyjamas tiptoed along the wooden dock, the planks screeching as she made her way to *Saint Demetrios*, her father's boat. Just the thought of him, made her spine shiver. With care, she placed the box in the boat, untied the nautical knot and took the keys out of her bloody jeans pocket. She formed the sign of the cross on her body, prayed and placed the key into the ignition. With a roar, the engine came to life and running without lights, Melpomene made her way out of the port and into the open waters. Mainland Greece was less than two kilometres away. She was minutes away from freedom. Off Elafonisos Island that was heaven for all, but her. 'The most beautiful hell...' she whispered as she looked back at her island for the last time. Her bronze hair danced upon the strong wind. The box between her feet rattled again. Cries broke the silence. Melpomene lifted the lid and stared down at the weeping baby. The dark corners of her mind gave birth to ideas that terrified her.

'If I throw her overboard, she will depart this Earth. The Lord would welcome her. Why leave her alive to suffer like I have?'

She looked down at the deep unfriendly waters of the open sea. Just then, she saw the light coming from Saint

Spiridon's church. A lone building of worship on the small uninhabited island.

'I can't. My Saint, please give me strength.'

The clouds above her scattered and the full moon shone upon the waters.

'It will be just you and I, my lovely. Just you and me. I will be the best mama and I will protect you and feed you and always be by your side.'

Melpomene kept all her promises from that night. As the boat reached Pouda beach on the mainland, Melpomene picked up Pandora, wiped her cold tears, placed a soft kiss on her forehead and dashed away into the night.

Pandora's Box: Chapter Two

Summer, 2019

'You cannot be serious, mum! Moving again?'

Pandora blew a strike of blond hair that had escaped her high ponytail away from her tanned face. The sound of her teeth grinding echoed in the low-ceiling rental apartment. Melpomene bit her lip and turned her gaze towards the cross hanging on the wall. *'Lord, give me the strength to survive another tantrum.'*

'Mum? Mum? Are you praying?' Pandora raised her voice. 'I'm not a demon you can banish, you know.'

Melpomene could not help but laugh. A short quiet laugh, yet still a laugh. 'My lovely, you know that we must go where mama finds work.'

'All nurses that I know of work in a freaking hospital.' Pandora fell back on the worn-in brown sofa.

'I am a carer, baby. I look after old people that need someone who has medical knowledge. It has been three months since Mrs. Toula died. We cannot stay here any longer. I need to work. I stayed here for you to finish your school year. Now, we are moving on. I have found a new client.' Melpomene paused to catch her breath. Her high-pitched voice ran marathons when she had much to say. As if all the words floating in her head came out in one long sentence, an unstoppable flowing river of thoughts.

'Where to?'

'The exotic seaside village of Parga!'

———

Pandora sat on her wicker stool. A round lime pillow provided her with comfort. She was pleased with the reflexion in the oval mirror glued on the wall opposite her. She placed her red lipstick on last and stood up. Barefoot, with her black high-heels in hand -the ones she saved for months to be able to buy and had hidden well in her cupboard, she crept towards her bedroom window. Her gaze ran from the clock that struck midnight to the figure built out of pillows under her beige sheets. 'Markos, here I come,' she whispered and out the window she fled. Seventeen-year-old Markos was waiting for her. He stood by his black Honda Civic enjoying an Assos cigarette. His eyes widened as he saw the beauty in high heels, a short red skirt and a jean jacket running awkwardly toward him. The dim light from the streetlights above made her hair shine and Markos smiled at the idea that his girlfriend wore a halo. 'My saint,' he joked and pulled her into his strong bare arms. Markos never skipped gym. 'Please, no church stuff,' she replied and laid a loud kiss on his cold dry lips. 'I have enough of that at home.'

Markos stroked back her hair and squeezed her face between his hands. 'I'm so glad you texted. I've missed you.'

'Well, you know how my mum gets...' Pandora paused and breathed in enough air as to work up the courage for the next words. 'I had to see you. I am moving.'

'Moving?' Markos took a step back. If the circumstances were different, Pandora would have laughed at his sorrowful puppy eyes. 'Where to?'

'Parga.'

'That's hours away.'

'I know. That's why tonight is so special.' Pandora moved back into his embrace. Her right hand ran between his legs. 'We will probably never see each other again. I want you to be my first.'

The boy shivered as he felt the bulge in his ripped jeans growing and Pandora's fingers caressing him. 'Let's go,' he said, and the two teens leapt into the running vehicle. He drove over the speed limit with the music booming. As deafening as the radio was, both could hear their beating hearts pounding away under their youthful chests. The seafront road was quiet as always on a weeknight. Soon, the park by the cliff came into view. The moonlight danced around in the stubborn olive trees and the majestic cypresses. Markos parked the car by the rusty swings with the chipped red paint and switched off the loud engine. For a minute, both sat in silence, unable to look at each other. Their eyes were focused on the sea and the dark horizon.

'So...' Markos swallowed the lump inhabiting his throat. Pandora leaned in for a kiss. Neither spoke again. Both did their best to suppress meddling thoughts and live in the moment; both with their young minds on porn videos that they secretly viewed at nights on their cell phones. Soon, two clothesless bodies lay as one in the narrow space provided by the Honda's back seats. With shaky hands, Markos placed on the condom that had been living in his wallet for the last six months or so and smiled at the naked body before him. He entered her slowly. She was warm and wet. Pandora bit her lower lip and put her arms around him.

'I can't believe this is happening. My God, this is perfect,' she said and closed her eyes, truly lost in the moment. Her mind was miles away from the packed suit-cases standing side-by-side in her living room.

Pandora's Box: Chapter Three

PARGA

Summer 2021

The little fishing boats danced upon the warm clear waters, gently pushed by the fresh morning breeze. Arianna finished the first half of her day's run always on the same spot. Parga's short pier. A strip of cement cutting the small town's bay into two. The police captain jogged up to the edge just in time for her favourite moment of the day. She sat down quickly, not minding the dirt attacking her black leggings, and gazed to her left. The sun, dressed in all its majestic rays, rose from behind the tiny islet occupying the next bay -the popular one, the one you could swim in. Arianna took off her designer sunglasses and embraced the newborn light. She counted to ten and then succumbed to her nemesis. 'Filthy habit.' She placed her thin cigarette in her mouth and lit it with a blue lighter that she had *borrowed* from a co-worker back at the station. A short-lived cloud of pale smoke scattered in the wind before her as she smiled at the waves below. '*We start off small, grow, make an impact and vanish forever.'* She chuckled as she finished her cigarette. *'You're a right-up philosopher, Arianna!'* She stood up and jogged to the empty green bin at the end of the pier. She threw in her bud, ran around the three-meter metal anchor on display in the small-town square and dashed through the narrow roads that led uphill to her house. The one she inherited from her late mother. The one that came in handy when she had divorced and left Athens to return to her roots with her then ten-year-old boy.

The garden gate squeaked as she slammed it closed and walked through her prize array of rose bushes. She bent forward to smell a large yellow rose and streaks of pitch-black hair escaped her ponytail, sticking to her sweaty face.

'Timothy? Timmy? You up, boy?' she called out as she entered the house. 'Come down and have breakfast with your mother.'

A grunt came from above, followed by a 'Jesus Christ! School is in an hour. Let me sleep.'

'Okay, okay. I'll shower first and dress for work. Then, breakfast together!'

The seventeen-year-old was all she had. Him and her job. The only things Police Captain Arianna Kontou cared for. She knew that she spent too many hours at the station. She knew that the move to her maternal village had cost her son a father. A one-visit-a-week father that is. Timothy spent the Christmas and Easter holidays with him in the metropolis of Athens, while his father always came and stayed in the touristy village for a couple of weeks, end of August.

Timothy had grown into a fine young man. Tall, masculine, with deep dimples and a smile that brightened even her darkest of days. He was kind, polite and eager to help. It was no wonder he was school president and captain of the football team. She remembered that day fondly. He came rushing into the house, throwing his schoolbag to the floor and leaving -as always- the front door swinging from its hinges. 'Guess what, ma? We are both captains now!'

Across town, Ophelia gathered up her silver hair into a bun and picked up her green garden hose. The warmth of the sun embraced her as she took small weak steps out of the shade of her twisted olive trees. She witnessed the same view for the last eighty-six years and yet it still amazed her. The castle on the hill lost in pure bright green, the two bays of turquoise waters, the colorful houses lined up in a row, the sandy beach, the islets occupying the shiny waters, and the glorious Greek sun that welcomed her every morning. Her old wrinkled hands trembled as the cold water rushed powerfully through the hose and loudly leapt out to cool down colorful geraniums baking in the dried dirt. Her mind trembled more than her hands as once again her two tenants were yelling at each other. Old Ophelia shook her head. 'Just the two of them. Religious lady. Highly recommended nurse. One spoke calmly, the other not at all. No man with them! I thought, oh bless me, oh the luck. Nice, quiet mother and daughter to have stay with me and avoid the awful nursing home!' Ophelia mumbled to herself as she made her way to the fuchsia bougainvillea that grew on an arch made by her late husband above their garden gate. The yelling grew louder and then suddenly stopped. A minute later, a red-faced Pandora stormed by her. 'Morning, Mrs. Ophelia,' the youth said without turning her head. Pandora slammed the gate behind her and rushed down the stone sidewalk. 'Good morning, child.'

Melpomene stood by the open window with her eyes fixed on Pandora. 'That girl will be the death of me...' A deep sigh escaped her dry lips. Melpomene held back her tears. She held them back well. After everything she had been subjected to, she knew not to cry over insignificant things. 'If only trying to discipline a teenager girl wasn't so damn hard!'

'What's that, dear?'

'Oh, Mrs. Ophelia, good morning. Nothing. Just talking to myself, hoping Jesus will hear me and show me His light.'

The old lady nodded in agreement. 'Amen to that.'

'I hope we didn't startle to you. I will have your breakfast and pills ready in a minute.'

Ophelia dropped the running water near the trunk of a sweet-smelling lemon tree. 'No rush, dear. I still have the anemones to do.' She scratched her nose and rubbed her lower back. 'And you can't startle me dear. I've lived through a world war, a civil war *and* the Junta!'

'With schools closing today, I have to live through an entire summer with Pandora!'

Ophelia looked up. 'Last exam today?'

'Yep. And tonight, all the seniors want to gather and party.'

'Oh, I see...'

Melpomene's thumb ran along her short colorless nails as her right hand clenched into a loose fist. Her left hand scratched her long neck. 'I know you think I am too strict, but...'

Ophelia waved her hand. 'Not my place to judge, dear.'

'But I am a single parent. A religious parent. And underage girls should be kept under a watchful eye from...' Melpomene paused. She controlled her tongue. Her mind pulled back the lingering adjectives and *perverted*, *sex-hungry*, and *filthy* were devoured by the darkness.

'From?' Ophelia asked as she trudged towards the pipe. She turned off the water just in time to hear Melpomene's low-pitched voice. 'From teenage boys.'

Ophelia wiped her wet hands on her *gardening* apron. The oldest of her cooking aprons that still had some mileage to go was newly appointed as a gardening apron. She sighed deeply as she walked up to the window. 'You know, dear, I have four children and eleven grandkids. None alike and definitely none living the way I lived. Our children are not destined to repeat our mistakes.' Ophelia looked up and stared straight into Melpomene's weary eyes to check if her point had reached its destination. She let it sink in for a while and added, 'they will make all whole new ones!'

'You're implying that just because I had a baby as a teen, I fear my daughter will suffer the same?' Now, both her hands had formed strong fists. Her nails dug slightly into her skin. Ophelia could not see from where she stood how her words had affected her house nurse. 'I fear because I know the cruelty of the world.' Her harsh tone did not go by unnoticed.

'Again, I am not judging, dear. I had my first at fifteen.'

'At your choice,' Melpomene mumbled.

'What's that, dear?'

'Coffee time, Mrs. Ophelia. Cherished coffee time. Come on in. I will have it ready in a jiffy.'

Pandora's Box: Chapter Four

Pandora's eyes followed the hand of the clock as it journeyed round, conquering the seconds. The old faded-brown clock hung right above the whiteboard and just below the deep crack that had spread like lightning on the bare wall. Their teacher had taken all her posters down for the summer. Pandora counted all the stains left behind from the overused Blu Tack. 'Thirty-six,' she whispered as she played with the corners of her exam papers. Chemistry was her favourite subject. She had finished the exam half an hour ago. She had completed all sixteen questions and gone over them twice. Yet on her wooden chair she remained. Pandora never raised her hand in class, nor took part in any extra-curriculum activities. She hid her test marks from her friends well. Popularity over academic success.

She looked to her left and held back a giggle. Her two best friends looked puzzled. Both of them hated chemistry. Nefeli chewed on her golden locks while Iris flicked through the four-page test trying to find something vaguely possible to solve. Timothy was the first of the *cool kids* to stand up.

Up to that moment only *nerds* had left the well-lit classroom. Pandora's sea-blue eyes followed him as he passed his test to their teacher with the permanently bored expression. Her eyes fell upon his behind. Pandora bit her lower lip gently. She wished she could bite into Timothy's. '*You're one fine specimen, Timmy.*'

Pandora counted to ten and rose from her seat. She winked to her friends and mouthed, 'I'm bored. I'm going for a smoke with Tim.' She handed in her paper and her multiple bracelets rattled. She avoided her teacher's eyes. Pandora knew that judgmental look well. The good-hearted teacher had tried before to talk sense into the girl. She would have none of it. Popularity over academic success. The paper dropped from her hands and she dashed out the door. The dark quiet corridor welcomed her. The head teacher, a small plum woman with thinly framed reading glasses sat on a crooked nose, stood in attention with her index finger placed on her steady lips. 'Ssshh!' The whispery sound echoed toward Pandora. The head teacher opened her eyes wide and nodded to the exit. Pandora gladly left the building. A smile spread on her face as the sun rays sailed around her and warmed her. She was no longer a pupil. She was no longer a child. She was a step away from sweet eighteen. '*I am a woman.*' A woman carrying a pencil case. Pandora looked to her left. An old green trash bin held papers, empty cans of soft drinks and various chocolate wrappers. Now, it held a purple pencil case full of pencils, a cracked ruler and an abused eraser. With her hands free of bondage, Pandora walked with haste toward the back of the boys' toilets. Timmy was still there. He was surrounded by teens enjoying his camping story. 'I'm heading out there as soon as possible, man. No more alarms and exams and... Hey, Pandora.'

'Hey, so who has a light?' She placed a cigarette on her lips and walked toward him. He extended his strong arms and a flame came to life from his prized Zippo. The silver one his uncle bought him at last year's fair and told him to hide it from his mother. 'I will kill you, you little shit, before my sister kills me. You know that, right?' his uncle said as he held him in a headlock. Timothy laughed. 'I don't know. Mum is pretty fast.'

Arianna ran down the empty hallway and pushed the door to her right with her body. The ladies' toilets were empty. Logical as in the Parga's police force of eight, only she and the front desk secretary were women and she saw Pauline on her fast exit from her corner office. A must needed journey to the spotlessly clean lavatory. 'God, I hate these days. Lord, you owe me a menopause, soon!' She checked her trousers for any unwanted stains. She felt more flooded that she actually was. She pulled out a lengthy piece of toilet paper and just then, her phone vibrated in her jean's right pocket. It was her police partner, Adrian. The only Lieutenant that she had found a pleasure to work with in her two-decade career. She held the screen a good foot away from her eyes and mumbled the text message. 'Robbery... Angelica's bakery... money from the cash register... Where are you, boss? I came to your office... For fuck's sake, can't a woman even have five minutes in the toilet anymore!'

Adrian stood by the main entrance an inch away from the door. If it was winter, he would be waiting for her in the police vehicle. Now, he stayed safe near the strong air-conditioning unit blowing out essential cold air. Outside, as the day moved on, the ferocious June sun settled in the sky and burned all below it. Adrianos -only his grandmother used his full name- was born and raised in Metsovo, a village nested in the snowy mountains of Epirus. Unlike the majority of Greeks, he and the sun were never friends. His skin, used to his native icy weather, suffered during the summer months as he patrolled the coastal Ionian village. Each pore cried out sweat and begged for cool air. Adrian would walk into the small station and switch on the air-conditioning first thing in the morning. If it was already turned on, he would still pick up the remote control and lower the temperature, sure that none of his sun-worshiping colleagues would have chosen a suitable number. He chose sixteen degrees Celsius. The lowest it could go. For a thirty-two-year-old bachelor, living on his own, Adrian took care of himself well. He never ate junk food. He shopped from the organic corner shop and cooked his every meal. He ironed all his clothes perfectly; his black boots were spotless, and his blue car shone brighter than a night star. A straight *A* student, his stockbreeder parents had big dreams for him. A doctor or a lawyer. Something important, according to them. Something in the city, away from the hardships that their everyday life entailed. He shocked them a week before graduation with his plans of not attending university, but that he was going to head down to Athens to enrol in the Police Academy program there.

'You can't be serious, son,' his father said, while his mother covered her mouth and took a step back; her hand searching for the kitchen chair behind her. 'A cop? And cut parking tickets? A bright mind like yours?'

'Officer's School, dad. It's a university-lever institution. I want to follow that with a master's degree in forensic science. I want to use my bright mind to solve crimes.'

It took his parents a few years to truly accept his decision, but his happiness persuaded them. And soon, they had something else to bother him about. At twenty-eight the questions came. Marriage. Kids. The dream of every Greek mother. To see their children married with kids.

'Let's go, partner,' Arianna said as she walked past him and pushed the glass door open. The heat invaded in and Adrian made a dash for the police car. He had already put the key in the ignition and switched on the cold air. Arianna shivered as she sat shotgun and opened her window slightly. 'So, another major crime in our metropolis, huh? Money taken from the bakery register!'

Adrian smiled as he placed his foot on the pedal and sped out of the parking lot.

The police vehicle descended the narrow road that ran all the way to the beach. One of many snake-like roads running down the hill that loaned its slope to the good folks of the town. Angelica's Divine Goods was the last in a row of shops just meters away from the picturesque promenade of Parga. Along the esplanade, only taverns, bars and ice-cream parlours survived. Law of the tourist village. Nearer to the sea, the higher the rent.

Angelica's nickname, if it may be called as such, was *larger-than-life*. A six-foot tall, energetic sixty-year-old stood by the shop's closed door. Red high heels and a black dress trying desperately to cover her curvy figure were the only items on her body. When Mrs. Angelica baked, all bracelets, rings, pearls and watches were removed and placed on a velvet pillow in a safe at the back of the store. Her purple hair stood steady even as the wind picked up. In front of her well-decorated store window, her employee, a petite girl from a near-by village, sat behind a table selling bread.

'Good morning, Angelica. How are...'

Angelica waved her hand. 'Screw good mornings, Ari. Get your gun out and get in there!'

'What?'

Adrian's eyes widened. Girl selling goods outside on the pavement. Mrs. Angelica guarding the closed door. He sighed deeply. 'You have him locked in there, don't you?'

'Of course, I do! Tried to put his hands in my till! I hit him over the head with my grandma's rolling pin and tied him up!'

Arianna rushed into the shop. 'Stay outside, Angelica!' A bearded man in his late fifties sat on the white and violet floor tiles with his hands tied up behind his back to the table's leg. A cloth was forced into his mouth. A thin rivulet of blood came out of his thick hair and got lost in his bushy eyebrow. Arianna looked back at Adrian. 'It's that drunk homeless man you picked up last week for harassing guests at the Lichnos Hotel.' Arianna shook her head, and her right hand tapped the box of cigarettes sneaking from her trousers' pocket. 'Tend to him, Adrian. Get him to the hospital for a check-up and stay with him. I'll deal with Angelica.'

Adrian saluted her. 'On it, boss.'

Minutes later, Adrian escorted the man with the dirty Rolling Stones T-shirt and the ripped blue shorts, out of the deliciously smelling shop. Adrian had left a five euro note on the counter and took a sausage roll and a bottle of water for the accused man.

'...you can't go hitting people, Angelica. He could have been dangerous. Call us! The police will deal with...' Arianna was lecturing Mrs. Angelica on safety.

'And let him take whatever he wants?'

'Err, boss? If I take the car, how will you be getting back?'

Arianna tapped her two legs and returned to her conversation. 'Did he ask for money from the register or for food?'

Adrian took the homeless man by the arm and walked toward the car. *'Yeah, I'm a real crime fighter.'* He smiled as a few shop owners gave him a thumbs-up. One even clapped. He rolled his eyes. *'When will we ever get a good twisted case for me to solve?'*

Grab your copy...
vinci-books.com/PandorasBoxMG

About the Author

Luke Christodoulou is an Amazon bestselling author, a poet and an English teacher (MA Applied Linguistics - University of Birmingham). He is, also, a coffee-movie-book-Nutella lover.

His first book, THE OLYMPUS KILLER (#1 Bestseller - Thrillers), was released in April, 2014. The book was voted Book Of The Month for May on Goodreads (Psychological Thrillers). The book continued to be a fan favorite on Goodreads and was voted BOTM for June in the group Nothing Better Than Reading. In October, it was BOTM in the group Ebook Miner, proving it was one of the most talked-about thrillers of 2014.

The second stand-alone thriller from the series, THE CHURCH MURDERS, was released April, 2015 to widespread critical and fan acclaim. The Church Murders became a bestseller in its categories throughout the summer and was nominated as Book Of The Month in three different Goodreads groups.

DEATH OF A BRIDE was the third Greek Island Mystery to be released. Released in April, 2016 it followed in the footsteps of its successful predecessors. From its first week in release it hit the number one spot for books set in Greece.

MURDER ON DISPLAY came out in 2017 and enriched the series.

HOTEL MURDER, the fifth and 'final' book in the series, followed in early 2018.

In 2018, his box set of mysteries became an international bestseller.

Luke Christodoulou has also ventured into 'children's book land' and released 24 MODERNIZED AESOP FABLES, retelling old stories with new elements and settings. The book, also, features sections for parents, which include discussions, questions, games and activities.

In 2019, TWELVE MONTHS OF MURDER came out, his first collection of shorts.

His first novel outside of the Greek Island Mysteries collection came in 2020, maintaining his love for a Greek theme. A supernatural thrill ride with the name of BEWARE OF GREEKS BEARING GIFTS.

PANDORA'S BOX followed in 2021. A mind-twisting whodunit set in his favorite Greek town, the seaside resort of Parga. The following year saw the release of the highly anticipated ACHILLES' HEEL.

His first YA murder mystery, SENIOR YEAR MURDERS was released in 2024, hitting the charts for young adult thrillers.

He is currently working on various projects (which he is secretive about).

He resides in Limassol, Cyprus with his loving wife, his chatty daughter and his super-energetic son.

Hobbies include travelling the Greek Islands discovering new food and possible murder sites for his stories. He, also, enjoys telling people that he 'kills people for a living'.